AN AMISH HUSBAND
FOR TILLIE

AN AMISH HUSBAND
FOR TILLIE

AMY LILLARD

THORNDIKE PRESS
A part of Gale, a Cengage Company

GALE
A Cengage Company

Copyright © 2020 by Amy Lillard.
Amish of Pontotoc Series.
Thorndike Press, a part of Gale, a Cengage Company.

Thorndike Press® Large Print Christian Fiction.
The text of this Large Print edition is unabridged.
Other aspects of the book may vary from the original edition.
Set in 16 pt. Plantin.

LIBRARY OF CONGRESS CIP DATA ON FILE.
CATALOGUING IN PUBLICATION FOR THIS BOOK
IS AVAILABLE FROM THE LIBRARY OF CONGRESS.

ISBN-13: 978-1-4328-8443-7 (hardcover alk. paper)

Published in 2020 by arrangement with Zebra Books, an imprint of Kensington Publishing Corp.

Printed in Mexico
Print Number: 01   Print Year: 2020

An Amish Husband for Tillie

CHAPTER ONE

"Are you sure you'll be all right?" The
English driver looked down the narrow, red-
dirt road, then back up into Tillie's eyes.

She smiled in what she hoped was a
confident manner and nodded her head.
"I'm sure."

It wasn't too cold out, just enough to let a
person know winter had arrived in Northeast Mississippi. But he was talking about
something else entirely.

He hesitated once more. She held her
breath. She didn't want him to follow her
down the road to the house where she had
grown up. She knew he was only trying to
be kind and gentlemanly, but she didn't
want anyone to be a witness in case they
turned her away. She remembered her
father's reaction when Hannah had returned. He had not been pleased. He would
most likely be even less joyed that she was
back. Her mother would be happy, she was

7

fairly certain, but would it be enough to keep Tillie there? She didn't know. The shame of her return was more than enough to keep her running.

English Christmas music streamed from the car radio as the man considered his choices. "There's only Amish houses down that way," he said.

"Yes, I know."

"You used to be Amish?" he asked, taking in her English attire. His gaze swept her from head to toe. She was glad that she had fastened the middle buttons of the military coat she had found at the Goodwill. She would never get him on his way if he knew what she had concealed beneath her winter jacket.

"Something like that," she replied.

"If you're sure."

"Positive." She gave him one last smile that she hoped was confident enough to pass.

"Okay." He gave a final nod.

She had a feeling that if she'd had a couple of suitcases she wouldn't have been able to dissuade him. But all she had were the clothes on her back and what she had been able to stuff into her backpack.

She handed him the folded bills she had counted out for the ride home. It was all that she had left. The last of her money had brought her back to Pontotoc. She had no choice but to stay. For a while anyway. No choice at all.

With a sigh she hoped the driver didn't hear, she turned and looked down the road toward the house where she grew up. She couldn't see it, of course. It was down in a little valley surrounded by barns and out-buildings and the houses belonging to her brothers.

Behind her the car idled. She would have to take those first steps before the driver would be certain that she would be okay. Of all the people she had met in the English world, why did one of the sweetest and nicest have to be the last one she would see for a while?

Somehow she managed to take that first step. Why was it harder to walk toward home than it was to leave Melvin a note explaining where she had gone and why?

The sound of the engine changed. The tires crunched across the gravel as he allowed the car to roll forward. Two more steps, these easier than the one before, and the driver started down the road. Two turns and he would be back in town. A quarter of a mile and she would be on her parents' front porch.

Each step was a little easier to make than the last, but still it was rough going. Not so much because the winter had started to take its toll on the packed dirt road, but because she knew what was waiting for her at the bottom of the valley. Or rather, she didn't know what was waiting for her. Would they be welcoming or would they flatly turn her away? There was only one way to know, and it was a trial by fire.

She stopped at the top of the hill, next to the cabin where Jamie and his adopted son, Peter, had lived for a time when they first came to Mississippi. Maybe her folks would allow her to stay there. It was almost a home. They had built a room onto the back, upping the room total to two, but it would be enough for her and the baby.

Tillie adjusted the straps on her backpack, then cupped her hands over the growing mound concealed by the bulk of her coat. Just another month or so and she would give birth to Melvin Yoder's child while he remained in the English world repairing engines and enjoying the freedoms he couldn't have in their conservative Amish community.

But she couldn't stay there any longer. It was just so hard.

"Okay, baby," she said. "This is it." What

10

was Cindy at the day care always saying? *It's now or never.*

"Now or never," she muttered.

Lord, please don't allow them to turn me away. I know I've made more than my share of mistakes. But this child is innocent. She needs a home, a place to stay and be loved. Move their hearts and have them accept. If not for me, then for this baby. Amen.

Once again she started walking, taking in the subtle changes that had come to their little valley since she had left. There was a new tire swing in the large oak that sat next to the barn and horse corral. Someone had moved a washer up to her brother David's house. She supposed their *mamm* had gotten tired of washing her youngest son's clothes. A stack of bee boxes sat to one side of her brother Jim's house. A lot of changes, but none at all. Maybe it just felt that way because she was different. The English world had changed her, taught her life lessons that she could not have learned anywhere else.

As she entered the shared yards, a screen door slammed. She turned to see Anna, her brother Jim's wife, standing at the edge of their porch.

"Tillie?" Almost a whisper.

"Hi, Anna." She smiled, hesitantly, the

one motion asking for forgiveness from the start.

"Tillie?" The screech behind her had Tillie whirling around to face her mother.

"Abner! Come quick! Tillie's home."

After hugs from her brothers and her nieces and nephews, and a frown from her father, Tillie was led into the house and directly to the kitchen table. Of course her mother wanted to feed her straight away, but the roundness of Tillie's belly gave her *mamm* pause.

During all the welcoming and joyful tears, no one had mentioned her obviously pregnant condition. She didn't know if no one wanted to be the one to broach the subject or if they simply didn't know what to say. Or maybe it was because of the mixed company — men and children. Women didn't discuss such matters around men and children.

But now the clamor had died down. Everyone save Mamm and Libby, her brother Jim's oldest daughter, had gone back to their lives. Dat was most likely in the barn working on one of the sheds he sold to English and Amish alike. Jim was out with him, she was certain. Just as she was certain David had been sent to her sisters' houses to tell them the news. And to Gracie's new home. Leah had written her about Gracie's new family. She was delighted for her cousin. A family of her own had been Gracie's unspoken dream for so very long.

Mamm slid onto the bench seat opposite Tillie and shot Libby a look.

The girl immediately stood. "I'll go check on Mammi." In the blink of an eye, she was gone, bustling off toward the *dawdihaus* to see about the oldest member of their family.

Obviously Libby had been brought over to help Mammi. Tillie's grandmother had fallen and broken her hip a couple of years ago. Hannah had returned shortly afterward, using that injury as an excuse for returning when the real reasons were much more alarming — a dead, cheating husband and debts beyond anything they could imagine. Gracie had come to help at first and stayed until she married Matthew. If Tillie had been at home, Mammi's care would have fallen to her. As it was, it had become Libby's responsibility.

"Would you like to tell me about it?" Mamm's voice was soft and so gentle that tears sprang to Tillie's eyes.

No, she didn't want to tell her mother about "it," but what choice did she really have? None, if she wanted to stay for a while.

"The baby's due in January." Maybe not the best thing to start off with, but it was out and she had to be satisfied with it.

"And your Melvin?"

Tillie just shook her head. The lump in her throat took up too much room for her to speak around it. She swallowed hard and tried again. "He didn't want to return."

Mamm nodded, but the action was more resigned than agreeing. "And this is what you want?"

Tillie started to speak again, but her *mamm* beat her to it. "You've made peace with it?"

She didn't need to say the rest, that she would be shunned in their small community. Even though Tillie hadn't joined the church, the community would frown heavily upon her wandering from her faith and all the lessons that she had been taught in her life.

"I suppose," Tillie finally said. "I mean, I'm hoping he'll change his mind now that I'm here." And that was something. Her *mamm* had no idea how hard it had been to walk away from her job, the apartment where she lived with Melvin, and Melvin himself. But she'd had to. Even if she might not get to stay in Pontotoc. If she was to stay, Melvin would have to come back and the two of them would have to get married. It was as simple as that.

But with all the Christmas celebrations going around, Tillie had longed for home. She longed for her family, the traditions and people, the church where she felt loved. Home. And she knew that she had to return. For the baby. She wanted her child raised among the grace and faith of her Amish community. Even though what she wanted and what she could have were literally worlds apart.

When she told Melvin her plans, he scoffed. Maybe he even thought she was joking. That's why she had left in the middle of the morning, while he was at work, and made her way back to Pontotoc.

Her mother smiled, the same smile Tillie had traveled miles and miles to see. "Yes," she said. "You're here. Now," she continued, "let's see about getting you something to eat." She started to stand, but Tillie reached out a hand and laid it on top of her mother's.

"I'm — I'm sorry," Tillie said. Nothing else seemed to fit, but the words themselves were sadly lacking. She was sorry for so many things — for leaving in the dead of night, for going against the *Ordnung,* for coming home in shame.

But the one thing she couldn't be sorry about was the baby itself. It was a miracle. Not in the Biblical sense, but a miracle nonetheless. A life was growing inside her, a life that she and Melvin had made. She was sorry that they hadn't gotten married yet, but he always seemed too busy. Honestly, she thought the friends he had made at the garage had talked him out of marrying her.

And that was another thing she was sorry for: Melvin had changed.

Maybe she had too. But now all she wanted was to return home, be among her family, and spend Christmas in their loving embrace.

"I know, dear." Mamm patted her hand and made her way to the icebox. She pulled out a couple of containers of leftovers, dumped them out in two separate stainless steel pans, then lit the stove.

Mamm turned back to face her. Tillie tried to smile, but the action wouldn't come. She was tired. So very tired. It had taken her hours to get home, though it was only about an hour and a half by car between Pontotoc and Columbus. "It's not going to be easy, you know."

Tillie nodded. It was already difficult. Seeing the shame on her father's face, the shock on her brothers' faces. Only Anna had worn a sympathetic look. But that was Jim's Anna, always worried about the person next to her.

"I know," she said. "But —" She stopped.

"But what?" Mamm prodded.

"I had to come home."

Steaming pots forgotten, Mamm crossed over to her and placed her hands on either side of her face. She tilted Tillie's chin up until she had no choice but to look and listen, much like Mamm had done when Tillie was a child.

"You are home," Mamm said emphatically. "Never forget that."

After eating almost more leftovers than she could hold, Tillie donned her army coat and went out onto the porch. She loved sitting on the swing with her cousin Gracie, talking about boys and cooking and quilting and all the other things that young girls talk about.

"Tillie?" Libby eased the screen door open but stopped before letting it shut behind her. "Can I . . . can I come out and sit with you?"

Tillie smiled. "Of course." She scooched over and patted the seat next to her. She gave Libby an encouraging nod, though she really just wanted to be alone. She supposed there would be time for that later. Right now her niece seemed to have something on her mind.

Libby sat down next to her and tears once again filled Tillie's eyes. She missed her sisters so much. They had just come back to Pontotoc to live when Melvin had decided he had had enough of Amish living. What choice had she had but to go? She had loved him, after all — though now she wondered about that love. Was it really love if the person didn't seem to love you in return? She had thought he did, but things change. People change. Melvin changed, until she hardly knew him at all. But that wasn't the reason she had come home. No, it was Christmas. The chill in the air, everyone talking about buying gifts and wrapping them. All the ladies at the day care wanted to talk about their Christmas trees and when they were going to put them up. Those who didn't know her well also didn't know that she was Amish. She didn't have a Christmas tree or lights or ornaments. No stockings of red and white, no Christmas music, no singing Santa or dancing Grinch, the weird, green creature that didn't seem like Christmas to her at all. She had none of these things.

Up until that moment it had been easy to pretend that she belonged in the English world. Sure, she'd had to buy all her clothes at Goodwill, and sometimes she didn't match things up just right, but she was trying her best to fit in. Then came all the talk of Christmas, and one thing became so very clear: she was never going to fit in.

And that's why she had to come home.

"I'm glad you're back," Libby said, flashing her a shy smile. *Shy* was not a word Tillie normally associated with Libby, which meant something was up.

"I'm glad I'm back too."

Tillie waited for Libby to say more.

"Hannah and Leah will be so happy to see you."

"*Jah,*" Tillie said. Still she waited.

"And Gracie. You know she has five kids now? Can you imagine? And one of her own coming soon."

The last thing she wanted to hear about were her sisters' and her cousin's perfect lives.

"What's up, Libby?"

It was as if a dam broke. Libby turned toward her and grabbed Tillie's hand. "Does it hurt?" she asked with a pointed nod at Tillie's burgeoning belly. "Being pregnant?"

Tillie laid a protective hand over the

19

mound. "Why do you ask?"

Libby sighed, a frustrated sound. "No one will tell me. You know how the women are. They don't like to talk about things. I just want to know. That's all."

"Because of a boy?"

"Maybe." Another sigh, this one more wistful. "I'm growing up and everyone still treats me like a child. I just want to know things."

Tillie waited.

"Silas King." The name was almost like a prayer on her lips.

Tillie remembered Silas. "He's a little older, right?"

Libby sniffed. "Not that much older. Just five years. Anyway, he's been acting like he's going to ask me to court him, and, well . . ." She fiddled with one of her *kapp* strings, then shook her head. "You just got home. I shouldn't be bothering you with this." She started to stand, but Tillie reached out and held her in place.

"Don't run away," she said. "If you have a question, ask it." She would much rather people ask than stare at her and make her wonder what was going on inside their heads. No one paid her much mind in the English world, but now that she was back in Pontotoc, she knew that was going to change. Stares and questions — they were both coming.

"It's just marriage and relationships . . . I'd ask Mamm, but it's been so long since she and Dat got married I doubt she even remembers."

Tillie bit back a laugh. "You'd be surprised," she said. "But I wouldn't want to ask my mother about such things either."

"How do you know when you're ready? To . . . you know . . ."

"I do hope you're talking about getting married."

Libby sniffed delicately. "Of course." She really was still so young. A tender soul trapped in the body of a young woman.

"You'll know," Tillie said.

"Like you and Melvin."

Well, she had thought she knew. Now everything had changed. She had rushed in, been impulsive, gotten herself in a bit of trouble, and had come running back home. Part of her knew she should be with Melvin, talking to him about marriage and the early family they had started. But she had to be here, in Pontotoc, where she truly belonged. They might not give her a second glance when she was among the English, and she was certain to endure more than her fair share of gossip and disapproving looks, but

21

she needed to be here, with her family. For as long as they would have her.

"I don't know," she finally said. She wanted it to be true, but Melvin hadn't come after her. Not yet, anyway. Was that what she wanted? For him to swoop in and take her away?

No, she wanted him to come back too, and live with their families. Well, her family, since all of his had moved away. Leah had told her in one of her letters. But they could live here, she and Melvin and the baby. Maybe in the cabin up the drive. Or even in a house they had yet to build. But they had already started their family without talking all these things through. What was a girl to do with that?

"Just promise me one thing, Libby," Tillie said. "Don't be in a rush."

Rushing in had gotten her in the exact spot she was in now. And the place wasn't always comfortable. Not by far.

CHAPTER TWO

Levi Yoder pulled his gloves from his hands and made his way into the feed store. He hated coming into town. He hated stopping at the feed store. Too many men standing around talking about too many things that hardly seemed to matter. The weather, Thomas Byler's new carriage mare, and these days . . . Christmas.

Most of all, he hated Christmas.

And he hated himself for hating it.

"What can I get you, Levi?" the man behind the counter asked. Tyrone Getty had run the co-op for as long as Levi could remember. Like with a lot of folks of color, it was impossible to tell exactly how old Tyrone was. His wiry steel-gray hair bore testament to his years, but his dark face was devoid of wrinkles, smooth and unlined like that of a much younger man. He had been here when Levi was a child and it seemed that he would remain long after Levi had passed.

"Tyrone," Levi grunted, and slid a small piece of paper across the counter toward the man. With any luck the order would get him through, clear to the new year. But it seemed these days luck wasn't on his side.

"Gimme a minute," Tyrone said, never taking his brown eyes from the paper. The man didn't wear glasses — another thing that made his age such a mystery. "Help yourself to a cup of coffee." He nodded toward the old-fashioned sideboard that had been converted into a coffee station for the customers.

Levi started toward the station, then faltered. On a day like today, when the wind had turned off a bit chilly, the coffee was a welcome offering. It was the company that made him leery. Four men stood between the sideboard and the potbellied stove. He knew them all. George Williams owned the land next to the bishop's. Max Myron ran the Randolph Animal Shelter. They were the two English in the group. Jason Menno and Chris Lambert were both Amish farmers, members of the same church district as Levi, and they already wore sympathetic looks on their faces.

How much longer before people stopped

looking at him like he was something to be pitied? How long before he stopped feeling like a walking sack of grief? Who knew?

Just another reason why he hated to come to town.

But they had spotted him. Jason moved from in front of the coffeepot and the men stood and waited for him to come near.

What choice did he have? Levi recovered his steps and started toward the station. On the way he passed an endcap of Christmas lights and another with some sort of inflatable creatures to place on the front lawn. A reindeer, a Santa, and a snowman. Like there was any snow in Northeast Mississippi. Not this early in the year, and hardly ever enough to build a snowman. Then he passed a dancing Santa that moved to its own music every time someone walked by it. A dancing Santa. Why was that necessary in a feed store? It wasn't. Just like all the strands of shiny garland that looped and swooped around the ceiling. Or the silver and gold snowflakes that hung from fishing line and paper clips. None of it needed to be there, and it only served to remind him that they were gone.

Mary. And the baby he never got to hold.

Gone in an instant.

"Levi."

One of the men spoke. He wasn't paying attention as to who it was. He just wanted to get his cup of coffee and back away to allow them to finish their conversation on Thomas Byler's carriage mare or the weather, or Strawberry Dan's last boring sermon. Whatever it was that they had been talking about before he arrived and everyone's day was shattered with sadness.

Levi nodded in their general direction, poured himself a Styrofoam cup full of coffee, and wandered away without making eye contact with any of them. He didn't want to talk. He didn't want them to ask him how he was doing. He answered those questions every day, every time they had church or he had to run into town to get supplies. Each day when at least one of the good members of their community came to visit, bringing food and company he did not want. The lies were weighing heavy on him. People asked, but they didn't want to know the truth. They didn't want to know that he was having a hard time accepting what all would say was God's will.

God's will. He almost snorted coffee up his nose at the thought. Thankfully it slid down his throat instead and saved him from drawing all their attention once again.

He had been taught that the Lord controls

all things. That He has a plan and His will would prevail. The idea of God's will seemed perfectly logical when talking about other people's problems. He had even been able to accept that it was the reason for his brother Daniel's death. But not this. Not his Mary and his baby.

And lying to everyone when they asked him how he fared and telling them that he was good and God's will would shine through made him choke. How could the death of an innocent who had yet to draw a first breath be a part of God's will? What kind of God would will that? None that he wanted to follow. Which stood to reason that God's will wasn't a part of Mary's death. Something else. Maybe punishment for a crime of his youth. He didn't know. He only knew that it couldn't be God. If it was . . . heaven help them all.

He took another sip of his coffee and unbuttoned his coat. It was warm in the store. Or maybe it was the eyes that watched him that had him warm beyond normal. He knew they meant well. And normally he would have been able to handle it. But not while surrounded by blow-up snowmen and dancing Santas.

Without looking at the other men, he headed back to the counter. A small bell sat next to the cash register and was used to summon a clerk, mostly Tyrone, if he wasn't right there already.

Levi tapped the bell with more vigor than he had intended. Tyrone appeared in an instant.

"Something wrong?" the man asked without hesitation.

Had he rang the bell that urgently? No matter. "No. *Jah.* My order," he finally managed. "Double it." Then for sure he wouldn't have to come back into town before the Christmas celebrating was over and done.

Levi managed to avoid the four men, as well as the two others who came into the feed store while he waited for his increased order.

Just after he had asked for the extra supplies, he had second thoughts. It would eat up a lot of his savings, and with too much feed on hand he would run the risk of rats getting into it. Or moisture and mold. But it was done and he wasn't changing his mind now. He just stayed to the side and out of the way, hoping that no one noticed him there.

He listened in while the men talked but didn't join their conversation. He had nothing to say about a new mare, an old bull, or the fact that Melvin Yoder's girlfriend had returned without him.

He remembered when they had left. Sort of. Levi was a little older than Melvin and Tillie, the girlfriend, but he knew her brother, David. They were in school together, and in the same youth group. He had spent many a summer afternoon at the pond behind the Gingeriches' house fishing and lolling about in the sun. But that had been before a sweet girl named Mary Byler had captured Levi's attention and stolen his heart away.

He swung up into his wagon and snapped the reins to start his horse. He was glad he had brought the wagon into town today instead of his buggy. He would never have been able to get all this home without the extra room.

And now another trip to the feed store was one less thing he had to worry about. The next hurdle was church. Tomorrow was Saturday. He had one day to prepare for the kind looks and sympathetic twists of the ladies' mouths as they gazed at him. Having the entire congregation to deal with was so much worse than the pitying looks of the one or two daily visitors. It was maddening.

It had been two months since Mary had died. A brain aneurysm, they had called it.

He supposed that was a fancy way of saying that her brain had started bleeding for no reason. Well, none that they could say for sure. It could have been the strain of the pregnancy. Or something she was predetermined to suffer from. He wasn't so sure about that. Wasn't that a scientific way of saying *God's will*? Even then, none of it mattered. Understanding what had happened to Mary wouldn't bring her back. So he'd only halfway paid attention when they were telling him. Or maybe it was the sheer weight of his grief that had wiped it from his memory. What did it matter, now that his Mary was gone?

She had been six months pregnant, and he couldn't help remembering that if she were alive today, she would be as round as an apple and glowing like the other women he had seen this far along. He was certain she would be crocheting this or that for the baby, planning, but not too much. It wouldn't do to appear arrogant, like they were taking God's blessing for granted. And they had wondered if maybe . . . just maybe . . . the baby might come a little early and be born on Christmas Day, sharing a birthday with Jesus. Now, he had heard some of the men in town debating on whether or not Christmas Day was actually when Jesus was born, but it didn't matter. It was the day when everyone celebrated, and that was enough for Levi.

And he missed her. He missed Mary every day. He had hoped some of the pain would have eased by now. Or maybe he was expecting too much from himself. Right now he just wanted to go home, away from all the talk of Jesus and Christmas, away from all the pretty red poinsettias and English chatter of Santa Claus and hide away until it was all over.

He turned down the dirt lane that led to his house. The road needed to be graded. It was "rough as a cob," his grandmother would have said. He smiled at the memory. Just one more person he had to miss this holiday. He should go back into town in a day or so and find someone to help him with the road. But he wouldn't. It could wait.

When he saw the buggy parked in front of his house he almost pulled back on the reins and turned his wagon around.

Miriam Elizabeth Yoder, most always known as Mims, stood next to the buggy, hands planted on her hips. His sister. His nosy, busy, bossy sister who meant well, but liked to bully him, and anyone else who would allow it.

"Levi Yoder." Her look was stern, her mouth set in a thin line.

He cringed as he pulled the horse to a stop. "Mims." He gave her a nod and hopped down from his wagon.

"Where have you been?" she asked.

"Town." He didn't mean to be curt, but like half of his family, she treated him as if he were a fragile piece of china that would shatter if a person looked at it too hard. The other half acted like nothing had happened. He didn't know which was worse. He was struggling to find his way, and as much as he loved his family, they were not helping in that process.

"I came over."

"I can see that." He pulled the fifty-pound bag of dog food from the stack of supplies in his wagon and carried it toward the barn. Puddles waddled out from inside, her tail wagging her entire body despite the added weight around her middle.

"Le—" Mims started, then broke off. She shook her head. "I was concerned about you."

"I'm fine." He shifted the bag of food to his shoulder and reached down to pet the freckled dog on the head. Puddles, an Australian cattle dog, had been Mary's dog, and the pooch grieved for her mistress almost as much as Levi did. "Come on, girl," he said, then led the way into the barn.

He half expected Mims to follow him, but she didn't. Yet she was still waiting there by her buggy when he came back out.

"We should talk about this, you know." Her words were like a puzzle with a few missing pieces, but he understood her meaning.

"There's nothing to talk about." He picked up the sack of feed corn. It wasn't his best solution, but he hoped it would keep weight on the few heads of cattle he had decided to keep during the winter. He supposed if they preferred to roam for grass, he could feed it to the chickens and the ducks. And he wasn't coming up with things to think about, so he didn't have to sit around and miss Mary.

"You can't just lock yourself away."

He didn't know why not. There were several members of their community who were committed to staying at home on all days except for church Sundays. Granted, they were eccentric at best, a little off in the head at worst, but he could deal with that label. In truth, he didn't care one bit what people thought of him.

Well, maybe a little, but since he had lost Mary, he cared less and less.

He made his way into the barn and out again before answering. "I'm not locked away. I just went into town."

She looked into the back of his wagon. "This looks like it was bought by one of those English people who thinks the end of the world is coming."

"It is. One day." He picked up the bag of alfalfa pellets and hoisted it onto his shoulder.

"Levi. It's a wedding. He's our cousin. Everyone will be devastated if you don't come."

"I doubt that." In fact, he was pretty certain that his cousin, who was widowed and getting married for the second time, wouldn't notice if Levi was there or not. Maybe if he was cousins with the bride it would be different, but men didn't put as much importance on things like weddings. To men like him, the marriage was more important, and his marriage was gone. His not wanting to go to the wedding had nothing to do with the fact that his cousin was starting over while to Levi the concept of a new beginning was as foreign as the moon.

"Then do it for Mamm."

The words stopped him. His mother. She was one of the ones who acted like everything was just as it had always been. He appreciated the fact that she was trying, in her own way, to help him move forward, but so far, her efforts had been in vain. He was stuck.

Maybe when the holidays were over. How could he move forward if all he could think about were the things that were gone?

"Mims." The one word said it all. How she wasn't playing fair, how she needed to think about his feelings too, and how family came first, but some things were delicate.

His sister propped her hands on her hips in that sassy way of hers, but her eyes softened. "Lee."

"Fine." He sighed. There were some things in this world that were too tough to fight, and Mims was one of them.

"You won't regret it." She beamed at him. "I promise you."

That was strange, because he regretted it already.

He shook his head. "Don't just stand there. Help me get these things in the house." He pointed to the bag of cat food. It was by far the smallest of his supplies, and he knew that Mims was a strong woman both in her head and in her muscles, but he didn't really need her help. He was hoping that once he got her body occupied, she would stop trying to find things to tell him to do.

She picked up the bag and toted it toward the house. "Why are you buying cat food?" she asked. So much for his theory. "You don't have a cat."

Levi gathered up the remaining supplies and started behind her.

"Are you going to feed every stray that comes along?" Mims sighed. "You'll have a hundred dogs and twice that many cats before next fall."

"I can't watch an animal starve, Mims." But he wasn't the one who had started feeding the strays. That had been all Mary. But how could he stop? They came to the house needing comfort and food, sometimes even shelter. How could he turn them away?

She shook her head as he opened the door. She pushed her way inside and headed for the kitchen. "You'll definitely need to get remarried. Or you'll end up being that crazy old man with a thousand pets."

"I'm not getting remarried," he said before he even realized the words were in his head. "Not ever."

"You don't mean that." She eyed him warily as if he was about to do something no man should even think about.

"I do."

"Levi." There went her cajoling voice again. She had perfected that when they were children, and she used it regularly to get whatever it was that she wanted.

"If it's God's will that my wife and son are gone, then it's surely God's will that I remain alone for the rest of my days."

CHAPTER THREE

"This is too much," Tillie whispered as a car pulled up outside her family home. Her sister Leah; Leah's husband, Jamie; and their son, Peter, hopped out of the car and waved.

Beside her, Tillie felt, rather than saw, her *mamm* smile. "It's just a family dinner."

Just a family dinner. To most, that meant the family members in a household gathering around the table for a quick meal. For Eunice Gingerich, that meant everyone she could fit in her house. For Tillie, it was completely overwhelming.

Hannah and Aaron had arrived some time ago with their three children. Jim, Anna, and their five had walked across with Dave, who at this point Tillie was glad had no children.

"Gracie and Matthew should be here shortly," Mamm said with a smile as she returned Peter's enthusiastic wave.

And that was another six. Add in Brandon, his friend Shelly, Mammi, and everyone else, plus Tillie made twenty-nine. That many people did not add up to a simple family dinner. Not even among the Amish.

"Mamm —" Tillie started.

But her mother shook her head. "Hush now, girl. We're just happy you're home."

And she was happy to be home. Wasn't she? Except she didn't feel all that happy. It wasn't that she missed Melvin. She did. But she didn't miss the life that they had built.

Tillie touched a quick hand to her belly. Everyone seemed content to ignore the fact that she was nearly eight months pregnant.

Or maybe they don't care that you sinned.

If that was the case, she was sure it was because they loved her. The rest of the community wouldn't be so forgiving. And it was only a matter of time before her family would have to shun her as well. They wouldn't be able to eat with her, take money from her, or even talk to her. A time of reckoning was coming, and she both wished it was already there and dreaded it, all in the same instant.

"Everybody's bringing food," Mamm said. "And we've got paper plates and plastic cups. All we have to do now is eat and enjoy ourselves."

Tillie smiled. If only that were the truth. "We'll still have to wash the serving spoons and the silverware," she joked.

"I think we can handle that." Mamm's eyes twinkled the same way they had when Hannah had come home. Suddenly Tillie felt horrible about leaving in the first place. She had made such a mess of it all.

Tears rose and blurred her vision. Tillie blinked them away.

Mamm took Tillie's face into her hands and looked into her eyes. "This is a happy time," she said, her voice firm. "We'll have none of that."

"Right." Tillie sniffed. She wouldn't cry. Not tonight, but she knew there were a lot more tears in her future.

To say the house was full was an understatement. It seemed that wherever she stood, she was surrounded by babies, children, or siblings It was a warm feeling for certain, and one that she hadn't felt in a long, long time.

With so many people in one house, there was no eating around the table. Libby made Mammi a plate and took it into her room. Jim and Anna's youngest son, Samuel, followed closely behind with his own supper. A couple of years ago, he had gotten "lost" and ended up in Mammi's room. He'd only been two at the time and hadn't realized the stir he had caused when he disappeared. Hadn't known that the entire family was looking for him. But ever since then, he and his great-grandmother had had a special bond.

Even with two tables, one in the dining room and one in the kitchen, a third table had to be set up for the smaller kids. And still that left the teens to find their own place to eat. Brandon, Shelly, Joshua, and Libby took their plates into the living room, leaving the adults at the two tables. In typical Amish fashion, the women ended up at one table and the men at the other.

Tillie didn't mind. She would have loved to talk to David a little more, but the men being in the other room meant her father took his disapproving stare with him. Abner Gingerich was a good man. He provided for his family and always had. He worked hard, feared God, and walked the line. But he was Amish through and through. He hadn't said as much, but Tillie knew: he was ashamed of her and her actions. The worst part of it all was there was nothing she could do about it. The rules were the rules and she had broken them. She was pregnant and soon to have a baby. She wasn't married,

41

and she couldn't bring herself to apologize for her situation. Somehow this child she had never met had become so important to her. She couldn't call it a mistake. If her having a baby was part of God's will — and how could it not be? God controlled the world — then how could His will be a mistake?

"Don't you think, Tillie?"

"Huh?" She looked up at Hannah, realizing only then that she had been daydreaming at the table.

"I told you she wasn't paying attention." Leah pointed her fork at her sister.

"What?" she asked. "I'm sorry. I just didn't hear." Far from the truth, but she certainly couldn't share her thoughts with them.

Then who can you share them with?

"I was just telling Leah and Gracie that since the weather is supposed to be cooler next week, we could mix the lotions here in the house."

"I don't know if that's a good idea," Leah countered with a shake of her head.

"But if we don't make some more soon, we won't have enough to fill any after-Christmas orders."

"Will there be many after-Christmas orders?" Gracie asked.

42

"Yeah," Leah said with a grin and a nod.

"Your sisters and cousin have made quite a business for themselves while you were away," Mamm said, directing her speech at Tillie. She said the words as if Tillie had merely been on some sort of mission trip and not off consorting with the English.

"Jah?" She looked from Gracie to Hannah and Leah. Her older sisters might be twins, but they were about as different as two women could be. Hannah had brown hair and hazel eyes, much like Tillie's own. Leah was the true beauty in the family, with her dark, dark hair and green eyes. And they had each been through so many different life experiences. Both had left the Amish long ago. Leah had soon after joined the Mennonite church, while Hannah had married a wealthy Englisher. A couple of years ago Hannah had returned, widowed and broke. But her story had a happy ending when she reconnected with her longtime love, Aaron Zook, and now they were married and raising his three children in the Amish way.

She had tried to tell her, Tillie thought. Hannah had tried to tell her that the English world was hard, but Tillie had foolishly thought that she and Melvin would have it different than Hannah had. After all, she and Melvin had each other. So much for that theory.

Gracie gasped and her eyes went wide. "You can join the business now that you're back."

She started to protest, but Leah interrupted. "Don't even say that you can't. We have so many orders for Christmas that I even have Brandon and Shelly working on them."

"If you want me to," Tillie murmured.

"Not officially, of course." Leah gave a wink. "But as long as you're here, I see no reason for you not to help."

This might be the hardest part about coming back, the love and welcoming. For she knew it would be short-lived. She expected nothing less from her family, but it was hard all the same.

The rest of the community wouldn't be so easy. That was why she was waiting until after the baby was born before she told everyone that she wasn't staying. She figured Mamm had already worked that out for herself. But Tillie needed some time with her family. Despite the fact that she couldn't stay. Not unless Melvin changed his mind and came after her. And if he didn't . . .

It was something she didn't want to think about. Not until she was faced with the choice. "What kind of business?" she asked. Much better to keep on the current subject.

"We've started selling Mamm's goat milk products in Leah's store in town," Hannah said.

"Gracie has them in her shop in front of the house, and Mamm has a few out here," Leah added.

It was common in their community to have small stores in the front of their houses in which to sell homemade goods to the public — fresh vegetables and fruits in the summertime and canned goods, potholders, and other nonperishable items all year round.

"Sales drop in the winter," Gracie went on. "So Leah set us up with a website." She shook her head, but her smile remained in place.

Hannah laughed. "We had no idea people from all over would want to buy lotion and soaps made by a couple of Amish girls —"

"And one Mennonite," Leah interjected.

"— from Mississippi," Hannah finished.

"So you really need my help?" Tillie asked.

Hannah gave her sister a sympathetic look. "We really need your help."

"But the *Ordnung,*" Tillie protested. Hadn't they violated the rules enough?

"Pah," Hannah said.

Tillie blinked back the tears that prickled at the back of her eyes. This was a happy moment, and yet all she seemed able to do these days was cry. She supposed everyone would blame it on the hormones, but Tillie herself knew the truth. She was simply very, very sad — torn between two lives. And now that she had managed to get herself in a family way, she belonged in neither of them.

"I'm sorry," she mumbled, then stood up and raced from the room.

She heard them talking as she left, but she didn't understand their words. Just their tone. Worry. Concern. Love.

Despite the cool temperatures that the nighttime brought, Tillie headed to the front door. She stopped on the porch, stunned and a bit embarrassed. She shouldn't have run out on her family. She should have explained. They loved her, and they would understand that she was overwhelmed. But the deed was done. She would need to stay gone for a few minutes, at least to give time for the dust to settle on her departure.

She collapsed into the swing, rubbing her arms as the cold started to seep through the loose weave of her sweater. She couldn't remain outside for long. Not without a jacket.

The screen door creaked open and Leah

stood there, one of their *mamm*'s crocheted afghans in her arms. "You okay?" Leah asked. She stepped onto the porch as Tillie nodded. Behind her, Gracie and Hannah pulled on their coats before heading out after her.

Only three of them could fit on the swing. Leah and Hannah flanked Tillie while Gracie pulled up a chair and settled her girth into it. Her beautiful cousin rested a hand on her own rounded belly, and Tillie was filled with love and happiness for her. All Gracie had ever wanted was a family. Not only had she married a man with five children, she was due to have her own sometime after the new year, if the size of her belly was any indication.

Leah spread the afghan over the three of them while Gracie pulled her shawl a little closer around her shoulders.

How many nights had they sat out here just like this? Too many to count. Some with all four of them, then, later, after Hannah and Leah had gone, just Tillie and Gracie. She knew for a fact there weren't many problems in life what couldn't be solved on their front porch — her current state being one of them.

"So," Tillie started before anyone else could find their words to ask her about her

47

flight from the supper table. "You and Matthew Byler, huh?"

In the dim golden lamplight that filtered out from the front window, Tillie could see Gracie's cheeks fill with color.

"*Jah,*" she said, "me and Matthew Byler."

"Funniest story ever," Leah added.

"No." Gracie shook her head. "We're not going to start —"

"So you remember Matthew's wife, Beth? Well, she died," Leah continued without waiting for Tillie's answer. "That's not the funny part. Anyway, Gracie goes over to Matthew's to take him a pot of stew —"

"It was a casserole," Gracie corrected.

"It matters," Leah said with a scoff. "Anyway, she took him a casserole and then asked him to marry her."

Tillie had been rocking the swing back and forth using the heels of her feet, but at this revelation she stopped dead. "You did that?"

If she wasn't mistaken, Gracie's color deepened until it was almost the same burgundy hue as her dress. "I was feeling a little desperate."

Desperate or not, that was a very bold move for an Amish woman.

A moment of silence fell between them all before Gracie started up again. "It's just

48

that Matthew can be a bit stubborn," she explained. "And he didn't think he needed any help with the children. I knew that he did, but I also knew that the only way I would be able to truly help was as his wife."

She didn't need to say how much she wanted a family of her own and how hard it was to find a man in Pontotoc that they weren't related to. It was a challenge they had all faced at one time or another.

"Well, I'm impressed." Hannah used her feet to restart the swing while Tillie studied her cousin.

Gracie made tiny little folds in the fabric of her apron. She had seen what she had wanted, and she had gone after it. Bold; scary; commendable.

Tillie'd had that brashness once. It too had gotten her in the family way, but she didn't have a home, a husband, and five little children to round out the one she carried. She hadn't built the family that they had all been dreaming of since they were old enough to talk.

"Tillie." Leah's voice cut through her thoughts. "Is Melvin coming back?"

"No," she quietly said. "I don't think so." She didn't add that she hoped he would. This trip had been all about that. Making him realize that he wanted to return. Even if he didn't know it right away. But as much as she loved him, she'd had to come home.

"I don't suppose . . ." Hannah let her question trail off.

She didn't need to finish for Tillie to know what she was asking: whether she and Melvin had gotten married. "No."

She didn't have to say more, that since she and Melvin were not married, if he didn't come back and marry her, they would be shunned, excommunicated. And that would defeat her whole purpose in returning. She might be able to live close — it was still a free country — but she wouldn't be welcomed by the church, by the friends, neighbors, and family that she loved so much.

"So what now?" Gracie asked.

"You know we're here to help and support," Hannah explained.

"That's right." Gracie nodded, and Leah followed suit.

"I know," Tillie replied. She knew that they would help her in any way possible. That's what sisters did. And even if by birth Gracie was their cousin, she was like a sister to them all. "But that's all I know." She wished it were enough. Love and support would help her through, but they wouldn't make the tough decisions she now faced.

"Let's talk about something uplifting," Leah suggested.

"Tell me more about Peter," Tillie asked, grateful for the change in topic. "When did he start talking?"

When Jamie had first come down to Pontotoc to live, his nephew Peter was so traumatized by the fire that killed his mother, his father, and his baby sister that he didn't speak a word. He too had suffered, with burns that left scars too big to hide and gave him a permanent limp. He had been understandably sullen and sad, but the little boy that Tillie had been reintroduced to this evening was a sight different than the one he had been when she had left.

"Let's see," Leah mused. "I guess it was right after Jamie and I got married."

"Another thing you need to tell me all about," Tillie demanded. She would much rather talk about her sisters' triumphs and joys than her own heartache.

"Tuesday," Leah promised. She looked around at them all. "Jamie wants to get Peter a new puppy for Christmas." She went on to explain for Tillie's benefit how Peter's first dog had died in the fire that had killed his family. Peter himself had been injured trying to save his dog and her pups. Then, after they had moved to Pontotoc, Jamie

51

had taken Peter into town. He and Brandon had found a stray, matted and dirty, outside Leah's store. They had posted signs, and someone had claimed the pooch as their dog. But not before Peter had fallen completely in love. To help combat his obvious grief over losing yet another thing he had begun to care about, Jamie had taken Peter to the Randolph Animal Shelter. "And I promise you, he picked out the oldest dog in the place," Leah said with a laugh. "But they bonded, and there wasn't any changing Peter's mind. But despite his age at adoption, Duke lived a good long while. He died this summer."

"Did Peter take it hard?" Tillie asked. If he had, the loss seemed not to have set him back any. Which, as far as everyone was concerned, was a good thing.

"Hard enough. But he's had time to grieve. Jamie thinks it's a good time for another pet."

"You're not doing the whole Santa thing with him, are you?" Hannah asked.

Since Leah was a Mennonite, she celebrated Christmas a little differently than the rest of them, something Tillie hadn't thought about until now.

"Do you have a Christmas tree?" she added before Leah could answer. She might be Amish, but she thought Christmas trees were about the prettiest thing she had ever seen. When she went into town as a child, she always had to be careful not to stare. If she lingered too long in front of some of the windows boasting the trees, she got a sharp reprimand from her father.

"No to Santa. Yes to a Christmas tree, though I'm not sure Jamie quite approves."

"How does Peter feel about it?" Hannah asked.

Leah smiled. "He loves it."

"You're staying, right?" Gracie asked.

Tillie whipped her attention around to her cousin. "Staying?"

"At least through Christmas," Hannah clarified.

"Jah," Tillie said, doing her best not to sigh with relief. "Through Christmas."

CHAPTER FOUR

Levi trudged back into the house from the barn, food bowl in one hand and Puddles at his heels. Judging from her size, she was going to whelp those pups any day now, and he would rather she be outside than in. But tonight it was going to be a little colder, and he couldn't have them all freezing to death.

He let her into the house and led her to the kitchen. There was an old pillow there covered in an even older towel where she had been sleeping these last few cold nights. With any luck she would stay right there and have those pups if she happened to do so during the night . . . while she was inside the house. If luck was on his side . . .

Yet when had luck ever been with him?

"Dinner, then bed," he told the dog. It was much easier to blame everything on luck — or the lack of it — than to try and figure out God's plan.

He placed the filled food bowl next to her bed, then went back out to fetch her water. He had already filled the bowl and it was waiting by the outside spigot. Back in the house, he set it next to her food.

Puddles looked from the bowl to his face. She whined and thumped her tail against the floor.

"I'll get something to eat later," he promised her. Heaven knew he had enough in his icebox to last through the new year, but that was Mims and the rest of the church ladies at work. Someone was always coming in and out, though he knew he was not fit for company. All he really wished for was to be left alone. On top of all that, Mims came over every other day or so and fussed at him for what he hadn't eaten, made more, and gave him strict directions on when and how to eat it — along with glaring looks that clearly conveyed what would happen if he didn't. He barely got through one container before she was shoving in three more. And he ate plenty.

Well, enough to keep him alive. That's all that mattered right now. That and making it through Christmas.

He sighed. Christmas. Everyone said this was the hardest time of year and the first one was the worst by far. He sure hoped so.

He couldn't go through this year after year.

In fact, if he had his way, he'd pull the shades and lock the door and not come out until January.

Puddles whined a little but continued to eat as Levi made his way down the hall. He slowed at the first door. The room that Mary had said would be the nursery.

He stopped, touched the doorknob. He hadn't been in the room since the funeral. Right afterward he had shut the door and vowed that he would, one day, go through all the things that remained, baby things that he no longer needed. But Christmas was not the time to execute such a chore.

His heart beat a little faster as he turned the knob and stepped inside, reaching for the chain on the propane-powered lamp. Not many folks in their district had them. This was their only one, but Mary had insisted. She wanted a quick light in the middle of the night when the baby needed attending.

Levi pulled the string, and a golden circle of light cascaded across the wall and part of the floor. The room itself was still dim, but he could make out shapes. The crib was pushed against the far window. Mary had debated on the sun bothering the baby but had decided that, since the window faced north, the baby wouldn't be too hot from the position in the sun or too cold in the winter. Even then, the day before she died, she had asked him if he thought she should move it. He had smiled indulgently and told her to do what she wanted.

He should have given her a real answer. He had no idea what that answer would have been. Would the close proximity to the window be an issue? He had no idea. But he still should have given her an answer instead of brushing off her question since he had heard it so many times.

There was still a lot of work that needed to be done to the room. But Mary's family had been bringing things over since the day she told them that she was having a baby. Some of it was hand-me-downs and bags of diapers, both cloth and disposable, along with a few toys, blankets, and tiny little clothes that were impossibly small.

Mary hadn't wanted to do too much to the room, but she had to have a place to store the items. She hadn't wanted to appear arrogant about the baby. It was always a worry, that balance between excited and haughty.

He really should take some of the things to church and give them to the people he thought could use them. Or maybe even into town to the shop on Main that had secondhand Amish and Mennonite clothing.

But he couldn't. Not yet.

Mims had been talking about making a shadow box to hang on the wall, a memorial to Mary and the baby. Something to remember them by, always remember them.

He knew when he did that he would be conceding that Mary and the baby she carried were really and truly gone. He wasn't ready for that just yet.

He cut off the light and shut the door on the memories, but they followed him back into the kitchen. He had been headed to his room for something, but for the life of him, he couldn't remember what it was.

Puddles had finished her meal and had laid down on the large pillow bed he had made for her. Her tail thumped against the floor when she saw him return.

She whined. The cow dog had been Mary's idea. She had wanted a dog to signal when someone came onto their property. Since he did most of the leatherwork in the district, the community, even, it was good to know if someone was around.

"I'm getting something," he told the dog. He opened the icebox and pulled out a container. Chili. Easy enough. Though he wished he had a pan of Mary's corn bread to go with it. Mary always made the best corn bread, and for the duration of their marriage he had carried an extra five pounds around his middle as testament to that.

But Mary was gone. There was no corn bread. Crackers would have to suffice.

He got out a pan and lit the stove. Even that reminded him of his wife. Of just after they had just gotten married and she had singed her eyebrows off because she had turned the gas up too high before lighting the match. It had scared him half to death at the time, but when they had looked back on the incident, they had laughed about it. He would give anything to be able to laugh with her about it just once more. Or to spend this last Christmas with her.

A sigh escaped him as he dumped some chili into the pan and set it on the burner. Puddles whined once more. She laid her chin on her paws and looked up at him with those innocent brown eyes. Her brows were wrinkled in doggy worry.

"I know, girl," he said. He needed to get himself together — if not for his own sake, then for that of his dog. Mary's dog.

He scratched the pooch on the top of her head, and once again her tail thumped against the floor.

"It's going to be all right," he told her. Though he wasn't sure he believed it himself. Christmas would come and Christmas would pass. Then the new year. February, then March. Time would move on, and folks assured him that with each passing day it would get easier. He wouldn't miss Mary quite so much. Wouldn't think about the things that could have been. How old the baby might be.

He even had people telling him that before long he would start thinking about getting married again. His eyes closed at the thought. He couldn't imagine. He and Mary had been a couple from the very first time he had seen her. He couldn't say it was love at first sight, but he had known even then that she was the one he would marry. They had immediately been best friends. Inseparable.

Until death do you part.

From that first moment on, she had been a part of him. He had felt it in his bones, his heart, his very skin. She was the one God had intended for him.

He wasn't sure he would ever feel that way about anyone ever again. But before he could even entertain the idea, he had to make it through Christmas.

And the new year.

February, then March.

Was she staying?

She wanted to, how she wanted to, but she never dreamed that coming home would be this hard. Or that Melvin really wouldn't follow her back.

Tillie stared up at the darkened ceiling. She had forgotten just how dark it was here in Pontotoc. In the city there were lights. Always lights. Even in a town the size of Columbus. It wasn't like they had gone to New York City, or even Jackson, but there always seemed to be some sort of light or another. Streetlights, car lights, porch lights, and the ever-present lights of the signs that tried their best to lure a person in to taste what they offered. Low prices, pizza, roast beef, cheap gasoline.

Tonight she found the darkness both comforting and disarming. She was comforted knowing that she was home, but a little shaken in thinking about staying. *How long are you staying?* they asked, as if they expected her to leave, and soon. She knew that without Melvin, she wouldn't be allowed to stay, but she had hoped . . . hoped that he would follow. Hoped that her family would toss the rules out the window. But she knew. It was only a matter of time before they were forced to adhere to the *Ordnung* or be shunned in the way they should be shunning her.

They couldn't keep it up for long. Perhaps they were biding their time until she left again. It was a ridiculous thought. They were her family. Of course they wanted her to stay. Even in her present state. But in the darkness the doubts still crept in.

Tomorrow was Sunday, and from all the talk at supper she knew that it was a church Sunday for their district. In the morning everyone would be stirring around and getting ready for the service. But tonight no one had asked her if she was going.

Leah had her own Mennonite church to attend with Jamie and Peter, but everyone else save Brandon and Shelly would be attending the Amish service. Did they expect her to go?

If she stayed — and part of her really wanted to — she would have to get back into the habit of Amish church. Well, it wasn't like she had been gone that long. She still knew what was expected of her. But she didn't want to go tomorrow.

Chicken.

Even in the darkness the word echoed inside her head. She was a chicken, no two ways about it. But she didn't want to face the entire district. Wasn't ready for it.

A quick check told her that the next church Sunday would be on Christmas Day. That didn't happen very often and was surely something she didn't want to miss, spending Christmas morning with all her family and friends celebrating Christ's birth. But tomorrow? That was too soon. She just needed a couple more days to come to terms with all that was her life now.

Was that too much to ask?

A soft knock sounded on her door. Before she could answer, light from a lantern filled the now open doorway.

"Who is it?" Tillie whispered into the darkness. She couldn't see who was behind the light, though she figured it was her *mamm*.

"Me," a hesitant voice said. "Libby."

Tillie awkwardly pushed herself up into a sitting position. It was perhaps the thing she hated most about being pregnant. Everything took so much effort. Then she remembered Gracie's serene face over supper. It seemed her cousin didn't suffer from such thoughts.

"I thought you went back to your house at night," she said.

Libby shrugged. "Not always. Dat thought

it would be good for me to spend more time with Mammi." She gave a little cough. "My *mammi,* not your *mammi.*"

Tillie smiled and patted the bed in front of her. "I understand."

Libby smiled gratefully and eased onto the bed near Tillie's feet. She was dressed in a nightgown, her long blond hair pulled back into a ponytail at the base of her neck, just the same as Tillie's was at that very moment. She may have gone to live English for a while, but she hadn't adopted all of their practices.

Once Tillie's eyes had adjusted to the light, she could see Libby's face much clearer. "Secretly, I think they just have their hands full with Joshua right now and they don't want me to know so much about it."

"What's wrong with Joshua?"

"Nothing. Just running around."

"But I thought —"

Tillie wasn't allowed to finish that sentence. Not that she had been certain what she was going to say. That she thought Joshua was a good son? If she said that, did it make her a bad daughter? Maybe *I thought Joshua was happy being Amish.* But hadn't she been before Melvin convinced her to go with him out into the world so he could repair English motors?

"Do you remember Benuel King?"

Tillie nodded. "Leah's old boyfriend."

"Right. Well, he married Abby."

"Our cousin, *jah*."

"Silas's father." She couldn't be certain in the darkness but she thought she saw Libby color. She did toss her ponytail over her shoulder.

"Jah," Tillie said, using the one word to urge her niece on.

"Bethie Ann's father."

"And Joshua likes Bethie Ann," Tillie asked, catching the connection between it all.

"Joshua likes Bethie Ann, but she likes Sam Yoder."

It didn't happen like that often in their district. They were small enough that there wasn't always a big choice in who a person might date. Yet it seemed Bethie Ann King wasn't plagued with such limitations. And she was using that to its full advantage.

"Acting the fool, is he?"

Libby sniffed. "I told him to just leave it be. If she wants to be with Sam, then what can he do about it?"

"Nothing."

"Then he told me that with thinking like that I'd never land Silas, and . . . that hurt my feelings."

"That doesn't sound like Joshua," Tillie said.

"He's changed a lot since you've been gone."

"I guess so," was all Tillie could say. As if Jim and Anna didn't have enough on them with six kids still all living at home.

"Anyway," Libby said, bouncing back from her melancholy like a rubber ball against the pavement. "I came to ask if you'll help me make Christmas candy this week."

Tillie blinked at the change in subject. "*Jah.* Sure."

"I'm not the best in the kitchen, and I don't want to ask Mammi."

"Why not? She's about the best cook around."

"*Jah,* but then she'll want to know why I want to make the candies and then —" She abruptly stopped.

"And then you'll have to tell her what?" Tillie urged.

"That I want to give them to Silas King as a Christmas present."

"You don't want to give him something at the singing tomorrow night?" The youth always held a singing on Sunday nights after the church service. Once a boy or a girl turned sixteen, they could attend. Tillie had

66

gone to many in her teenage years. It was where Melvin had first captured her attention.

Libby shook her head. "There's a card exchange next week. I thought I would give them to him then."

"Are you sure? I mean, if he leaves the card exchange with more than cards . . ."

"Everyone leaves the card exchange with more than cards. At least they did last year. Sarah Yoder gave him homemade Christmas cookies." She made a face.

"But they're not dating?"

"She's not a very good baker."

Tillie bit back a laugh. "Okay, then. Christmas candies next week. Maybe Thursday?"

Libby beamed. "*Danki*, Tillie. You're the best auntie in the whole world."

Tillie returned her smile. "I'll be sure to tell Leah and Hannah."

"You wouldn't!" Libby looked playfully horrified.

Tillie just shrugged.

Libby stood and gave Tillie a one-armed hug. "Thanks." She placed a kiss somewhere to the side of Tillie's ear, then she released her and started for the door.

"One more thing," she said once she got there. "Will you help me with my hair tomorrow? I want it to look extra good for the singing."

Tillie smiled and eased back down into the bed. "Of course."

"Really the best," Libby said.

"You know it," Tillie replied, then Libby was gone.

Tillie sighed into her pillow. She had needed that. She needed the distraction. She needed to know with everything going sideways in her life that there were other people with other problems. Those might not seem as big to her as her own. But they were important to the people they affected. Joshua, Libby, even Anna and Jim.

And somehow knowing this made her own problems seem a little more manageable.

Now if she only knew what she was going to do once Christmas passed.

CHAPTER FIVE

Church. It was the one and only thing that Levi couldn't avoid. It wasn't that he wanted to skip out on God. He simply wanted to get away from all the sad looks cast his way. All the pitying stares coupled with other people's obvious happiness over the upcoming holiday made him miss Mary all the more.

He didn't blame the others. It was all him. Therefore he should be the one taken out of the equation. He would be better off if he stayed at home. And he wondered how others felt when they spotted him. Did he ruin their holiday spirits? He supposed it was inevitable. He couldn't manage a smile. Hadn't been able to since they had placed his Mary and their child together in the ground. Everyone else would be better off if he stayed at home. They could talk about gift giving and parties, present exchanges and every other festive thing they had planned, without accidentally catching sight of his melancholy face. When he had said as much to Mims, she had told him that he was being melodramatic.

Maybe, but it was how he felt all the same.

He buttoned the last button on his vest and headed back to the kitchen. Puddles had gone outside for the morning. She hadn't given birth during the night. He was wondering if she was overdue to have the pups or if she was merely carrying a large litter. Only time would give the answer.

The clock above the sink told him he had fifteen more minutes before he had to leave. He didn't want to get to church any earlier than he had to. He was only going because it was expected of him. As far as he was concerned, he could stay in his rocking chair all morning, praying and reading the Bible, and get just as much connection with God as if he had ridden all the way over to Strawberry Dan's.

Dan Swartzentruber was the minister for their district and about the worst preacher Levi had ever heard. Not that he was trying to be mean, but he had such a hard time staying awake when Dan was delivering their Sunday message. It wasn't that the man had nothing important to say. He took his allotment as minister very seriously and studied his Bible every chance he got. As a result he knew the Lord's word forward and backward. He just wasn't a good speaker. With any luck though, Dan wouldn't be preaching today and Levi wouldn't have to worry about his mind wandering to places where it shouldn't go, which it seemed to do most of the time these days.

Once Christmas was over, he told himself. Surely things would settle down for him once Christmas was over.

He poured himself one last cup of coffee and leaned a hip against the sink. As he drank it, he looked out over the yard. He could just see the barn off to the right, his toolshed on the left, and the road just beyond the large tree that sat at the entrance of his property. Mims and Mary had planted it years ago, when he and Mary had first gotten married. The two women had decided that they needed a tree there for shade when they were trying to pull out onto the road, and it would block curious passersby from taking pictures or just gawking.

Opposite the tree was the little shed where Mary had sold pot holders and button necklaces to the English who happened by. She had also canned pie filling and pickled vegetables — okra, beets, and cucumbers. One wall of the shop had been reserved for

71

his smaller leather goods. Key chains embossed with every letter of the alphabet. They were always popular. Dog leashes, dog collars, and braided bracelets. The last one he had to get special permission to sell, but when the bishop saw that the bracelets were made from the scraps from other projects, he approved them since they represented a lack of waste. Their community was nothing if not frugal.

Levi took another sip of his coffee and let his gaze wander a bit more. Behind the shop and just between it and the barn was his leather shop. It was almost as big as his barn, since he had to have room to hang leather that he was dying or stretching. He also had to have plenty of room for saddles. He did saddle refurbishing and repair for the English and Amish alike. Though truth be told, not many Amish owned a saddle. When they wanted to ride a horse, most Amish kids simply grabbed a handful of mane, hoisted themselves up, and rode bareback.

His coffee had cooled and his fifteen minutes were up. If he didn't leave now, he would be late. Just on time was okay, but late not at all. Levi poured the coffee down the sink and set the mug upside down inside it. He'd wash it when he got back home.

72

He made sure all the lanterns were extinguished — a habit, really. He hadn't lit any when he got up, but Mary had always done the same. Maybe it made him feel closer to her to perform her rituals. Or maybe he was avoiding the inevitable as long as possible. Coat, hat, and he was ready to go. As ready as he could be, anyway.

His horse was hitched to his buggy and tied to the post. She stood, ready and waiting for him to come out of the house. Levi shut the door behind him. The mare snorted and stamped her foot as Levi approached. Her breath was steamy in the cold December morning.

Church today. Then two weeks of quiet and solitude — Mims and well-wishers aside — and it would be Christmas. As unusual as it was, Christmas fell not only on a Sunday, but on a church Sunday. Maybe it was for the best. He would have to go unless he fell ill, but at least he wouldn't have to spend Christmas morning with his folks and his sister thinking about how much he missed Mary and how, if ever, he was going to heal from the heartache.

"You're not dressed."

At her *mamm*'s words, Tillie looked down at herself. She was dressed in perfectly ac-

73

ceptable clothing. For the English world, that was. She had on a long skirt, boots, and a sweater that may have molded a little too closely to her belly, but finding modest English clothes was a chore at best. Trying to find modest English clothes when you were pregnant was almost impossible. It seemed that English women were proud of their growing bellies and liked to wear clinging shirts and dresses to show them off.

"You're not dressed for church," Mamm corrected before Tillie could say a word.

"Church," she murmured. She wasn't dressed for church because she wasn't going. Her arrival in town had caused enough of a stir, she surely didn't want to shock everyone out of their shoes by showing up at church. But how did she tell Mamm that?

"I don't have a dress." Relief washed over her. She couldn't go to church without a proper dress. And even though Amish dresses were pinned in order to give a woman a little more room, one of her old dresses surely wouldn't be big enough to accommodate her large belly.

Mamm seemed almost resigned as she looked her up and down. Then she snapped her fingers, her face lighting up like the sun. "I know. Anna."

Tillie inwardly groaned. Her sister-in-law.

74

Jim's wife. It had been a few years since she'd had a baby, but she was still in those years and surely she wouldn't have gotten rid of maternity dresses.

Before Tillie could protest — not that it would have done any good — Mamm bustled out the door and over to her brother's house.

It only took a few minutes for her mother to run to Anna's and come back with a beautiful purple dress. Only a few minutes, but long enough that Tillie knew there was no getting out of church.

She sighed a bit as Mamm handed her the dress. Then shook out the white cape and apron for her to put on next. "Let me know if you need help pinning it over your middle."

Tillie nodded.

"Breakfast in ten." Her mother smiled and Tillie stopped obsessing over what everyone was going to say at church. Going was making her *mamm* happy, and that's all that mattered. Though she did worry just a bit.

She took the borrowed clothing back into her bedroom and started to undress. Christmas was two weeks away exactly, which meant that after this morning, the next service would happen on Christmas. And as much as she dreaded going today, she was sort of looking forward to church on Christmas Day. In her entire life she never remembered that happening. Church and Christmas and all her family there. All but Leah, Jamie, and Peter. It was good for them, but a little sad to Tillie that her sister had joined the Mennonite church. She had such fond memories of sitting next to her, sometimes between Leah and Hannah, sometimes not, as they waited for church to be over. At the time they were old enough to know that they needed to be paying attention, and they did their best, but three hours was a long time even if it was broken up with songs and prayer.

The soft purple dress slipped easily over her head and adequately covered her midsection. The fabric smoothed over her like a caress, like the touch of an old friend, even though she had never worn this particular dress before. But being back in Amish clothes felt good, proper. As if she had made the right decision by coming back. Even if she couldn't stay.

To say it hadn't been easy to walk away and leave the new life that she had built with Melvin behind was an understatement. Yet as hard as that was, she knew English life wasn't for her. Returning in shame hadn't been a cakewalk either. But she was here now. And going to church. She just wished Melvin was here too.

She pulled her hair down from its simple bob and refixed it into the style she had worn for most of her life. Then she pinned her prayer *kapp* into place. Slipped into a pair of thick black stockings. Her church shoes were in the closet where she had left them. She put them on when instead she really wanted to wear her black lace-up boots. They were much more comfortable. Or maybe it was an act of rebellion.

Once her outfit was complete, she turned in front of the mirror to view herself from every angle. Anyone who hadn't heard the news that she had returned was going to be in for a big surprise. The thought made her giggle, though it shouldn't have. There would be those who would say that they always knew she was going to end up with a shamed life. That running around with Melvin Yoder had been her first mistake. Let them talk. She was here now, doing her best to make amends. No one could fault her for that.

A light knock sounded on the door just a moment before her mother peeked her head inside. "All set?"

Was she? *"Jah,"* Tillie said, though she wasn't entirely convinced that she was telling the truth. She needed to be all set. This was going to be her life from here on out. With any luck though, most people would be too busy during the meal after church talking about Christmas and all the things they had planned to notice Tillie Gingerich and her new, altered state.

That would never happen.

But the thought was nice.

Her mother slipped a hand around her shoulders and pulled her into a one-armed hug. Tillie met her mother's gaze in the mirror's reflection.

"I'm sorry," she said, tears stinging her eyes. "I never meant to cause you shame."

Mamm kissed her high on the forehead. "Hush that. You may have made mistakes, but once you ask for forgiveness then all will be forgiven."

But not forgotten. Never truly forgotten.

And without Melvin . . .

"Jah," Tillie managed. She wasn't sure what else to say. Without Melvin at her side she wouldn't be allowed to remain. What did she think was going to happen? That she would ask forgiveness and then be allowed to raise her child, the only single mother among the Pontotoc Amish? Single and never widowed. Even if by some chance that happened, she would be permanently

shamed. She knew. Parents would point at her and warn their children about the perils of the English world.

No. She just needed Melvin to care enough to come after her.

And stay.

It seemed like with all the trials she faced her plan would be a little more involved. But God had a plan. That much she could be sure about. What that plan could be was a different matter altogether.

Levi shifted in his seat and tried not to appear too uncomfortable. But at times like this all he could think about was being back at home. It shamed him to think that he couldn't stay among his friends without wanting to escape. He wondered when those feelings would end.

Strawberry Dan droned on and on about the dangers of the world and the decisions and the mistakes that people made.

Levi did his best to absorb God's word, but it felt like the sentences were flying over his head, missing him entirely. It was a fanciful notion, but it seemed that's where he spent most of his time, in those crazy thoughts that sometimes had him worrying about his own self. Time, everyone said. He needed time to adjust, to mourn, to come to terms with everything and all the changes that had happened in his life. It would be better after the holidays, better once Christmas had passed. Better when there was more time between now and the tragedy. But time always seemed to drag on more slowly each day, each hour, each minute. Or maybe he was just tired.

He hadn't slept well in weeks, months. Not since Mary had stood up from the rocking chair on their front porch and collapsed into his arms. She hadn't spoken, just looked up at him with those crystal blue eyes of hers as the life seeped out of her.

Tears stung his eyes. He blinked them back, ashamed that he had allowed his mind to wander so much during church. He was supposed to be receiving God's word, and every time he came to church he prayed for understanding. Still it hadn't come.

And Strawberry Dan continued to talk about the dangers outside their community.

Levi had never been tempted by the English world, never thought once about it. Maybe because he had Mary. But even now he had no desire to leave, though today could be the perfect day to preach on the subject.

It wasn't often, but times did arrive when the sermon didn't quite pertain to him. And it made it harder to sit and listen and be patient and not just walk out. An unforgivable thing to do.

That seemed to be where he lived these days. On the line between acceptable and not acceptable. He supposed he still had his reasons. It had only been two months since he lost Mary and the baby. But that two months would soon be three and then four and then enough time that any transgressions that he had, any eccentric behavior that he displayed, would not be as easily forgiven.

He shifted in his seat and let his gaze wander across the room to where the ladies sat. He had always found it a bit of a distraction to sit opposite the women of the district. Or maybe it was just sitting opposite Mary. He would look over and see her, and she was always enthralled by what was being said. Or maybe she was merely obliged to be interested. Then, as if she knew he was looking at her, she would turn to him. She would give him a little smile. He would smile back. Then she would look away, look down at her lap, lean a little closer to her mother, and the moment would be broken.

His gaze stopped at the spot where Mary used to sit. Tillie Gingerich. He knew her, sort of. Though he almost didn't recognize her. She was David Gingerich's younger sister. He and David were good friends, or they had been before Levi had married. David had never married, and consequently they no longer hung with the same crowd. Was it easier never to have loved at all? And he wondered why David had never married. It was much easier to think about that than his own troubles. David had always been a little slow. Levi thought he had some trouble reading, but he was a good man with a good heart. He had his own land, worked with his father and brother at the shed company, and otherwise had a good and godly life. Levi had never understood why David remained a bachelor. Maybe he hadn't found the girl for him. Or maybe he wanted to avoid the chance at the heartache that was now Levi's very existence.

But this was Tillie. He didn't know her that well. As well as he knew anyone in Pontotoc. It was a small community. He knew she was the youngest of the children. She ran with Melvin Yoder, no relation to him that anyone could remember, and a few months back, he couldn't remember when, she had run off with Melvin so he could build engines and fix cars in the English world. If she was back, Levi supposed that hadn't worked out so well. But he hadn't seen Melvin. Not that it mattered.

Melvin had always liked to fix engines. Some of the gas-powered engines that they were allowed to use. But in their conservative community there weren't many. A man couldn't make a living out of repairing engines alone. Even Levi couldn't make a living out of just leatherwork. He still farmed peanuts and soybeans. He didn't have a big crop; just enough to keep his family going. It was the way with most of the Amish in the area. They had their little shops, farming, a special trade like leatherwork or furniture making. All those things together made for a successful farm. Levi shifted his gaze to the men in front of him. He was seated in about the middle, so there were just as many behind him as in front, but he didn't see Melvin Yoder among those before him. He could just as easily be behind, or still back in the English world. Levi wondered.

It wasn't that it mattered, but thinking about other people kept his mind off his own problems.

His gaze wandered back toward Tillie Gingerich. He wasn't sure why she drew his attention again, but there she was. As if sensing his stare, she looked to him. Her hazel eyes were questioning. She didn't smile like his Mary would've done. She merely looked away. The moment was further broken when they were asked to stand, kneel, and pray.

It was the last prayer before they were dismissed. It was cool outside, so everyone would meet in the barn to have their after-church meal, not that Levi was staying. He was headed out just as soon as the crowd started milling around.

Time, that was what he needed. Time. And to leave as soon as he could. With any luck he could scoot away when everyone was talking and milling around before they ate and no one would miss him. Not even Mims.

That wasn't true. He had other family that would wonder where he had disappeared to — a grandfather, a father, and a mother. And there wasn't much at all his sister missed.

"Where do you think you're going?"

Levi stopped and closed his eyes, then he turned to face Mims. "I'm going to get my horse." He should leave it at that, get his horse, hitch her to the buggy, and get out of there while he still could. But he couldn't handle the disappointment in Mims's eyes. He loved his sister; he didn't want her saddened. Even if it meant he was having a tougher time than she.

"You can't keep running away, Levi. The people here care about you."

He knew that. They cared, and some cared almost too much. It was him, that was the problem. He got upset with people who didn't talk about Mary. He got upset if he thought they talked about Mary too much. He got upset when people told him that grieving took time, and he got upset when people told him that soon it would be time to move on. That it would be time for him to find his way. And he couldn't do it in the shadow of conflicting advice, conflicting looks, and his own conflicting thoughts.

Levi sighed. And Mims smiled. She knew she had him.

"Let me get you a cup of coffee," she said. She reached out a hand to him.

Levi started toward her. "One cup of coffee," he said.

"And a plate of food," she added.

"One cup of coffee, one serving of cup cheese with pretzels. Then I'm out of here."

Mims slipped her arm through his. "One cup of coffee, one peanut butter sandwich with cup cheese, and a slice of cherry pie."

"Cherry pie?" No one brought cherry pie to church; only snitz pie.

"At Mamm's." She smiled and patted his

arm. "You can't hide out forever."

Great, he thought. Except that hiding out was exactly what he wanted to do.

CHAPTER SIX

Tillie stood in the yard, her coat wrapped as tightly around her as she could make it. She crossed her arms over her middle, like that hid anything. But at least it made her feel a little better, as crazy as that thought was.

"What are you doing way over here?" Hannah.

Tillie turned to her sister. "Just waiting."

"If you've got to be outside and not in the barn, you should at least get close to one of the heaters."

The day was sunny, bright, and clear, but there was a hard chill in the air. A few brave souls had spilled out into the yard, but most of them were collected around the gas heaters on the hardpacked drive. Huddling around a heater meant huddling around with people, and Tillie just wasn't up for that. Not yet. And she had no idea when she would feel differently.

Hannah scooted in close to her sister. "Did you get something to eat?"

Tillie nodded. She had eaten a little. And only to say that she ate something. But being among all the friends, family, and church members with all their watching eyes took her appetite away. Maybe when she got home . . .

"Not much changes here," Tillie mused.

Hannah glanced around the yard, then back to Tillie. "Nope. Not much at all."

"Except for you and Aaron."

Hannah gave a knowing smile and small shrug. "I guess."

It was a big change. Hannah had left the Amish when she was eighteen or twenty — Tillie couldn't remember — and she hadn't come back until just a couple of years ago, bringing with her an English son, Brandon. As if that wasn't enough shock for the community, Aaron discovered that he was Brandon's father and not Mitch, Hannah's English husband. Mitch had died, leaving Hannah and Brandon in serious debt and without any means to pay it off. And then she had been faced with an angry Aaron who had missed the last fifteen years of his son's life. But it all worked out for the best, Tillie supposed. Even with anger and hurt feelings, they managed to pull themselves together and become a family. Aaron's wife Lizzie had gone to her reward a year or so before, leaving behind three girls and a boy who needed a mother as much as Hannah needed a reason to come back home.

"And Leah and Jamie." Hannah smiled.

"Don't forget Peter," Tillie added. She resisted the urge to cup her belly. It was an instinctive motion meant to protect, but all it would do in the yard full of all these people — friends, churchgoers, and family — was point out that her belly was huge, that she had sinned, that she was ashamed, and all the other things that she didn't want to attract attention to.

"So is this where the party is?" Gracie waddled up.

Tillie had never seen her cousin happier. In her arms she carried baby Grace, her youngest child. Tillie had already heard the story of how Grace had been increasingly unhappy until Gracie came and took over as her mother. Though she didn't know all the tragic events — or rather, all the details of the tragic events — surrounding Matthew's wife's death, she had heard enough to know that it was indeed a tragedy. Yet it was one thing that no one seemed to discuss. Kind of like Tillie and the baby she carried now.

"We're talking about how not much changes here."

Gracie looked around. "I don't know about that. I think a lot of things have changed."

Hannah shrugged. "I guess. But it seems there are some things that don't ever change." She nodded her head toward Nancy B, who had dragged the minister, Strawberry Dan, away from the warmth of the heater he had been standing by and over to a private spot just south of the barn. Nancy B had never married; never even pretended she wanted to. And Strawberry Dan felt that all women needed to be married, that all family needed to be made. It was something he preached about often and something that Nancy B felt just as passionate about, though on the opposite side.

Tillie couldn't help herself; she chuckled at the pair. It was a common sight to see them talking after church. Nancy B usually had something to say about the sermon, and not always something complimentary. It was true what they said when it came to Nancy B — being selected a church leader was just as much of a curse as a blessing. Or at least it had been for Strawberry Dan.

"And then Levi Yoder," Hannah said with a sad shake of her head.

90

Levi Yoder. She'd seen him in church. He had been staring at her. Or maybe not. He'd simply been looking, and she caught him and then looked away. She figured that like everyone else in the district, he was assessing her, wondering why she came back, pregnant and unwed and with all the other horrible, shameful things that had happened. Things that she would ask forgiveness for, but things that would never be forgotten.

"What about Levi Yoder?" It was so much easier to focus on someone else's problems than her own.

"His wife Mary died a couple of months ago," Gracie said with a shake of her head. "It was tragic."

"What happened?"

"Aneurysm," Hannah supplied. "She was pregnant at the time."

"And the baby?" He wasn't holding a child in church, but it could've just as easily been with his sister or his mother, or even Mary's parents.

Gracie just shook her head.

Tillie gasped.

"I shouldn't have brought it up," Hannah said.

Tillie shook her head. "No, I'm glad you told me." Maybe that was why he was looking at her in church. He must've seen her before, must've heard about her situation. Though she was certain he didn't understand the twist of it all. Mary and Levi were married and had their baby taken from them. And she was taken from her husband. Here Tillie was, unwed and on her own, and her baby was just fine. Was God playing tricks on them all? Unwed or not, she wanted this baby with all her heart.

Lord, please forgive me my uncharitable thoughts toward You and Your plans for us. Amen.

She wasn't trying to be testy, but the hormones had been getting the better of her for some time. In fact, she was starting to wonder if they might have been the cause of some of the problems between her and Melvin. But that might be oversimplifying it. She had wanted to come home. She wanted to spend Christmas with her family. No matter how much time she spent with the English, Amish country would always be home.

But already, she had grown weary. She was tired of being there, tired of being at church, tired of being watched, tired of everyone wondering, of them whispering when they thought she couldn't see them or hear them. As much as she wanted to be home, she didn't belong there. Not now. Would she ever again?

It took some doing, but Levi finally managed to give his sister the slip and headed home. He had done what she wanted, gotten some food, but he was not committing himself to going to his parents' house today, sitting around, eating pie, drinking coffee, and acting like everything was just the way it should be. It wasn't. Things were wrong, terribly wrong, and he hadn't come to terms with it yet. His mom would want to make Christmas candy and cookies and cakes and the like to share with neighbors and anyone who happened to stop by. Just the smell of cinnamon made him think of Christmas. And ginger from the gingerbread and all the other traditions and smells that went along with the holiday. No, he'd much rather go home and hide from all those familiar, heart-wrenching things, and pretend Christmas wasn't just two weeks away and his Mary wasn't gone.

But he knew Mims would never let him get away with that. He had no sooner gotten his horse brushed down and back in the stall before Mims pulled up in her own buggy.

"Levi Anderson Yoder," she called as she

hopped down from her buggy. She hobbled her horse and marched toward him. "Why did you just leave like that?"

Levi shrugged. "Because I wanted to." But he knew it was an excuse Mims would never accept.

"You worried Mamm and Dat and even Dawdi."

Levi shook his head. "I didn't mean to worry anyone. Everyone should know by now, I just need time."

"We know that. But you also need things to go back to normal."

Nothing would ever be normal again. Levi hooked one arm over his shoulder and motioned his sister to come into the house. He didn't wait for her response, simply trudged up the porch through the front door. Of course, she was right behind him. She looked around at his house. The house he was supposed to share with Mary. Had shared with Mary for many years.

"Where's Puddles?"

"Kitchen," he said.

She gave him a sigh and an exasperated look. "You know, you could speak in complete sentences."

Jah, he could. But some things just seemed to take too much effort these days. Not that Mims would understand any of that. His sister was bossy to the core.

Without waiting for an invitation, or even asking for one, Mims marched toward the kitchen.

She returned a few moments later. "Nope, no puppies yet."

Levi gave her a cunning look. "You gonna take one?"

Mims's eyes opened wide. "Am I going to take one? Where am I going to put a dog?"

"In the barn like everyone else."

Mims laughed. "Your dog is in the kitchen."

He grunted. "*Jah,* well, it's cold outside." And it was Mary's dog, named Puddles because when she was a puppy that's what she made every time a person greeted her. Little puddles on the floor. Thankfully she had outgrown the habit; just not the name.

"If I don't take one, I suppose you're going to want me to help you get rid of them."

"What are sisters for?" He ambled into the kitchen, knowing that Mims would follow.

"You want me to make some coffee?" Mims asked.

And if she stayed for coffee, she might not leave till almost dark. Did he really want company? On the other hand, could he really chase his sister away? Other than

95

Mary and perhaps even David Gingerich, Mims was his best friend. But he and David had fallen out of touch years ago, and Mary was gone. Mims was all he had right now.

He adored his sister. Not that he would ever tell her that. They'd gotten closer after their brother Daniel had died. It was a freak accident where he had been trampled by a bull in the pasture. They'd been trying to cut the beast from the herd. But something about Daniel had angered the bull, and he charged.

It was a terrible death, but understandable, obvious. He could see Daniel's injuries, the blood, broken bones. But Mary's death had been so different. She hadn't had a mark on her. Maybe that's what made it so hard to take.

"You have cookies?" Mims asked. "Did you make me any cookies?"

"You know, I'm not going to do this forever, right? Come over here and make sure you got enough to eat and that you're eating it? You'll have to do this on your own soon." But he knew she was all talk. And she was right — he should do this for himself. He couldn't rely on his family forever.

"Just give me until Christmas." *Or maybe the New Year,* he silently added. He knew.

96

He knew one day he wouldn't feel quite the same heartache and loneliness like he felt then, but he couldn't say when that time would be.

Mims started the coffee and began opening the cabinets one by one. Upper for flour and sugar, lower for the mixing bowls and cookie sheets, then into the icebox for butter.

"What are you doing?"

"Speaking of Christmas," Mims started, "are you going to decorate any at all?" She didn't say as much, but he understood the unspoken *You know Mary would've at least put up some pine boughs on the fireplace mantel. Nothing like fresh pine and a few sprigs of holly to put a person in the holiday spirit.* "Making cookies."

Levi sucked in a breath; this was Mims. Busy, nosy, bossy, busybody, sweetheart. "I'm not going to decorate for Christmas. And isn't making cookies a little much like work for a Sunday?"

She already had half the ingredients dumped in the mixing bowl when she turned around and gave him a sly grin. "I won't tell if you won't tell. And wouldn't you like to have some snickerdoodles this afternoon?"

And there was the cinnamon. He might

be able to handle the sentiment, but pine boughs and cinnamon would definitely do him in. No, he wanted to pretend that Christmas wasn't coming.

"Snickerdoodles sound wonderful," he said. It was the truth and a lie all at the same time, but he wouldn't hurt Mims for anything.

She continued to smile as she turned back around and attended the dough she was mixing.

"Remember that time that you and I went to the woods to get some mistletoe?" She laughed a bit at the end.

Levi couldn't help but chuckle a little himself. "Mamm was so mad."

"She thought you were going to use it to try to kiss people in town."

He shook his head. "Wonder why she would think that?"

Mims shot him an innocent smile. "I have no idea." Just like that, he once again knew his sister had set him up.

CHAPTER SEVEN

Maybe if she found herself a husband . . . But since Mims was approaching thirty, he might have to find one for her.

Levi watched as his sister flitted around the kitchen. When snickerdoodles weren't enough, she started on chili and a pot of stew.

"You don't have to do this, you know," he said. "I have enough food for the week in the icebox already."

She waved away his protest and continued to stir the two bubbling pots on the stove. She tapped the handle of the wooden spoon against the rim and laid it across the top. Then she grabbed a pot holder and peeked at the cookies inside the oven. "I can't have my only brother starving to death."

Levi shook his head. "That's hardly going to happen."

Mims pulled the tray of cookies from the oven and set them on the hot pad waiting on the counter. Even with as much of a pang of nostalgia as the aroma of the cookies gave him, he had to admit they smelled delicious. The hardest part about snickerdoodles was waiting until they were cool enough to eat. "They're calling for storms, you know."

He had heard some talk of the matter at church but hadn't paid it much mind. Some men chose the color of their shirt depending on which way the wind was blowing. He wasn't one of those. He kept up just enough to keep his soybeans and peanuts growing. Other than that, the weather was up to God.

"That's what they say," he said.

"Well, if it storms, I won't be able to get out here to feed you. And then you *will* starve to death."

He shot his sister a look. "I'm a grown man, and I can get myself something to eat when necessary."

She shot him a cloying smile. "Of course you can." Her voice was syrupy sweet. "I'm just trying to make it a little easier for you."

Levi sighed. It was an argument he wasn't going to win. In fact, not many arguments with Mims were won by the other party.

"I just love you, you know." She had the cookies served up on a plate and at his side. The playfulness was gone from her tone,

and in its place, a look of worry and concern.

"I know." He touched her hand. "I love
you too. And I do appreciate all that you're
trying to do for me. But it's too much." Too
much on a lot of levels. Too much for one
person to take on, too much traveling back
and forth between her house and his, and
too much time that forced him to spend
with others.

The sparkle returned to her blue eyes.
"It's not enough," she said. "Now eat up."

Mims three, Levi zero.

She made it. Tillie bit back her heavy sigh
as her father pulled the buggy down the
drive. Behind her she could hear Hannah
and Aaron in their buggy. Gracie and Matthew had opted to go home. Henry was in
trouble again, but as far as Tillie could tell
it wasn't anything unusual. He seemed to
be something of a stinker. But she loved his
mischievous smile and the ornery twinkle in
his eyes. Maybe because it reminded her a
little of Melvin. He had never quite fit in
either. And truth be known, she had never
wanted to leave. She only left for him, and
a lot of good it did her.

"We should do something Christmassy,"
Hannah said.

"Like what?"

Hannah shrugged. "How about making Christmas cards? We used to always do that."

"Christmas cards?" Tillie asked.

Everyone had climbed down from the buggy. The women headed toward the house as the men took care of the horses. They would be a while, Tillie knew. Most men in their district liked to take time to talk about the weather and other things. A lot like she'd seen English men do — not so much in Columbus, but in Pontotoc, in town on Main Street. Sometimes right outside Leah's store.

She nodded. "We can get the kids to help," Hannah said. "Then we can take them over to the nursing home, or even the veterans' hospital. They always love things like that this time of year."

That was true. She knew there were a lot of people who didn't take the time to make cards or go visit or anything like that. "Do you have a visit planned?" Tillie asked. A lot of times youth groups and buddy bunches would plan the event, then take the cards to the designated place on a certain day. The lucky recipients got the cards, Christmas cheer, and an unexpected visit all in one.

"No," Hannah said. "I thought it might

be fun for the kids."

Essie, Aaron's eight-year-old daughter, jumped up and down in place. "I want to color cards. I want to color cards."

Laura Kate, the oldest of the Zook girls and by far the most serious, gave her sister a reprimanding look. "We all want to color cards, and see? We don't have to yell about it."

"Do I have to?" Andy was fifteen now and way too grown up to do something as silly as color cards for another person. That is, unless there was a girl his age involved. Then he might want to.

Hannah smiled at her son. "Not if you don't want to, but I have a feeling that when Brandon and Shelly get here, they'll color cards with us."

Andy idolized Brandon. Tillie was certain he was probably about the coolest thing Andy had ever seen. Brandon had been raised English, drove a car, had a girlfriend he still claimed wasn't his girlfriend, and went to school on the computers in the public library in town. She was certain that to Andy, Brandon's life was about as interesting as could be.

When Hannah had come back to Pontotoc, she rejoined the Amish church and married Aaron, and Brandon had moved in with Leah. Now he lived with Leah, Jamie, and Peter in a little house near town. He helped out Leah in her shop — he and his not-girlfriend Shelly, that is. There was an apartment above the shop that was now empty, but Tillie figured once Brandon graduated from high school, he would move into the apartment himself. He was independent that way, like a lot of English kids. And she had to admit he took his mother's return to her religion fairly well, though she had a feeling he was still dealing with the fact of learning that Aaron, not Mitchell McLean, was his father.

"If you say so," Andy said and headed for the kitchen.

"I'll get all the things," Tillie said.

Mamm helped Mammi into her room and got her settled down with a puzzle book and a cup of tea while Hannah gathered the girls plus Andy around the table.

"Mom?" Brandon yelled.

"In here," Hannah called.

A moment later Brandon and Shelly appeared in the dining room doorway.

Hannah immediately went over to hug her son. Tillie could only imagine how hard it was for Hannah to give up Brandon so she could follow her convictions and marry Brandon's real father. Hannah and Brandon seemed to have a special bond. Maybe it was just everything they had gone through after Mitch's death, but Leah adored Brandon almost as much as his mother did, and Tillie was sure that it was a comfort to her sister to know that her son was well taken care of.

Hannah squeezed Brandon tight, then gave a quick hug to Shelly as well.

"What are y'all doing?" Brandon glanced around at the supplies Tillie had placed on the table. There were Christmas stickers of all sorts, some glittery, some puffy. Most were snowmen and wreaths made from sprigs of holly, but she noticed that a few sheets had Santa Claus faces on them. But they were giving the cards to people who perhaps had once believed in Santa, so what was the harm in that? She wasn't sure the bishop would see it that way, but it was done now. Kind of like the baby she carried.

Then not at all.

"Your mother wanted to do something Christmassy," Tillie said. "Then she came up with the idea of making Christmas cards to take to the veterans' hospital or the nursing home."

Brandon clapped his hands together and rubbed them in anticipation. "I love making

Christmas cards." Definitely not something Tillie would've expected him to say before he met Shelly, but he was a smart boy in doing things his girlfriend liked even though she wasn't his girlfriend.

Hannah shot Andy an *I told you so* look.

He shrugged and pulled out a chair, plopping down next to Laura Kate.

Once everyone was settled around the table with markers and colors and glitter glue and stickers and everything else they had available to create Christmas cards in order to make someone's holiday a little brighter, she felt the baby kick. It wasn't an unusual phenomenon. She had heard that being up and about rocked the baby to sleep, so babies tended to be less active when the mom was active. Now that she was sitting still, he, or she, woke up and demanded a little attention of her own. Tillie rubbed her belly to soothe the child.

"Everything all right?" Hannah shot her a sharp look.

Then of course all eyes turned to her.

"I'm fine," Tillie said.

"So when are you going to have that baby?" Essie asked without even taking her eyes off her picture. She colored with focused intent, her tongue sticking out one side of her mouth.

"Esther Zook, that is not a polite thing to ask someone." Hannah turned a stern look toward her youngest.

Essie stopped coloring and looked up. Her gaze traveled from Hannah to Tillie and back to Hannah again. "If I don't ask, how am I supposed to know?"

Hannah pressed her lips together, to keep from laughing Tillie was sure. That was Essie, something of a pistol. "You don't always need to know. We don't talk about such things." At least not mixed company. Women talked a little, but not much. And definitely not like the English women did at the day care center where Tillie had worked.

"If you say so," Essie said, clearly not convinced.

"I say so," Hannah said.

Everyone continued coloring their pictures, drawing holly and candles. Brandon and Shelly even drew Christmas trees with ornaments on theirs.

"When you're done with that," Mamm said from the doorway, "you can go out into the woods and pick some pine boughs to decorate the mantel."

Shelly nodded enthusiastically. "It's a good day for that."

"They're calling for storms," Brandon said.

Hannah shook her head. "They always say that and then it blows over. I'll believe there's snow when I see the snow." But they all knew snow in Mississippi was a rare thing, especially this early in the year. They were more apt to get ice than snow, and having an icy Christmas just wasn't the same.

The baby kicked again and Tillie decided it was time to walk around a bit. She wasn't sure if the baby didn't like her being still or if she was enjoying the time of playing imaginary kickball when Tillie sat down.

"Finished?" Hannah asked.

"Jah."

Hannah stood as well. "Okay, everybody finish up, and then we'll find a snack."

Essie clapped her hands. "I like snacks."

Tillie bit back a smile as she ducked into the kitchen. Essie was the kind of kid who liked everything.

"Did you see Levi Yoder today?" Mamm asked.

"Jah," Hannah said as Tillie nodded.

Mamm pressed her lips together and shook her head sadly. "He's having a hard time."

Hannah nodded. "I know what it's like to lose a spouse, but Mitch and I had grown apart before he died. So it's not quite the same."

"*Jah,*" Mamm added. "He looks thinner every time I see him."

Tillie rubbed her belly while the baby's kicks subsided.

"I know for a fact Mims goes over there every other day or so," Hannah said.

"She's a good sister," Mamm said.

"I've offered to help, but she says she has it all under control," Hannah said.

"I guess these things just take time," Mamm said.

Time. Everything needed time. Time to heal. Time to grow. Time to mourn. Time to change. It was all about time. And for some reason, since it was Christmas, it seemed to go by slower, each day a little harder than the one before. If time was so valuable, shouldn't its passage make the loss or even the change easier? But Tillie didn't ask her sister or her *mamm.* It wasn't a question that truly needed an answer. It merely was. And she certainly didn't want them to know her own struggles. As Mammi would say, she made her bed; now she had to lie in it.

Levi Yoder needed time. Tillie needed time. She supposed they all needed time at some point or another. But today, seeing all the looks, the people who shook their heads not knowing that she saw, the people who didn't care that she knew they disapproved — altogether it made her wonder if she would be able to make it through this transition. Times like this morning at church made her wonder if there was enough time at all to get back in the good graces of the Amish in Pontotoc.

The combined scents of pinecones and vanilla would forever be Christmas for her. Tillie lit the fat white candles her mother put aside for Christmas each year. To Tillie they smelled heavenly, like home. Times like these she could close her eyes and imagine that everything was just as it should be, even though it wasn't. Or maybe it was. That was the hardest part of all for her to understand. Were her sin and shame part of God's plan? Would God plan something like that? How was she supposed to know? And who was she to ask? If she went to the bishop, it would appear that she was being manipulative, twisting things to suit her own purpose. And that surely wasn't what she wanted. No, what she wanted was direction. And despite daily prayers, she had none. She was merely floating, getting through to Christmas and then on to the new year. Who knew what would happen after that? Well, she would have the baby. And if she were to stay in Pontotoc, she would have to marry Melvin and join the church. Her transgressions were definitely new to their community. No one just left, got pregnant, and came back unmarried, even for a short while.

Sudden tears pricked her eyes. They were sharp and fell before she had a chance to blink them back.

"What's wrong?" Of course Mamm was behind her. Eunice Gingerich had a talent for knowing just when one of her kids needed her, whether they wanted her there or not.

"I was just thinking about Levi Yoder." Now where had that come from? Thinking about Levi Yoder was a sight easier than thinking about her own problems. But that didn't mean she had really been thinking about him. So why had his name popped onto her lips so easily? "I was just wondering if he had any Christmas decorations up."

It might've been the most ridiculous thing she had ever said. Why would Levi have up Christmas decorations? He lost his wife two months ago. His wife and his baby. Tillie was certain he dreaded Christmas almost as much as she did.

It wasn't Christmas so much that plagued her, but the story of Mary having a baby, being a virgin. Joseph willing to raise that child. Having to travel so close to her due date, giving birth in the barn. Somehow Tillie felt more kin to Mary than she ever had. And yet she had never felt further from God.

"I suppose if he has any Christmas decorations it's because Mims has gone over and put them up for him."

"Jah," she said. "I suppose you're right."

"Why all the worry about Levi?" Mamm asked.

Tillie only shrugged. "I don't know. Just you guys talking, I guess."

"I suppose it wouldn't be a terrible idea if you wanted to ride out there tomorrow and see if he has Christmas decorations or needs something done in the house."

"We could, yes." The thought of helping Levi Yoder, of maybe cleaning his house, putting up some Christmas decorations, doing their best to add cheer to the place, somehow that made her feel a little better. Like she was indeed going to be able to come back into the community, be a part of it, be accepted. If nothing else, perhaps it was just a bit of atonement that she needed.

Mamm nodded and smiled. "It's settled,

then. First thing tomorrow morning right after breakfast we'll head over to Levi Yoder's and help out a neighbor."

Tillie returned her smile. "It's a deal." A wave of warmth washed over her. Christmas spirit? Or merely the thought of doing something good after all the shame she had brought her family?

Or perhaps because of the shame he wouldn't want her within ten feet of him. The thought was sobering, and she remembered his stare from earlier in church. She had no idea what was going on behind his eyes as he stared at her. She wasn't even sure why he was looking at her with a room full of other faces to view.

CHAPTER EIGHT

"How long do you think it'll be before the bishop comes to visit?" Tillie asked.

As decided on Sunday they had headed out to Levi Yoder's house first thing Monday morning after breakfast. Libby had begged to go with them, but Mamm had insisted she stay behind in case Mammi Glick needed anything.

"When do you think the bishop's coming?"

"I wish I knew. I thought he would have been here before now, but . . ." She trailed off with a small shrug.

They both knew that the bishop would be knocking on their door one day soon to get things straightened out. A woman couldn't just come back pregnant and expect everything to fall in line. The only holdup, as far as Tillie could see, was Christmas. Either the bishop was trying to be kind and allow them Christmas in order to get things together or he was merely too busy with his own celebrations to give her more than a passing thought. For now.

"Well, he's coming," Mamm conceded. "I just don't know when." They rode along in silence for a moment. The day was bright and cool, just like the previous day had been, even though the weatherman continued to warn about storms. It was all the talk at church yesterday afternoon and all the talk at supper the night before. It seemed that all the men could talk about were the storms coming, rolling through Northeast Mississippi and promising weather that they hadn't seen in a long time. Honestly, Tillie thought most of the men were a little dramatic when it came to the weather, but there was no telling farmers that. Even in the wintertime.

Mamm drew in a deep breath and let it out slowly. Tillie's heart sank. Every time her mother did that it meant something was coming that perhaps neither one of them was going to like. And that's when she knew that her *mamm* had told Libby to stay behind not because Mammi Glick might really need something but so she could have Tillie all to herself. "About Melvin."

Tillie shook her head. But she didn't say anything. The last thing she wanted to talk about was Melvin. She would rather talk about the baby and what she was going to do after it was born. She had at least a little bit of control over the baby. A baby she could love, hug, dress, and feed, and Melvin . . . Melvin was a grown man. With his own mind. He had made his own decisions, and she had made hers. Right or wrong, good or bad, even though it went against every grain of her Amish upbringing, Tillie did not want to go back to the English world. How could anyone ask her to? How could anyone expect her to? It wasn't a matter of sins and transgressions; it was a matter of making two of the biggest mistakes she had ever made in her life. Mistakes that had lasting consequences, mistakes she would spend the rest of her life dealing with, and mistakes that caused her to be carrying a child who was no mistake at all.

How could she view her child as a mistake?

But how could she stay?

There was no answer to it.

Life wasn't going to be easy. In fact, she knew it was going to be awful hard. But it was her life, and she would live it through.

"I don't think Melvin is coming," Tillie said for what seemed like the hundredth time. Anytime anybody got her by herself it was the first thing they wanted to know: was Melvin coming to live with her and if so, when? Was Melvin coming to visit? Was Melvin coming when the baby was born?

No.

She had asked him, begged and pleaded with him, sobbed, then cried herself to sleep, waiting for him to change his mind, to tell her that they were going to return to Pontotoc, to their home. But he told her then that his home was no longer in Pontotoc. Her family might live there still, but his had moved away shortly after they left. He had no one in Pontotoc save a distant cousin. But Tillie had left the English anyway, praying that he would follow. Yet she'd been gone for days and he hadn't come after her; she could only assume that he wasn't going to.

"The bishop's going to ask, you know," Mamm said.

"I know." The bishop could ask, but it wouldn't change one thing. It wouldn't change how she felt. It wouldn't change how Melvin felt. It wouldn't change one single thing.

And she would be forced to leave. Shunned, excommunicated.

"Two weeks till Christmas," Mamm reminded her.

Tillie nodded. "Are you telling me for Melvin? Or the bishop?"

Mamm took her eyes from the road for a moment and settled them on Tillie's face. Her mother's gaze was like a soft caress. Kind and loving. "It's just . . ." Mamm turned her attention back to the road. "It's very complicated."

You can say that again. "I'm sorry." Her voice caught on a sob, hitched, and raised an octave. She coughed and cleared her throat to ease the tears back down.

"I know." Mamm's voice was gentle. Soothing. Understanding. It made her want to cry all the more. How had she messed up so badly in such a short period of time? And what could she ever do to make it right?

"What do you think he'll do?" Tillie asked.

Mamm shrugged. It was a unique situation Tillie found herself in, to be sure. Any couple caught in a compromising position before they were married were made to wed immediately. The bride wasn't allowed to wear her white apron and cape and there was shame on the family. But this was something much, much worse, and heaping insult onto injury was the fact that the father of her child was gone. People could say that he would change his mind. People could say that they would talk to him. But she didn't want Melvin to stay with her out of obligation. There was enough of that going around as it was.

So what did she want?

She wanted to live Amish, but she wanted to have her baby with the peace of the English girls who got pregnant without a husband. And again she thought of Mary on the road to Bethlehem. It was never that simple.

"Here we are." Mamm pulled on the reins and turned the buggy down the narrow drive. A large tree stood at the entrance. Tillie remembered coming here once before, when she was little. But the property had belonged to someone else then, she couldn't remember who. One of her friends' families maybe. Then they had moved up to Adamsville to be closer to Ethridge, like so many did. Then when Levi had married Mary, they had bought the place and set up farm.

Mamm pulled the buggy to a stop and hopped down. She hobbled her horse and nodded toward the box of goods sitting on the back seat of the carriage.

"Can you grab that box?" Then she shook her head. "No, I got it."

Tillie sighed. "I'm pregnant, not crippled."

Eunice shook her head. "You're testy, prickly as a cactus," Mamm said. "I didn't want you to get it because I want you to get the sack."

The cool wind slapped against Tillie's heated cheeks. "I guess you're right. I'm sorry."

"Matilda Sue, stop apologizing. We are a family, and we will get through this no matter what. Because that's what families do. *Jah?*"

Tillie had to blink back tears once again. *"Jah."*

A screen door slammed and they both turned toward the sharp sound. Levi Yoder stood on the porch in his shirtsleeves. With his hat covering his dark hair and his beard shadowing the lower half of his face, he looked a bit menacing standing there, unwelcoming, like a bear who'd had his hibernation disturbed. It was so very obvious that the man was grieving.

All the more reason to be neighborly, Mamm would say.

"Hello, Levi Yoder." Mamm waved cheerfully at him.

He raised one hand in a return salute. "Eunice Gingerich, what brings you here?"

"My daughter and I came out to make sure that you're set for Christmas."

He nodded but didn't move from his place in front of the door. It was almost as if he was blocking them from getting any closer to his house. "I am. *Danki.*"

Mamm was not to be deterred. "Well, now you'll be extra ready." She grabbed the box from the back of the buggy and started toward Levi Yoder.

Levi wasn't sure whether to help the ladies in order to expedite their trip or to go inside, lock the door, and hope they just went away.

Jah, he wanted to be left alone. *Jah,* his sister came out on a regular basis and aggravated him beyond belief. *Jah,* the rest of the women in the district had looked after him as well. And for that he was truly grateful. But what did a man have to do to be left alone for a couple of hours around here?

But he had lived in Pontotoc his entire life, and he knew the force that was Eunice Gingerich. If she set her mind to help someone, she did it. It seemed as if today, she had set her sights on him.

The worst bother of the company? It was Tillie Gingerich.

Tillie and the baby she carried.

He expelled a sigh that even to his own ears sounded a little more like a growl and made his way down the porch steps. He met her halfway between the buggy and the house. "Let me take that."

She relinquished the box to him without argument. Wonderful smells emanated from it. More food. Perhaps the one thing he didn't need. He had half a mind to take it down to the bridge under the freeway at the edge of town and leave it for some of the homeless people to have. He hated the thought of it going to waste almost as much as he hated the thought of having to eat it all himself. There was only so much a man could force himself to do.

"Are you ready for Christmas?" Eunice gave him a bright smile.

Levi grunted and he hoped it passed for an answer.

Tillie didn't say a word, just trailed behind them as he led the way up the porch steps and held the door open for them. Eunice's youngest daughter carried a sack full of what looked suspiciously like limbs from a cedar tree.

It was a full-on invasion, and Levi settled himself for a morning of company. With any luck, since Mims had come over the day before, she wouldn't come today.

"I got some coffee on the stove if you have a mind for a warm-up," Levi said. He might be hurting, he might be in mourning, and he might wish that the world would go away, but he still had his good manners.

Tillie set the sack down next to his couch and rubbed her hands together. "Coffee would be wonderful."

He expected they would talk about him as he left the room and went into the kitchen, but to his surprise, they followed behind him. They had coffee poured before he could even tell them where the cups were stored. Or, rather, Eunice did. Tillie hovered around the doorway as if she would rather have been anywhere but in his kitchen.

Was his inhospitable nature that obvious to her? Or maybe she had her own reasons for not wanting to be there? He handed Eunice the container of snickerdoodle cookies that Mims had made the day before, then studied Tillie Gingerich.

She was beautiful, he supposed, in the way all pregnant women were. Even though no one was allowed to talk about it. She was round and serene, even if she did look a bit unhappy. Or maybe the word was *uncomfortable*? Her eyes held a knowing light as if now she knew the secrets to it all. It was one thing about women — mothers — that amazed him. Once they gave birth, it was as if they knew more about the universe than any man alive.

He shook his head at himself.

123

"No?" Eunice asked. "You don't want a cookie?"

She seemed crushed that he wasn't going to eat one of his own cookies, so he grabbed one from the container.

"Let's sit," Eunice said.

If he didn't know any better, he would think that Eunice was trying to do a bit of matchmaking between him and Tillie. But that was impossible. Or maybe he was just too incredibly sensitive now that the holidays were here. Had he ever gotten a chance not to be sensitive? No, not since Mary died. He hadn't had the chance at all.

With any luck though, this visit would be short. Just neighbors trying to be neighborly, helping out someone they thought was in need. He supposed that to most he was in need. But to himself, he needed only peace and quiet.

"Your dog . . ." Tillie started, then trailed off.

"*Jah,*" Levi said. "Any day now, I think."

As if she knew they were talking about her, Puddles thumped her tail against the floor without raising her chin from her paws. It seemed she laid that way most times these days, and it made Levi wonder if it was the only comfortable position the poor dog could find. From the look of her, she was going to have ten or twelve pups running around very soon.

"I've always liked cattle dogs," Tillie said. Her voice held an amusing tone, almost wispy and whimsical.

"You can have a puppy if you have a mind."

Tillie snapped her gaze from Puddles's place near the potbellied stove back to Levi. "No," she said with a shake of her head. "That's very kind of you to offer, but —" She didn't finish the rest. It wasn't so kind of him to offer. He was going to have a bunch of puppies to find homes for soon, but more than anything it was what she didn't say. She wasn't going to have time to look after a puppy soon, and about the time Puddles's litter would be ready to go to homes, Tillie Gingerich would have a newborn baby to look after.

Levi waved away his words. "If you know someone."

Eunice smiled. "It's a shame she didn't give birth earlier. You could have had great Christmas presents for people. I know a lot of kids in the area would love to have a puppy for Christmas."

Tillie sat up a little straighter in her seat. "Mamm, what about Peter?"

Levi searched his brain to figure out who

Peter was to the Gingeriches but couldn't come up with an answer. "They won't be ready to go home in time for Christmas," he said unnecessarily. It was less than two weeks away.

"But if he has the promise of a puppy . . ." Tillie left the rest unsaid.

Eunice beamed her daughter a huge smile. "I think that's a great idea." She turned to Levi. "Could you save one for a little boy who would take very good care of it?"

"Of course." It was one less puppy to have to worry about when the time came.

"You remember Leah?" Eunice asked.

Levi nodded. He did. Leah was Hannah's twin. They were a little older than he and David, but in a community the size of Pontotoc, most everyone knew most everyone else. Leah had gotten married a couple of years back to a man named Jamie, if he was remembering correctly, who had a son named Peter. Right. There was more to the story, but for the life of him Levi couldn't remember it all. Just that Jamie — if that was his name — and Leah were Mennonite, and Peter was their son. Or he was now. And it seemed this boy needed a dog, like most boys do. He would have kept one of Puddles's puppies as his own, strictly for the baby Mary carried. He had known after

126

everything was said and done that the baby was a boy. His son. His son would've had a puppy to grow up with. Now he would keep a puppy because he wanted it. Perhaps even more than one, depending on whether or not he found them homes. Not that it mattered overly much. What was a farm without dogs?

Eunice drummed her knuckles against the tabletop. "It's settled, then. I'll send word to Leah when we get back home. *Danki,* Levi Yoder."

"You're welcome." A smile touched his lips. It felt strange there, and he realized it was the first time he'd smiled in a very long time.

"What happened in here?" Mims stood in his living room and whirled in a circle.

"It's not that bad." In fact, Levi had just about gotten used to it. Almost.

"Are those cedar tree boughs?" She eyed the mantel suspiciously.

"Cedar is very festive this time of year."

Mims propped her hands on her hips. "Cedar might be festive, but my brother isn't. What happened?"

Levi sighed. "Eunice and Tillie Gingerich." Well, mainly Eunice. Everyone in their district knew that Eunice meant well and all that. But when she set her mind to something, there was no getting her off of it. Case in point, his living room.

Trimmed, fresh cedar boughs lay across his mantelpiece, with white candles dotted throughout. When he lit them, they smelled like cookies. Tillie had said they were vanilla scented, but to him that was the same as cookies. They had brought red pillowcases to cover any throw pillows he had on his couch and a red, white, and green afghan that Mammi Glick had crocheted. When he had protested that it was too much, Eunice waved away his concerns. Ever since Mammi Glick broke her hip a few years back, she hadn't been quite as agile as she was before. Now she spent most of her days crocheting and working word puzzles. Eunice assured him that her mother would be greatly offended if he turned down her gift of a Christmas afghan to brighten his holiday season. So there it was.

Actually, he kind of liked it. Even though he didn't want to be reminded that Christmas was so near, something about the small little touches that Eunice and Tillie had left in his house had him feeling a little more comforted about the upcoming holiday.

It was ridiculous, of course, but he was going with it.

128

Mims immediately lost her starchy attitude. She smiled at him, her eyes twinkling with that sisterly love. "I'm proud of you, Levi," she said. "Who knows? Before long, you won't be a curmudgeon after all."

CHAPTER NINE

"You really think I'm a curmudgeon?"

Levi did his best to make his voice sound nonchalant. It was Tuesday, and he and Mims were on their way to their cousin's wedding. He had searched half the morning trying to come up with an adequate excuse not to attend, but his conscience kept coming back, telling him that he had promised. So there he sat on a cold morning, headed to a wedding he didn't really want to go to with a sister he loved almost more than anything else in the world. The things she got him to do.

Maybe that was the secret: stop hanging out with Mims. But he figured that would break his heart. She was his best friend, after all.

Mims stared straight ahead as if she hadn't heard his question.

Or maybe she was ignoring it.

Or maybe she doesn't want to tell you the truth.

"I'll take that as a yes." The thought shouldn't hurt Levi's feelings, but somehow it did. Never in his life had he wanted to be a curmudgeon, only a husband, a father, and eventually a grandfather. Nothing special, nothing more than a leatherworking farmer. Or maybe that was the problem — maybe he hadn't thought past occupation to attitude.

"You didn't used to be," Mims finally said. Still she looked straight ahead, so intent on what was in front of her that it took Levi a second to realize that she really had spoken.

"I miss them, you know. Mary." And he missed the baby. The thought of the baby. The planning and dreaming, and everything else that went with being an expectant parent. He supposed first babies were different than second babies, but he wasn't sure. He hadn't had a chance to go through either.

"I know." Mims patted his knee. "I just worry that you're going to miss a few opportunities because of it." She chose her words carefully, he could tell. She was worried that he would become too angry, too wrapped up in his own problems to be able to see salvation when it came.

Salvation? Was that what he was after?

131

Fanciful words.

"It's only been two months."

"I know," she said. "And in just a few more weeks it will be three. Then, before you know it, a year." She shifted in her seat and once again kept her eyes straight ahead. The cold had turned her nose red, and her breath crystallized with every exhale. "I worry about you."

"No need to worry," Levi said. He injected as much cheer into his voice as any curmudgeon could. And he was proud of the effect, even if he did say so himself. He sounded downright jovial.

"But you can't lock yourself away."

"Mims." His tone was both warning and beseeching.

"You can't stop living, Levi."

Couldn't he? He felt like he had whether he wanted to or not. Though if he was truly being honest with himself, each day was a little easier. That was, until Christmas. "Just let me get through the holidays. I'll go to as many weddings and get-togethers and what-haveyous as you want. Whatever else you want me to go to. But after Christmas."

"You think waiting will help?"

He didn't really have an answer for that. But he was saved having to come up with one as they pulled into the drive at their cousin's house.

The crowd had already gathered, of course. Family members who came early to help. The attendants and such who had spent the night before. Buggies were already parked in neat rows at one end of the pasture. It was a lot like church. People came, stayed awhile, clear to the afternoon, even. At least second weddings didn't last as long. It was one more thing he had to be grateful for.

He pulled the buggy alongside the others and hopped down. Another cousin greeted him, took the reins, and unhitched the horse while he talked about the weather and whether it was going to come a storm like all the English meteorologists claimed. To look at the sky today a person would think it had never snowed in the history of that sky. Clear blue and bright. He supposed John David couldn't have picked a better day to get wed. And still Levi wished he was somewhere else.

It was a definite toss-up. Tillie glanced around the crowd of people gathered for her cousin Amanda's wedding. Everyone seemed intent on having a great time, celebrating with the special couple, but it was definitely a fifty-fifty split when it came to people noticing her and her enlarged state. She was fairly certain that after all was said and done and everyone went home and the wedding escapades had been recounted once and then again, talk would turn to her. Or maybe she was just overly sensitive. She spent the morning pinning and re-pinning the maternity dress her *mamm* had borrowed from Anna in order to make her growing girth not quite so obvious. But even as she went about the exercise, she knew it wasn't worth the effort. Too many people had already seen her, too many people already knew that she was carrying a baby, and too many people had already told someone else. She could try and hide it as much as she wanted, but by the time she left the wedding today, everyone in Pontotoc would know without a doubt that she was going to have a baby. And soon.

"You look like you could use this." Hannah sidled up next to her and presented a small plate of desserts to her. Spice cake, iced cookies, and chocolate-covered cashews.

Tillie tried to smile. Wasn't dessert the best part of any wedding celebration? She supposed so, save the happy couple and the two souls bound together in love and harmony and God. Seeing as how she had

134

missed her wedding and would probably never have one now, it made it a little harder to see all that joy. Or perhaps she was just being selfish.

Time. Wasn't that what everyone said was needed? Then maybe that's what she needed as well. Just a little more time. Who knew? In a couple of years, maybe ten, everyone in Pontotoc might not care that she had come home pregnant and unmarried and the father of her baby hadn't cared enough to follow behind.

"Quit thinking about it," Leah said. Tillie hadn't heard her sister come up on the other side, most likely because she'd been too lost in her own thoughts about her own problems. It was becoming something of a habit these days, and she needed to shake herself out of it lest she get mired down in all the wrongs with her life. She knew when that happened she would forget all the good things that were around. Those were what she really needed to concentrate on.

"I'm sorry."

"And stop apologizing," Hannah admonished. Her voice was gentle, loving, and Tillie immediately wanted to apologize again. What was it about her transgressions that made her so apologetic? Perhaps the fact that there was no making up for the

135

pain and sorrow she was causing her family.

"Maybe I should go," she said.

"Home?" Hannah asked. Her voice rang with the unspoken *We just got here,* though in truth they had been there a couple of hours.

Their community, in particular, was small enough that most everyone was in attendance. They were a conservative district and did not have a lot of outside activities available to them. Weddings were definitely a bright spot in all their social calendars, and everyone looked forward to them and the entertainment they provided.

"I have the car," Leah said. "I can take you home and come back. Are you feeling okay?"

Tillie shook her head. "That's not what I mean. Maybe I should go back to Melvin."

"No!" her sisters exclaimed simultaneously. Their voices were loud enough that they drew the attention of several people standing close by. Leah waved away their exclamation as if it never happened and turned back to Tillie. "You can't go back yet. You just got home."

"I know, but . . ." She couldn't finish that sentence. She knew she had just gotten home, but she also knew that her baby needed a father. She knew that. She knew also that the community would never forgive her without a husband. She *knew,* but was what she was doing really what was best for all involved? Or was she just being selfish? Wishing for things to be impossibly different?

"Don't," Hannah said. She wrapped her fingers around one of Tillie's arms, and Leah got the other. Together her sisters marched her through the house and out the back door. There were a few other wedding goers outside, milling around. Some of the men were smoking, and a few of the kids in attendance were sitting under the tree swing and playing some sort of game.

And now that they were out in the fresh air, Tillie sucked in a deep breath. It felt a little better to be outdoors; not so confining.

"Why don't you tell me what this is all about?" Hannah said.

"And don't tell us what you think we want to hear. Tell us what this is really about," Leah interjected.

Tillie shook her head. "I can't explain."

"Try." Leah pinned her with a sharp look. "None of that watered-down stuff that you tell Mamm."

"What if Melvin doesn't come?" Tillie asked. The question fell between them like a dead goose. She had told them that Melvin wasn't coming, but she had been waiting for his return all the same. And with every day that passed, it seemed more and more unlikely that he would ever come.

"I don't know," Hannah said.

Leah shot their sister a look that could melt wax, then she turned back to Tillie. "You know."

They all knew. She would have to leave. She would have to go back to the English world. She didn't have to return to Melvin, but she couldn't stay there.

"You just need to sit down with the bishop and work through this. Maybe he can help. There is a solution. There is an answer."

She knew that, though she dreaded speaking with the bishop more than anything else she could think of. But she knew as well as her sisters that without that conversation, she would have no peace. She supposed she should settle that as quick as she possibly could. But knowing something and being able to do it were two very different things.

Hannah grabbed Tillie's hand in her own. Leah laid hers on top of theirs.

"Just promise me one thing," Hannah said.

"Don't do anything stupid," Leah interjected.

"Hasty," Hannah corrected her impetuous twin. "Don't do anything hasty. There's always an answer."

"Have you prayed about it?" Leah asked.

Tillie shot her a look. "No, I hadn't thought about that."

Leah laughed and pinched the side of Tillie's face in typical sisterly fashion. "You're cheeky. I like that."

"He hasn't answered."

"Melvin?" Hannah asked.

Tillie shook her head. "God."

"Well, it is Christmastime. He's probably busy," Leah quipped.

"Give it time," Hannah said.

There was the word again. Everything needed time. She just wasn't sure how much of that she had.

"Gift time!" someone called from the back door.

"We better go back in," Hannah said. She and Leah turned toward the house.

Tillie waved them away. "Go ahead. I'll be right behind you."

The sisters exchanged a look. Tillie knew they were both reluctant to leave her behind.

"Go on," she said. "I'll be there in a minute."

"You got five," Hannah said. "Then we're coming after you."

She just needed a breath of air. She had forgotten about all the differences between the English world and the Amish world. There were so many things that were so hard to adjust to when going from one to the other. All the things a person needed in the English world — electricity, water, money for gas. Food was more expensive. And everything seemed to be more spread out. Even a couple of English parties that Melvin had dragged her to weren't as busy and noisy as one Amish wedding. She just needed a little more space. But she knew that if she took too long, her sisters would indeed come back for her.

Most everyone from outside had gone into the house. She was grateful for the added privacy, and yet at the same time she felt strangely alone. She rubbed a hand over her belly, something she didn't allow herself to do often when she was out like she was right then. But there wasn't anybody around to see her.

"We'll get through this, baby," she murmured. Some people would think she had lost her mind, talking to a baby that hadn't even been born yet, but she couldn't help it. She almost felt a stronger kinship with this child than she did her own sisters. Hannah and Leah had been through their own trials, but not the same as Tillie's. This was something she and her baby were going through together. And even though the child wasn't born and didn't know, one day she would. Or he. Though Tillie was secretly beginning to think that the baby was a girl. And that made it all the more important for her to be among the Amish. The English world was just too rough on girls. Everything seemed to be a struggle and a fight. She knew people who thought the Amish way of life was confining. But she considered it to be delineated. She thought that was the right word. Maybe *outlined.* She knew what she was supposed to do, where she was supposed to be. She knew how she was supposed to act, she knew what she was supposed to wear. She knew what her job was. Always. She should be a wife and a mother, and there was no need to be anything more. What was so wrong with that?

Nothing, as far as she could see.

She rubbed her belly again, and the hair on the back of her neck stood up. She looked up to find blue eyes watching her. The blue eyes that belonged to Levi Yoder. He studied her for a moment. She didn't breathe. Just stood there, chin lifted, one hand around her middle. She hated that she'd been caught acknowledging her pregnancy by a man, but it was done now.

I'm sorry sprang to her lips, but she bit the words back. What did she have to apologize for? She had thought she was alone. Why wasn't he inside with everyone else?

He stared at her for what seemed to be an eternity. Then he turned and made his way in through the side door of the house.

Tillie almost wilted on the spot. She wanted to go home, avoid any more of the embarrassment that she faced. But she knew that if she left now, her sisters would worry about her, and she loved them enough not to want to cause them unnecessary concern. It was just the look in Levi Yoder's eyes — almost a resentment. As if he had been asking God why. Why was his baby gone when her baby was still growing? It wasn't fair; she knew it as well as he. But how many times in the English world had she heard of this same unfairness? Of couples who would give a baby a wonderful home with two loving parents but couldn't have one of their own while a drug addict on the street gave birth to one and left it for someone else to raise. That was one thing her time in the English world had shown her. There was nothing about life that was fair.

Not caring if she was alone still or not, Tillie rubbed another hand across her belly.

"It's okay, little girl. We'll find our way."
She wasn't sure how, but she would make it
right.

"Are you ready to go?" Mims asked.
I thought you'd never ask.
"*Jah,*" Levi said instead. It'd been a trying
afternoon. Aside from the fact that he
simply wanted to go home to peace and
solitude, it had been an afternoon of celebration that he didn't feel, talk of the
weather that he was starting to get tired of,
and heart-wrenching glimpses of Tillie Gingerich.

As he and Mims made their way to their
buggy, she chatted in her typical Mims way.
The color of the dresses, the desserts offered, the recipe for chicken and filling. He
understood the need for tradition, but
sometimes it could be a little overdone.
Having the same food at every wedding only
led to talk of recipes and who took whose
and other rivalries that sprang up when
people lived so closely together. But all he
could think about was Tillie. He must've
seen her a dozen times. Alone, together with
her sisters. He could hardly stand to look at
her. The sight of her hurt his eyes. Not
because she was ugly or even not beautiful.
She was . . . beautiful. She seemed hesitant

143

and confident at the same time, unsure and yet determined. It was like a magnet drawing him in, but he could hardly stand it when his gaze fell upon her.

For even as much as she drew him in, she scared him. She was the embodiment of everything he had lost. And each glimpse of her reminded him of that loss. Of the things he'd once had, then an unmerciful God took away. A God he was struggling with daily. He hated those thoughts. He didn't want them. Day by day he was losing his faith, inch by slow inch, and he couldn't seem to stop. Even though he was trying, and he was praying.

"Are you even listening to me?" Mims asked.

Levi swung up into the carriage next to his sister. He took up the reins before answering. "*Jah.* Blue dresses. Chicken and filling."

Mims harrumphed.

He knew what she was thinking. He would have to live again eventually. Eventually, but maybe just not right now. Right now, he was struggling. He was praying. Even when he wasn't sure he could believe, he still prayed. Then his mind started to wander and he lost his focus. The thing that bothered him the most was once that happened his mind was filled with Tillie Gingerich. And that wasn't helping at all.

CHAPTER TEN

"And you do this every Wednesday?" Tillie looked around her mother's dining room. The table itself was covered with mixing bowls, little brown bottles of essential oils, and plastic bottles waiting for product. The sideboard had stacks of labels that Leah had printed out on her computer.

"Tuesday," Gracie corrected with a smile.

"Right," Leah said. "It's only Wednesday this week because we went to the wedding yesterday."

"So yes," Hannah said. "We do this every week."

Tillie couldn't believe the number of lotion bottles, cakes of soaps, and other skin care products her sisters and cousin created each week. It was a booming business.

"I still think we need a few more of the Christmas scents," Leah said. She picked up two of the small bottles of oil and examined them. "Especially cranberry vanilla and honey cinnamon. People will use those even after Christmas."

"You're right, of course," Hannah said. "But we still have to get the rest of these orders filled before we can make bottles to just put up for sale."

When they held cousins' day, Gracie's children went over to play with Anna and Jim's for the afternoon. Baby Grace, who had become accustomed to more people since having Gracie in her life, went to stay with Mammi Glick in the *dawdihaus*. Brandon took care of the shop in town, allowing Leah to have a day off, and Hannah's kids were in school. The only limitation was that she needed to be home soon after them in order to make sure Essie and Laura Kate didn't somehow start a revolution.

"Just tell me what I need to do," Tillie said. "I want to help, but I'm a little lost." And she couldn't help thinking she wouldn't have been lost had she been here the whole time. Had she never left. She had talked over the idea of leaving the Amish with her sisters, and they had told her that it was a lot harder than most thought and that she would do well to stay right where she was.

What was that saying? *Hindsight is twenty-twenty.* She supposed it was, but to want to go back to before that time would mean she wouldn't have the baby she carried. She wasn't sure she would be okay with that. It might be that the pregnancy was causing her a great deal of grief at the present time, but she would not and could not call her baby a mistake. She would much rather think of it as a miracle. Maybe not a Christmas miracle. But still a miracle. Though it might be a miracle if she got through this without completely losing her mind.

"We sort of do an assembly line. So if you'll get down on the end and make sure the labels go on the right product and look nice, that would be a great help," Hannah said.

To Tillie it seemed like the least important job of all, but if they did indeed have as many orders as they talked about, she supposed they didn't have time to teach her all about the business.

And what would be the point if she was going to leave again anyway?

She wanted to stay past Christmas and on into the future, but she wasn't kidding herself. She knew that it would be hard. Leaving and coming back was one of those things that left a blemish. And unfortunately, she couldn't pretend like it never happened.

"I was surprised to see him there," Gracie

148

said, picking up their earlier conversation about Levi Yoder. "But I suppose Mims can be a little . . ."

"Bossy?" Leah supplied.

"Forceful," Hannah said with a sharp look at her sister. "Mims is forceful and is somewhat accustomed to getting her way." Though nobody knew exactly how that came about.

"I just felt bad for him," Hannah said. "He looked like he would have rather been anyplace else."

"Well, John David is his cousin," Leah said.

"I know," Hannah replied.

He had been as obliged to go to the wedding as she had, Tillie thought. Why did they do that to themselves? It certainly wasn't for the bride and groom. That much Tillie knew for certain. There were enough people at the wedding that neither she nor Levi would have been missed had they not attended. The people who knew they were both there would be the other people, other guests, attending the wedding. They would know if someone was missing and needed to be there. So that was the reason people like Tillie and Levi subjected themselves to the torture of the niceties dictated by their community.

It wouldn't do any good to say that it wasn't fair. It was simply the way it was.

"I heard you and Mamm went over to his house Monday and put up Christmas decorations for him." Leah's words took Tillie completely off guard.

"I . . . *Jah,* I mean, not . . ."

"We'll take that as a yes," Hannah said.

"We were just trying to bring him a little joy," Tillie explained. But even to her own ears it sounded weak. *Lame,* Brandon would say. It sounded like an excuse just to go over to his house. And all because his name popped up on her lips at the most inconvenient time.

"Whew!" Leah waved a hand in front of her face. "And this is why we usually do this outside," she said.

"Even in the winter?" Tillie asked.

"This is the first winter that we've had this many orders, thanks to somebody's website," Gracie said.

"We needed a website," Leah returned.

"Who knew it was going to take off like this?" Hannah shrugged. "So we hadn't planned on making this much lotion. Now we know to start earlier next year."

"And crack a window," Gracie said.

Leah rose to her feet and made her way across the room to the window at the front

150

of the house.

"It's really gotten cold out there." Hannah rubbed her arms as the first gust of wind swept through the room.

"It's either cold or overwhelming smells," Leah said.

Hannah laughed. "I'm sure Mamm's got a sweater I can borrow." She stood.

"Get one for me too," Tillie called.

"Make that three," Gracie added.

Hannah stopped at the door and looked back to Leah.

Her twin shrugged. "It's unanimous."

"Check," Hannah said and disappeared down the hallway. She returned a few moments later with a sweater for each of them.

"It's supposed to get bad tomorrow or the next day," Hannah said. "I heard Aaron talking about it."

Leah passed a stack of labels to Tillie and nodded. "I'm not sure how bad it's really supposed to get, but they have everybody worried. I went to the store this morning — no bread, no milk. I've got a growing boy at home who is not happy if he can't have a peanut butter sandwich for lunch."

"Don't they get a shipment in on Thursdays?" Gracie asked.

"Gracie Glick, you're the only person I know who would keep up with such a thing." Hannah laughed and shot her cousin a sweet smile. She meant no disrespect or harm.

"Everyone knows that. Besides, I've got *four* growing boys at home. I have to keep up with that sort of thing. Especially since Henry has taken a liking to cheese crackers. He thinks he has to have them every day, and if he runs out . . . . Well, you know Henry."

Tillie didn't know Henry as well as Leah and Hannah, of course, but she had seen him a couple of times. He was what their *mamm* would call a stinker. But so adorably cute everyone somehow forgave him his daily transgressions. *A handful,* that's what Mammi Glick would say. Henry Byler was a handful.

"I suppose we'll have to be there at the crack of dawn in order to get any if everybody else knows they're getting a shipment," Hannah said. She didn't say as much, but she had growing kids too. They all did. In just a short time everyone around the table had gained family, husbands, life mates.

Everyone but her.

She pushed the thought away as Leah continued, "You think there's going to be a white Christmas?"

Hannah handed a bottle of vanilla-scented essential oil to Leah. "And when is the last time you remember a white Christmas in Mississippi?"

Leah tapped her chin thoughtfully. "Sometime in the nineties?"

"I'll tell you when," Hannah said with a firm nod. "Never. That's when."

"Surely we've had one or two," Gracie said. She stood and started mixing lotion, using the mixed scents Leah had been carefully concocting.

"Well, there's a first time for everything, right?" Tillie asked.

"I suppose so," Hannah said. "But I'm not holding my breath on this one."

"I'm with Hannah," Leah agreed. "I'd suspect an icy Christmas over a white Christmas around here."

"You are staying through Christmas," Gracie asked with a hesitant look at Tillie.

She nodded as all eyes turned to her. "*Jah,*" she said. "I'm staying through Christmas." For now anyway.

"Have you heard from Melvin?" Hannah asked.

Tillie shook her head. There wasn't a good way for Melvin to get in touch with her, nor she him. The only phone shanty in the district was just outside the school. If an

Amish person wanted to use the phone, they had to borrow one. No one wanted to bother their English neighbor with something that wasn't an emergency. It wasn't like Melvin could just pick up the phone and call.

It wasn't like he *would* call.

Tillie pushed that thought away.

"You think he'll come back?" Leah asked.

That seemed to be what was on everyone's mind: Was she staying? Was Melvin coming back?

"I don't know."

"Do you want him to?" Leah's question caused a hush to fall across the room.

Did she want him to? She didn't have an answer for any of this. She just didn't know. All she knew for certain was that she wanted to raise her baby and live in peace and not have to worry about what everyone thought. And for that to happen she needed Melvin.

"Uh-oh," Leah said. "I know that look."

"I just want to raise my child in peace," Tillie said.

"The only place you're going to get that is in the English world."

Tillie hated the thought of it, but Leah was right. There were too many restrictions with the Amish for there to be no censure of her wrongdoings.

They had warned her before she had left. She didn't need to hear it again.

"Why?" Tillie asked even though she expected no answer. "Why is it just so hard?"

She supposed Hannah had it a little easier, since she had married an English man with money, but deep down she knew that wasn't true.

"Why is everything a struggle?" Tillie and Melvin had struggled. They struggled with the bills, struggled to get along with each other, struggled to survive.

"There are different kinds of struggle," Hannah told her.

Tillie knew. They all did. That Mitch had been unfaithful. That he hit her once. And that she had been planning to get away when he died, leaving her without a cent to her name, just Brandon's car. And she only got away with that because it was in her son's name and technically belonged to him.

"Melvin loves you," Leah said. "That's worth a lot."

Tillie didn't answer.

"What?" Gracie asked. "What is that look on your face?"

"You don't think Melvin loves you?" Hannah asked.

Tillie sighed. "I guess so, but I know that

he loves being with his friends. He left here to drink beer, fix motors, and a bunch of other things that the English world has to offer. He doesn't see the struggle as a struggle. He thinks it's just the way the world is. I don't feel like we struggle here."

"We do," Leah said. "Everyone struggles everywhere. The world is full of struggles."

Tillie knew she was talking about Peter and Jamie and all the struggles they had been through to get where they were today.

Gracie gave her a small smile. Tillie knew she meant for it to be encouraging. "It all depends on how you handle them."

And that was the problem. Tillie didn't feel like she was handling these problems very well at all.

Their talk plagued her for the rest of the day, on in the afternoon, past supper, even when Tillie was getting ready for bed. It affected her prayers. She could hardly concentrate on what she needed to say — maybe even should say — to God. These days, when she talked to God, it felt like all she did was ask. She asked for peace, she asked for understanding. Asked for forgiveness. Asked for hope. So far, she had been delivered none of these things. She was beginning to think God was sending her a message back: some of it was up to her.

Even with all of the decisions and pressures waiting on her, Tillie had enjoyed the day she spent with her sisters and Gracie. She enjoyed being with them and talking about their problems, other people's issues, and which scent was going to turn out to be the best for the season. It was more than just about making soap and lotion; it was about the four of them being together. She wondered if that was what caused the success of their brand. As if somehow the customers could sense the community and love that went into each bottle.

"Do you have anything planned for the day?" Mamm asked as they finished the breakfast dishes.

"No," Tillie answered. She picked up the stack of plates and set it back into the cabinet. She didn't have any plans at all — except to muddle through the mess that had become her life.

"I thought we might make some cranberry Christmas bread," Mamm continued.

Cranberry Christmas bread had been a Gingerich tradition for as long as Tillie could remember. When Leah and Hannah had returned home, the tradition had grown into what it had been before: all the Gingerich ladies in the kitchen baking together.

Even Anna came over. And since Libby was now eighteen, Tillie figured her young niece would be included in the mix.

The thought was both comforting and exhausting. Everything seemed to be exhausting these days. She wasn't sure if it was the pregnancy or the stress. As much as she hated to admit it, she was fairly certain it was the stress. She had come back for these times with her family and yet now they seem to wear her out — just one more of the trials she faced but hadn't anticipated. Coming home was supposed to be easy. It was usually the right answer.

Mammi would tell her the opposite. A lot of times, the right decision was the hardest one to make. Now when faced with that sort of tough decision, it was equally hard in either direction, and she didn't know which way to turn. She had left Melvin a note and told him she was headed back to Pontotoc. In that moment she had felt confident in her choice. Now she wasn't so sure. But that had nothing to do with her family and everything to do with struggles.

"I suppose everyone is coming over," Tillie said. She did her best to make her voice level, even upbeat at the prospect. She needed to, for any other day the idea would be appealing.

Mamm shook her head. "Now that the girls have their business going, it's too hard to get everyone together a second time."

"Oh." Tillie felt sort of deflated. Amazing how things changed. One tradition rose and another tradition fell. She knew life had to shift, but there were some things a girl needed to be the same.

"It's just for you and me. Maybe Libby. Anna has a little more time these days, but she's been trying to help David more for me."

And yet another adjustment.

"You don't suppose David will ever get married?" Tillie asked. She had never remembered any one girl being interested in David. And she never knew why. He was as handsome as Jim. He had a good job, a place to live, a stable family in the Amish community. She knew he had struggled in school and had a few troubles reading. And that he considered himself not as smart as most. Was that reason for him to not live his life to the fullest?

"Why do I get the feeling you're trying to change the subject?" Mamm asked.

Tillie laughed, then tilted her head to one side as a noise came from the front. "Are you expecting someone?"

Mamm dried her hands on her apron and

smoothed them over her prayer *kapp*. "No." She headed for the front of the house, Tillie on her heels.

Mamm stopped abruptly just a few feet from the front door. She caught sight of the buggy through the front window in the dining room. The same window they had opened the day before to release the wonderful, yet overpowering, Christmas scents they had been mixing.

Tillie drew up short. The time that she had been dreading was finally here. The horse and carriage out front were an undeniable testament.

The bishop had come to call.

CHAPTER ELEVEN

Amos Raber walked like a man on a mission.

Tillie's breath caught in her throat as she watched the bishop make his way from his buggy over to the barn where her *dat*'s workshop was housed. Her brother Jim stood at the door, waiting to shake hands with the bishop. She supposed he had heard the rattle of the buggy as well and had come to investigate. A second after that handshake, David appeared, his own hand extended. Her father followed last.

She and Mamm stood there at the window and watched as the men conversed for a moment. They were too far away for Tillie to understand what they were saying; she could just hear the sound of their voices. But twice the men paused and looked back at the house.

They were talking about her. Tillie knew. She supposed there had been a lot of talk about her in the last three or four days. She had shown up at church. She had gone to a wedding. For all intents and purposes it looked as if she was staying in Pontotoc. She had hoped that with the holiday so near the bishop would delay coming to speak to her until after Christmas had passed. But she knew and had known all along that was merely wishful thinking. There were too many busybodies in their church for them to let it go.

If she had to guess who had complained about her, her choice would be Amelia Byler. She was some distant cousin of Gracie's husband, Matthew. Though who knew how many times removed. Amelia was one of those people who, despite the Lord's love, never seemed happy. Even as she thought the words, a stab of pain seared through Tillie. She had the Lord's love too, but she wasn't happy these days either. Maybe she should take a look at herself before she criticized. Though she wasn't truly criticizing, Amelia had been that way for as long as anyone could remember. She was almost the watchdog for the community. She had been at the wedding, and Tillie had caught Amelia staring at her after church. But Tillie knew that if it hadn't been Amelia, it would've been someone else.

"Here we go," Mamm whispered.

The men shook hands once more, then Amos Raber turned on his heel and started for the house. The Gingerich men looked after him for a moment, then all three of them ducked back into the barn.

Tillie's heart began to pound in her chest. Sheer anxiety. She looked down at herself as if somehow she could hide her condition. That was not happening. She looked around as if somehow there was an answer beside her. Mamm smoothed her hands over her ample hips and cleared her throat. Tillie supposed that was the least and the most either one of them could do. She should have changed her dress while the bishop greeted her father. Though the temptation to run into her bedroom and lock the door behind her, barricade it from the inside, and never come out was a little too strong. It was probably best she hadn't chanced it.

"Lord, give me strength."

Please, she added. *Please give me strength.*

All too soon, a knock sounded on the front door, then it creaked open. Mamm bustled from the dining room and into the entry way. "Amos Raber," she greeted. "Happy to see you today."

Tillie was shocked at how easily the lie

sprang to her *mamm*'s lips. They both knew this was inevitable, and they both hated it. Her *mamm* had told her as much.

"Eunice." Amos Raber nodded his head and removed his hat. He hung it on the peg by the door. Then another quick nod to Tillie, and he removed his coat.

"I'll get some coffee and pie," Mamm said and motioned for Tillie to follow her into the kitchen. That was Mamm. Everything could be solved with pie. Tillie wished. She didn't think she was going to be quite so lucky this time.

Amos hung up his coat and motioned for Tillie to go first. She did so, albeit reluctantly. She could already see the censure in his eyes. Amos Raber was a tough bishop. She supposed bishops had to be strict in the conservative districts. But she also knew that he was responsible for addressing the needs and concerns of his community. That couldn't be an easy job. And it wasn't one he had asked for. He'd been chosen by lot, by God.

Mamm waved away her offers of help, and Tillie eased into one of the chairs at the kitchen table. Amos Raber sat across from her on the bench.

"They say the weather is going to turn bad in the next day or so," Tillie said. She immediately regretted the words. Not that they were so controversial, but that she had drawn attention to herself. Still, she couldn't stand the silence. Even with all Mamm's banging and bustling, the room just seemed eerily quiet.

"That's what they say," Amos replied.

In minutes that seemed to take forever and yet went by all too fast, Mamm presented each of them with a slice of pie.

"I suppose you know why I'm here," Amos said.

"I believe so, *jah,*" Mamm said.

Tillie couldn't speak past the lump in her throat.

"There's been a lot of talk going around," Amos started. "About what plans you might have."

Tillie considered it ridiculously generous that he was giving her the opportunity to state her own plans. She supposed he just was trying to figure out what they were up against.

"I came back in hopes of raising my baby with my family."

Mamm shifted uncomfortably in her seat. Tillie couldn't move at all.

"And Melvin Yoder," Amos asked. "Where is he?" He paused for a moment. "I assume that —" He waved a hand in her general direction but didn't finish the thought. He supposed that Melvin was the father of her baby.

"Jah." Tillie felt the heat rise into her cheeks until she was certain they were as red as holly berries.

"Am I to understand that there was a wedding between the two of you?" Amos asked.

"No," Tillie whispered. It was perhaps the hardest word she had ever said. It was one thing to talk about such matters with her sisters and Gracie, or even her mother, but it was quite another to discuss it with the leader of their church.

Amos Raber leaned back in his seat and drummed his fingers against his chest. "That's what I thought." He sighed. "I've given this matter a great deal of thought," he continued.

Tillie's breath caught. Mamm stilled.

"Must I say it out loud?" the bishop asked.

Tillie shook her head. It was just as she had feared. She would have to leave. She wouldn't be able to stay in her Amish home. Not without . . . "What if Melvin returns?" she managed to ask, though her words sounded a little more like a wheeze than a sentence.

"I've never had anything like this happen

before. I don't remember anything like this ever happening before. If he comes back and the two of you were to get married . . . But that's the only way for you to remain here." He pinned Tillie with his fierce stare. Amos Raber wasn't a scary man, but he was a presence. Tall, thin, and intense.

She knew what he wanted. He wanted to know her plans. What she would do now. Like she really had any choice. She would have to leave. And soon. He couldn't allow her to stay and remain unmarried. As the pressures of the district increased, so would the pressures on him. In turn they would flow to Tillie. How long would she be able to stay, unwed to her baby's father? Not long.

"This is the sort of thing that divides communities," Amos continued. "We're young here. We have many moving to Adamsville so they're closer to home. There's been talk, a lot of talk. Something like this could bring the whole community down."

Tillie's heart sank. She shook her head. "I can't." Though she didn't say what it was that she couldn't do. She couldn't marry Melvin. She couldn't be responsible for everyone's decision in the community. There were a lot of things she couldn't do.

"And if Melvin comes back?" Mamm asked.

Tillie shook her head, but Mamm wasn't watching her. Her eyes were on the bishop.

"If Melvin comes back, they will both stand in front of the church and confess their sins and the mistakes they've made. I'll have to talk to Jonas, maybe Dan and the others here, but we could have a special membership ceremony to allow them to join the church. Then they could get married and serve their penance after."

To say it was harsh was an understatement. They would be shamed in front of their family and friends. They would be exposed, judged, then finally welcomed back. Yet how could she do that? Tillie wondered. How could she stand up and say her baby was a mistake? Even if she could get Melvin to come back, maybe it would just be better if she did leave. She was putting so much on her family by even being there. But if Melvin didn't return, then Tillie wouldn't be allowed to stay. It was that simple.

Tillie put a protective hand over her stomach. She knew it was just the way. It was the Amish way. She had known this going in, before she transgressed. She had never thought it would come to this. She'd never given a thought past her bond with Melvin, or maybe it was the pressures of living English. Wasn't that what they did? Loved each other without worrying over vows?

Amos stood. Tillie realized he hadn't eaten one bite of pie. Mamm had not noticed. She was on her feet a heartbeat after the bishop.

"I'll leave you to discuss it with your family. We'll talk again next week. But after that . . ." He tipped his head toward the two of them and started back toward the front door.

Mamm trailed behind.

Tillie followed a little slower. She knew Mamm wanted to say something. Her mother always liked to have things under tight control, and this was something neither one of them was going to be able to manage.

"If anything changes, you let me know," Amos said. He didn't outline what changes he was talking about. But Tillie knew he meant if she decided to go back to Melvin. It would be easiest for them all. She knew it; Amos knew it.

He donned his hat and coat and let himself out. Mamm stood facing the closed door for what seemed like a full minute. Then she turned to Tillie. The look on her face was enough. Tears welled in Tillie's eyes and seeped down her cheeks. These mistakes that were not mistakes at all — how did one go about correcting them?

A sob escaped her as Mamm wrapped her arms around her, and Tillie cried.

"Mims, really," Levi started. He looked at the three huge stockpots on the stove. "I'm not going to be able to eat all this food in the next month, much less between now and Christmas."

"The weather is turning bad, probably as early as tomorrow," Mims said. She stirred the last one, tapped the wooden spoon against the rim, and laid it across the top of the pot.

Levi sucked in a breath to protest further, then let it out in a sigh. When Mims got like this, there was no changing her mind.

"Maybe if you found yourself a husband you wouldn't feel so obligated to take care of me."

She whirled on him, propped her hands on her hips, and shot him a withering stare. "Married or not I would still need to take care of you, dear brother."

He had hoped to get more of a rise out of her. It was better by far than thinking about Christmas and all that he had lost.

"And this should be just enough food to get you through to Christmas." Mims wasn't taking into account the packages of food still sitting in his icebox. He had to admit to himself, if not to her, that he enjoyed the company. And he wasn't admitting that it would mean that he wanted company all the time. But sometimes he didn't want to be all alone. It was weird. When he was alone, he wished someone were there. When someone was there, he wished he were alone. He supposed that was unhappiness at its finest.

"And you need to eat it," she said with another stern look. "Your clothes are hanging off you. It's much easier to make food than it is new clothing."

He found no need to tell her that he just wasn't hungry these days. Everyone said that was simply grief and it would change. But he knew that it wouldn't until after he got past Christmas.

There had been a time when Christmas had been his favorite holiday. He loved everything about it: families coming together, good food, exchanging presents, preparing for a new year. To him Christmas was like the turning point of winter. After Christmas he started looking forward to a new planting season. In the spring, people tended to their horses to get ready for the new season. They needed new leather goods. It was almost like starting over, and it all stemmed from Christmas. Or at least in his mind it did.

"I do like your decorations though." Mims nodded toward the cedar boughs lying on the mantel. "I love the smell of cedar. Christmassy." She smiled at him as if encouraging him to agree with her.

How could he refuse? "Christmassy," he agreed. Mary had always decorated with pine boughs, so at least that part was different. At least that part wasn't so nostalgic for him.

"Do I see some mistletoe in there?" Mims asked.

"*Jah,*" he said.

Tillie and Eunice had found a few sprigs of real mistletoe and holly with red berries and placed it throughout the fragrant cedar.

"Don't you go off kissing anyone," Mims said with a laugh.

Levi couldn't help it; he chuckled, though the sound was rusty and unused.

"There's my brother." Mims turned away, but not before he saw the sheen of tears in her eyes.

He was worrying his family, and he was sorry for it, but he was struggling. Surely they understood that. "Just give me time, Mims."

"I worry," she said.

He nodded. "I know."

She started back toward the kitchen — to stir the pots once again, he was certain, even though it hadn't been very long that they had been unattended. "Don't do any- thing . . . stupid."

"I won't."

She didn't say what she really meant. She was worried he would hurt himself. Had he been that depressed, that his family would worry so about him? The idea was unthink- able. *Jah,* he missed Mary. He missed his baby. Or maybe the idea of his baby and the family that would never be. But he wasn't so far gone that he would forget everything that he had been taught his whole life.

And it was just so much harder at Christ- mastime.

He and Mary had talked about what would happen if she had the baby early, maybe even on Christmas Day. Their child would share a birthday with Jesus. And Christmas reminded him of the family of Bethlehem, which reminded him of the fam- ily he would never have.

Suddenly Tillie Gingerich's face popped

into his thoughts. He hadn't heard anyone say with any great conviction what was to become of her and the child she carried. It had ripped his heart out every time he saw her at the wedding, then he realized he was just being selfish. Tillie could no more help her circumstance than he could help his own. They were all at the mercy of God's will.

While Mims stirred the pots on the stove, Levi made his way into the living room. He sat down in the rocking chair and stared at the mantel that Tillie had decorated with her *mamm* just a few days before. He appreciated the effort. He appreciated the sentiment. Even though he didn't feel much like celebrating. He supposed Tillie probably didn't either. She had been the talk of the after-church meal; she'd been the talk of the wedding two days later. He was certain she was the talk of every quilting circle and Christmas party that was happening this week. Every get together, every cousins' day. Every casual meeting over pie. He supposed if they were talking about her that they would no longer be talking about him. But somehow that thought wasn't the least bit comforting.

CHAPTER TWELVE

There were too many people.

Tillie tried to find a corner that was a little out of the way, but everywhere she went there was someone. Baby Samuel, her cousin, her brother, always someone. It was nothing more than a family holiday get-together, but she couldn't get a moment alone.

She braced her back against the wall and faced the room as a whole. She stared out over the sea of smiling, laughing faces. Christmastime seemed to bring out the joy in most everyone. How could it not? It was maybe the best holiday of the year. And knowing it was coming sure made the cold weather easier to bear. But this year Tillie didn't feel quite the same about Christmas. Not now anyway. There were too many things at stake, too much to think about. Too many mistakes.

After the bishop had left, Tillie had cried

for a bit, then pulled herself together. She had made mistakes, shameful, shameful mistakes. But they were done and now she had to live with them. And as much as she hoped and prayed that Amos Raber would go to Ethridge to talk to the leaders in their parent community and come home with the perfect solution for what she was to do to get back in the good graces of God and the church, she knew that wasn't going to happen. They would demand that she marry Melvin. They would demand that he come back. They would demand a confession in front of the church, a kneeling confession while they laid their sins out for all to see. There was just one really big problem with that. She knew in her heart of hearts that Melvin was never coming back to Pontotoc. She'd been there almost a week and he hadn't come after her yet. A sad little part of her wondered if he knew that she was even gone. Even as impossible as it was, the thought made her breath clog in her chest in a knot that seemed to grow with every bit of air she tried to take in. She hated Christmas, she decided. She hated the party. She hated it all.

Again she searched the happy faces of the people around her. Her whole family had turned out, from Mammi Glick all the way to Leah and her new family. David, Jim and Anna and all their kids, everyone. And everyone there was happy.

Everyone but her.

And why? Because the whole idea was pointless, having a party to welcome her back home. She was never going to be allowed back into the community. Not without Melvin and wedding vows. And if she was never going to be allowed to return, what was she doing there now? Torturing herself? Torturing her family? Prolonging the inevitable?

She couldn't take it anymore. She had to get out of there. She swung herself off the wall and out the door. She thought she heard someone call her name, or maybe they were just talking about her. After all, she was the talk of the community. But going from one room to the next was not enough. The dining room was as crowded as the living room was; doubly so. She couldn't stay any longer. Without a second thought, she wrenched open the front door. She hurried across the porch, down the steps, then started up the long drive.

Her thoughts tumbled over themselves. She had to get away. She was never going to survive in Pontotoc. Melvin was never coming after her. She would never be allowed to join the Amish church. And they would not allow her to stay in her conservative community as a single mother. Her family was shamed. It was all her fault and the stupid choices she had made. The weight of it was more than she could bear. She just had to get away.

She walked with no particular direction in mind. Just away.

Away.

The word echoed inside her head. She had to get away. Away from her family. Away from Christmas. Away from everything that she loved.

Her tears started, hard and wet, leaving streaks where they ran. They were silent tears. Some sad, some angry. But the anger was at herself. The mistakes she had made. There were enough tears that at first she didn't feel the sting of the ice against her cheeks. Or rather, she didn't recognize it for what it was. That storm everyone said was coming had finally arrived.

Great. She had picked the perfect night for her escape. She ignored the cold stinging her cheeks and just kept walking.

She walked as fast as she could down the narrow lane, not paying any mind whether she turned right or left when she got to the end of the red dirt drive. *Away.*

Freezing rain continued to fall. It was dark, the only lights the glow coming from the Amish houses and the occasional security light at the English homes dotted throughout. Some lived in trailers; most lived on farms. It was early enough that people were still awake, and their lamps cast yellow glows from their windows. It was just enough to keep her going. She could hear the splat of the rain as it hit the leaves of the kudzu, the rocks, and the road.

Sleet might have been better. Or even snow. But the rain clung to her, wet the hem of her skirt, soaked through her stockings and shoes. Ever since she'd been back, since that first day at church, she had been dressing in the traditional Amish clothing, but who was she trying to kid? She was never going to be allowed to be part of their community. She pulled her sweater a little tighter around her shoulders, vaguely wishing she had grabbed a coat on her way out of the house. Even a light jacket. True outerwear was a definite necessity when trying to escape in the winter. She could just chalk that up as another of her grand mistakes.

She stopped in her tracks as a pain seared across her belly. She bent over double and rubbed the spot. It subsided and turned into an ordinary stitch in her side. She couldn't seem to get enough breath. She started to walk again, smoothing her hands over that spot to ease the sting.

She should have gotten a coat. She should have stayed in Columbus. She should have never left Pontotoc in the first place.

There went hindsight again. She pulled on the sides of her sweater, trying to draw it closer to her even though the rain had started to seep through. It was no easy task to hold the ends of her sweater together and still massage that cramping pain in her side.

Mistake upon mistake. She stepped wrong, her foot coming down on a loose rock. Her ankle twisted. She stumbled, nearly fell, then caught herself. The freezing rain was mixed with sleet now, but it was no better than it had been before. In fact, it was coming down harder. Her teeth began to chatter. She was freezing. She had to get inside. She had to find someplace for cover. It was too far to go back home.

Her ankle hurt as she hobbled on it. Stupid, stupid mistakes.

Lord, please. I've made more than my share of mistakes. I've not listened to the people who love me. And now I'm out here freezing. Please help me find the answers. Amen. But it wasn't just Tillie who needed help. She needed help for her child. If she froze to death, so would her baby, and that could never be. She had made mistakes in being with a man who wasn't her husband, leaving her family and the Amish behind, but she couldn't call the child she carried a mistake. She just couldn't. The child within her was a miracle, and she should treat it as such. She had to get herself and the baby someplace warm and dry. She could see the outline of something up ahead.

A mailbox. Where there was a mailbox it was certain that there was a barn or a house or some kind of outbuilding where she could huddle in for the night. She had thoughts of warm hay and softly breathing animals. The perfect modern-day Nativity scene, warm and glowing.

She turned down the drive. That's what she wanted. That's what she needed. Someplace warm, someplace dry. She could just picture it in her head. There was a light on in the window of the house. But she couldn't disturb whoever lived there. Then they would be witness to yet another of her mistakes. If they even took her in. Too many people in their community got one look at her large belly and turned away. They were shamed by her shame, and they could barely stand to look at her. Of course, they could talk about her, but that was a different matter. She didn't want to be turned away. It was better by far to sneak into the barn tonight and ride out the storm. Tomorrow everything would look different. Surely tomorrow everything would look brighter.

Or maybe tomorrow she should call Melvin and beg him to take her back, even though the last place she wanted to be was the English world. At least there, they didn't look at her like she was the greatest sinner of all. At least there, she was just another pregnant woman, no special story. She felt around the side of the barn until she found the door. Thankfully, it was open, and she slid inside, grateful to be out of the weather. Not that shelter alone was much good. It was still freezing in the barn. So much for those visions of warm and toasty hay in a manger at Christmastime. It was freezing.

Tillie found a lantern and lit it. At least now she had light to see where she was. Indeed, it was the main barn. She could hear the cows shifting, and close by the horses most likely used to pull the owner's carriage. She was sure there were a couple of Belgians stored somewhere inside to pull the plow, for most everyone in Pontotoc farmed, at least a little piece of land.

So far she was out of the rain and she had

light, but the lamp could not provide the heat she needed.

She slipped out of her wet sweater and pulled on the black coat hanging on a hook just inside the door. The sweater had provided little protection against the weather, and the rain and sleet had started to seep through and soak her dress.

But at least the coat would keep her warmer than a sopping wet sweater. Her teeth still chattered, and her hands still shook. Her fingernails were blue underneath.

She blew on her hands, hoping to bring better circulation back to her fingers. Surely just a little more time in the barn and she would be warm. Well, warmer. She would settle for warmer at this point.

She had half a mind to find the carriage horse and sneak into the stall with it. Perhaps she could steal a little of its heat to warm herself. But the idea seemed a little strange. She supposed it would work, but it still seemed strange.

Or she could take off her stockings and shoes that were soaked through. What would that help? She didn't know. She could be colder without them. Well, she doubted she would be much colder.

She blew on her fingers again, somehow

managing to bite her tongue as her teeth chattered. "Ow!"

What a mess she had made of things! She was out in the middle of who knew where, in wet clothes, in a freezing barn, and she had just bit her tongue. And she was pregnant. She had really done it this time.

Maybe she could find an empty stall filled with hay. Maybe just being in a smaller space would make her feel warmer. She could cover up with the hay and hope she didn't sneeze all day tomorrow. She supposed sneezing the day after was better than freezing the day before.

Before she could carry out this new mission, she heard a loud bang coming from the end of the barn. She jumped, the noise as loud as a thunderclap. The side door. She must not have closed it all the way when she came in. The wind caught it again and slammed it against the frame.

Tillie jumped once more. She blew on her fingers and hurried toward the door. It would do no good to stay in the barn if she let all the cold air in. Of course, her side still hurt and her ankle throbbed, the one she had twisted on the rock. So hurrying wasn't quite best the option for her. The door slammed twice more before she got to it. She reached out with a very cold hand to pull it closed when suddenly her fingers were caught in a vice grip.

"You!"

Tillie stared at her hand, then up into the angry face of Levi Yoder.

Levi couldn't believe the sight before him. Tillie Gingerich in his barn on the worst night of the year. Weather-wise, anyway.

"What are you doing here?" she asked. To hear her, a stranger would think it was her barn.

"I think that's my question to you."

She pulled her hand from his grasp, and he reluctantly let her go. She was frozen through. He didn't know how long she had been in his barn, but she had pulled his extra coat on over a dress that was darkly stained with water. The spots had a stiff look to them, as if they were almost frozen themselves. Her teeth chattered and her hair was damp. Her prayer *kapp* had crumpled to a mess of linen on the back of her head.

"How did you get here?" he asked. That was probably a better question.

"I walked."

He couldn't believe it. "You walked in this weather?"

"It wasn't like this when I started out."

"Without a coat?"

185

She waved away his question.

"Why are you here? Why did you come here?"

She pulled on the ends of his coat, her hands covered by the sleeves. He hoped it was warming. She had been so cold when he touched her.

"I didn't come here on purpose. I got caught in the storm."

"Again, why?"

She shook her head.

Fine. She didn't want to answer. It wasn't any skin off his nose if she stayed in his barn overnight. It wasn't like she was going to harm the animals or steal his coat. Though at this point he figured she needed that worse than he did.

"I just want to stay here till dawn," she said.

"There's a blanket in the tack room," he grumbled after a few moments of thought. The last person he wanted in his barn was Tillie Gingerich. The fact that he didn't want anybody in his barn was irrelevant. She was by far the worst person to be there at all. She constantly reminded him of everything he had lost. She constantly reminded him that Christmas was just around the corner. Somehow just by looking into her hazel eyes, he remembered how alone he was.

But he couldn't turn her out in the cold. He couldn't do that to anyone. Even his dog was sleeping in the house. He turned to go back that way. He could feel her eyes on him as he approached the door.

Even his dog was sleeping in the house. *Can you really do it?*

Could he let his pregnant dog sleep in the house and leave a pregnant woman out in the barn just because she reminded him of the things that he loved and lost?

His feet stopped at the door. He didn't tell them to; they just did it on their own. One more step and he would have been out of the barn. But there he stood. He sucked in a deep breath. Let it out. Turned to face her. "You can sleep in the spare room," he grunted. His voice sounded like it belonged to someone else. One of those cavemen he had heard the English talk about. It was gruff and coarse, more guttural than anything. But that was only because his throat was clogged with so many emotions.

If the last thing he wanted was Tillie Gingerich in his barn, then the *very last* thing he wanted was Tillie Gingerich in his house. But it seemed he had no choice in the matter.

"Come on." He motioned for her to follow him and didn't look back to see if she did.

He couldn't. He didn't want to be inhospitable. He didn't want to be unchristianlike, but he wasn't sure his heart could take it.

Oh, Lord, why are you testing me? What have I done? But even as he said that small little prayer, he knew he would have no reply. God just simply wasn't answering him these days. It was as if he was leaving Levi to fend for himself, like a sink-or-swim kind of thing. Sink or swim in life's tragedies.

Up the porch steps, across the wooden planks of the porch itself, into the front door, and there he stopped. He sensed rather than heard her behind him. Even with the ungainly belly she was carrying around, she seemed to glide wherever she went. Graceful, at least all the times he had seen her before. He sucked in a deep breath and turned to face her once again. "The spare bedroom is upstairs. First door on the right. I'll get some sheets. Maybe something for you to wear."

What was she going to wear? One of Mary's dresses? It should have been an easy yes, but it wasn't. How could he look at her in Mary's dress? He hadn't even been in Mary's closet since she died.

Lord, lord, why are you testing me?

"Danki," she murmured. Then she turned and started toward the staircase. Gone was the grace he had seen earlier. She was limping. Had she hurt herself on her walk there? She must have. He had never seen her like that before. He supposed it wasn't easy navigating back roads in the dark. So what was she doing out here at this time of night? What was she doing sneaking into his barn? And now that she was here, what was he going to do about it?

CHAPTER THIRTEEN

"She's got to be somewhere," Eunice said. As the words left her mouth, she sent up a silent prayer that they were true. Tillie had to be somewhere; didn't mean she still had to be at home. And the thought was becoming more and more obvious the longer they searched for her: she was gone.

Eunice just didn't understand it. One minute, Tillie had been there eating and drinking alongside everyone. And then the next she was nowhere to be found. It was almost as if she had vanished into thin air. It was an impossibility, of course, but Eunice had no better ideas as to what had happened to her youngest daughter.

"I'll go up to my house and make sure she didn't sneak off and go up there," David said.

"Me too." Anna nodded.

The two of them left to check their houses.

"What about the cabin?" Jamie asked.

"Good idea," Leah added. "I'll go with you."

Leah and Jamie grabbed their coats as well and headed out the door.

Eunice ran through her mental checklist. They had checked Mammi's room, in the kitchen, the back porch, the sewing room, the front porch, even the outhouse. And there was no sign of Tillie.

"She's just been acting so funny lately," Eunice said.

Hannah sidled up next to her and ran one arm around her shoulders. "I know."

They all knew. Tillie had been going through so much, and there was not anything anyone could do for her.

"The bishop came by this week," Eunice said.

Hannah drew away in surprise. *"Jah?"*

Eunice nodded, and tears started welling in her eyes. "Her situation is impossible."

Hannah seemed to think about it for a moment. Then she nodded. "I understand. But there's always a way."

Was there? Eunice hoped. But all signs were pointing to Tillie going back to the English world.

"It's starting to rain," Jim said.

Eunice looked at her oldest. Rain and sleet clung to his coat.

A sob escaped her. She knew she was overreacting, just as she knew Tillie was gone. Out there somewhere in the dark, in the bad weather, pregnant and most likely upset. As her mother, Eunice needed to do something.

Hannah turned to her son. "Brandon?"

The young man nodded. "I'm on it." He pulled out his cell phone and called the police. Eunice barely registered what he was saying. All she could think about was Tillie and the baby.

"It's starting to get bad out there," Matthew said. "Before long we won't be able to get the horses out in this."

"Horses?" Eunice hated the sound of her voice. It was no longer a word that she had said, but rather a screech. Her daughter was out there alone and they were worried about the horses?

"Mamm, breathe." Hannah rubbed her shoulders. "Tillie is a smart girl. If it has started to rain or sleet or whatever it's doing out there, she's found shelter."

Gracie nodded and took a step toward Eunice. "Hannah's right. And we don't know which direction she went. Or even if she truly left the property."

The front door opened and Abner came back into the house. His hat and coat were glittering with rain and sleet. He stamped off his boots and hung his hat on the peg. "She's not in the barn."

Eunice walked slowly to the couch and sank down into the cushions. The barn had been her last hope. There was a new litter of kittens out there, and the horses, of course. Tillie had always loved animals. Eunice had hoped she had gone out there seeking solace in the touch of their fur. And now that hope was shattered.

Lord, please take care of my baby girl, Eunice silently prayed. *Take care of my girl and bring her home.*

Tillie sat on the edge of the bed and took off her shoes. She peeled the wet stockings from her legs and hung them over the back of the chair to dry. The room was small, and the lantern she had carried up the stairs with her only illuminated a small part of it. Just enough that she could see the bed wasn't made and there were no clothes in the closet. She wasn't sure what she was going to wear, but one thing was certain: she couldn't stay in her own wet clothes. She would be much warmer naked and under the covers than she would in frozen clothing. But there were no covers. Not yet, anyway. She ran her hands up and down her arms, but it created no warmth for her.

A light knock sounded at the door, just seconds before it opened. Slowly Levi Yoder poked his head inside. "I have bedding. You can make the bed." He spoke the last sentence more like a question. So Tillie nodded.

She wanted to tell him that this was the last place she wanted to be as much as it was the last place he wanted her, but she kept her peace.

He cleared his throat. "And a dress," he said. "I have a dress." He didn't say whose dress it was, and she didn't have the words to ask.

His hands trembled as he set the clothes on the desk just inside the room. He was reluctant to leave the items. Most likely the dress. His late wife's dress. Tillie wished there was something else she could put on. She could see that giving her the *frack* to wear was taking a toll on him.

It seemed he wanted to say more, but he didn't. He just backed away, out into the hall, and shut the door behind him.

Tillie stood there for a moment, then pulled her dress over her head. She hung it on the hook to dry, then stepped out of her underwear and placed it next to her stockings. Hopefully both would be dry in the morning and she would be able to wear them home.

The dress he had brought her was blue. Just the simple navy blue that was so common in their district. It slipped easily over her head and fell softly around her calves. The sleeves were too long and the hem almost reached her ankles, but it was dry, and that counted for a lot.

Tillie took off her prayer *kapp.* The rain had practically destroyed it, but she sat it on the desk in hopes that it would at least dry by the morning.

Though Levi hadn't mentioned it, he had brought her a towel as well. She unpinned her hair and patted it dry as best she could. Then she went about the task of making the bed. She had never made a bed in a place she never wanted to stay. It was odd to need to do that chore and hate it at the same time. But she knew Levi didn't want her there, and that knowledge sat like a lump of clay in her belly. Unmoving, indigestible, just taking up space and making her even more uncomfortable than she already was.

She was reaching across the mattress to tuck in the fitted sheet when a twinge caught in her side. She rubbed the spot, the same spot where she had cramped up on the way there. She had heard the ladies talking about cramps like these. False labor, most the Amish said; *Braxton Hicks* or something like that was what the English called them, but basically it was just the baby getting ready to be born. She still had three weeks to go. But it seemed this new life was gearing up.

And then what are you going to do?

She pushed that voice away and shook out the flat sheet. It was hard smoothing it across the mattress. Her belly kept bumping the edge, and the twinge in her side tweaked every time she stretched too far. But she finally accomplished the task, as well as spreading the blankets on top. Levi had also brought her a thick afghan that wasn't as big as the bed, so she placed it over the spot where she thought she would lay. It would add extra warmth, and right now she could use all the heat she could get.

She moved the lantern over close to the bed and pulled back the covers so she could get under them. She was loath to turn out the lamp. It was one thing to be in total darkness at home and another in the home of a man who wished she were anywhere but there. But she couldn't leave it on all night. She doused the flame and laid her head on the soft pillow. She was tired, exhausted, but she couldn't seem to close her eyes. The room was so dark she couldn't tell if they were open anyway. So she made herself close them. She could do this. She would go to sleep tonight, and in the morning everything would look different. Surely the rain would stop by then. Surely her dress would be dry. She could change and walk home first thing.

Except her side still hurt. She hadn't been paying attention to her steps and looking at where she was going. She hadn't thought about how far she was walking. It was surprising that she made it all the way to Levi Yoder's house. How far would she have walked had the rain not started? There was no way of knowing that now.

Tillie turned onto her right side and rubbed the aching spot on her left. That's all she needed, a good night's sleep, and she would be right back to her old self, which meant of course worrying about what she was going to do next, all the while knowing what had to be done. It didn't matter about her good intentions. It didn't matter about the fact that she didn't consider her child a mistake. All that mattered was she wasn't married to her father's baby, and that man was Melvin Yoder.

Levi sighed and stared out into the darkness. Part of him wanted to sneak back up the stairs to check and see if she was really here. That was as childish as closing his eyes and pretending he wasn't visible. Tillie Gingerich was upstairs in his guest bedroom sleeping in one of his late wife's dresses while he lay awake and thought about it all.

So much craziness was stirring around inside his head. Thoughts of Mary and Joseph and the baby Jesus. Thoughts of his Mary and their baby, a baby boy who would have been born very, very soon had the Lord not seen fit to take them away. And thoughts of Tillie and the baby she carried. He wasn't one for gossip, though he knew men who were. And he heard them talk. Not about Tillie and the baby, but about Melvin. How they could understand why a man with his talents for engines would want to live among the English and work where the repairs were numerous. What Levi couldn't understand was why Melvin couldn't remain Amish and still work on engines. Levi himself loved leatherwork, and he made things for the English. It was all a trade. As an Amish man, all his life he had lived a bit separately from the English who surrounded them. They all did. And yet they couldn't live without them. They couldn't completely seclude themselves. Most of the people who came into Mary's store, her little shop where she sold jellies and necklaces made out of buttons, were English. The Amish made their own pot holders, their own jelly, and they grew their own tomatoes. They didn't shop at each other's stores. Those were strictly for the English, and it was a good relationship they had. For the most part. The English kept their distance and the Amish kept theirs. They could live together, side by side. So why did Melvin Yoder seem so bent on living English? The only answer he could come up with was that there was another draw to that world, more than just plentiful engines that needed his touch.

Maybe it was freedoms; maybe he had lost his faith in God — Levi had no idea, though there had to be something. But he couldn't think of anything that would make him leave his wife and child.

Not when he would do anything to have them back.

He flipped to the other side, but in the darkness the view was no different, and it wasn't any more comfortable. It had nothing to do with the bed, his pillow, or the sound of the tiny ice pellets hitting the glass panes of the window next to his bed. It had everything to do with the woman upstairs.

He wasn't being fair to her. He knew it as surely as he knew his own name. But his feelings were powerful. It cost him dearly to give her one of Mary's dresses to wear. And it shouldn't have. Mary was gone. She couldn't wear it anymore. Tillie was here and she needed it. But offering it to her was like pouring salt in the wound.

Lord, give me strength. Stand with me. Amen.

He said the prayer even though it had been a while since God had answered any of his requests. Maybe that was the problem. He was asking too much. Or maybe it was just that he was asking. Every man knew there was a time when you gave, you gave to the Lord. And there were times when you received. Apparently this was one of his giving times.

That's not what he wanted this to be about. He didn't want his life to feel like a chore, like a sacrifice to God.

Lord, give me strength, he prayed again.

Maybe if he asked for time . . .

Levi closed his eyes, only then aware that he had opened them again. Every little sound disturbed him. Puddles was in the kitchen next to the potbellied stove, where she had been sleeping these last few days. She was warm, and her puppies were still safe inside. And if she went to whelp in the house, it would just be another mess to clean. But the little cattle dog puppies would be warm and safe. The woman upstairs had a dry dress. She had a warm blanket, a soft bed, and a pillow to cushion her head. He had provided her a roof over her head and shelter from the storm. There was nothing more he could give her.

His animals in the barn were stabled. They had hay and water and everything they needed as the ice fell outside. So why did he feel like there was something more? Why did he feel like there was something he had forgotten?

Tillie woke in the middle of the night with a start. Somehow she had drifted off to sleep without being aware of doing so. But the thought that had awakened her was of her family. She had just walked out. She hadn't told anyone where she was going. At the time she hadn't known. And she certainly hadn't predicted ending up at Levi Yoder's house. She had simply started walking. But no one at her house knew where she was. As if her mother didn't have enough to worry about. Truth be known, Eunice Gingerich was something of a worrywart. But Tillie knew her mother just loved

her children. She wanted them safe —
wanted her children and her grandchildren
safe from harm.

They had been in the middle of the Christmas celebration. The middle of the family
party filled with games and laughter. And
Tillie had walked out. She was certain they
knew she was gone now just as she was
certain that the ice falling here was falling
there. No one would find her until tomorrow. No one would know where she was.
Her mother would worry unnecessarily. And
there was no one to blame but Tillie.

She had always been impulsive. The nature
of impulse had led her to where she was
today. Impulsively she had left her family
behind. Impulsively she had thought her
relationship with Melvin was secure enough
to break the rules she'd been taught her
entire life. Impulsively she had left him and
come home. And impulsively she was now
stranded at Levi Yoder's.

She could feel the anxiety building in her
chest. She'd never meant to worry her family. And she hoped and prayed that they
weren't beside themselves wondering where
she was. But she knew that wasn't the case.
She hoped no one got out in the messy
weather to look for her. Surely they would
figure out that she had found shelter. But

even with that thought, the anxiety built until she felt like there were bricks on her chest. She sucked in a deep breath, trying to calm the rising panic inside her.

But her breath caught as her side twinged again. This time harder, this time straight across. It went from left to right and felt like someone was tearing her in half.

Calm down, she told herself. She just needed to calm down. All this anxiety, all this panic, all this worry was doing nothing but upsetting the baby. Mammi Glick would tell her that she would give the poor child a birthmark worse than the mark of Cain if she wasn't careful, if she didn't stop worrying. So she tried again, pulling in a breath, shorter this time. It wasn't pain-free, but at least it didn't send fire across her body.

She turned onto her other side. Most of the pain was gone now, just a tight feeling and a lingering throb. It was hours till dawn and a few more until she would be able to let her family know that she was okay. Until then, there was absolutely nothing she could do about it. Until then she needed to get some rest. She needed to sleep. Staying awake and worrying was doing no one any good. And considering the look that Levi Yoder had given her before he closed the door . . . she knew she needed the night's sleep to combat that. She needed to keep herself together. Keep her chin up. Keep her pride in place.

Pride goeth before a fall in a haughty spirit before destruction.

And where had her pride gotten her? Nowhere fast. And now it was as if she was daring those around her to censor her. Pride could do that.

She thought she'd been ready to be on her own, but these feelings showed her how much she still had to grow. How much she still had to learn.

Her next breath caught in her throat as the pain seared across her once again.

False labor, she told herself. Too much stress. Too much walking. Too much cold. But the pain didn't begin and end as quickly as it had before. Something about it was different. She didn't have time to determine exactly what it was before she felt the warm gush between her legs. Her waters had broken.

The baby was coming.

CHAPTER FOURTEEN

Levi jerked awake, unsure at first what had disturbed him. Wasn't Puddles in the kitchen? Was she having her puppies? Or was it just the fact that Tillie Gingerich was upstairs in one of his guest rooms that made him feel something was off?

Or maybe he had been dreaming.

He lay back on his pillow and listened to the ice hitting the frosty window just as he had when he went to bed. It was a bad storm for sure. By now, most all the trees had to be encased in ice. Much more and the limbs would start breaking off. It would make for slow traveling tomorrow, if anyone could get out at all. And that meant another day of Tillie Gingerich and her rounded belly that reminded him of all that he had lost.

He closed his eyes again, exhaled, and tried to relax. Then he heard it.

Was it the wind? That low keening sound?

The wind through the trees covered in ice, maybe. Or Puddles. As cold as it was, he needed to get up and check on the dog. He threw back the covers and lit the lantern he kept by his bed. Then he slipped into his housecoat and house shoes and made his way to the kitchen.

Puddles looked up at him with those adoring brown eyes as he entered the room. But she didn't get up. Her belly was still swollen with pups and she thumped her tail against the floor as he came near. He reached down and scratched her behind the ears, and she licked his hand affectionately. "Good girl," he crooned. She thumped her tail harder. Puddles was fine. Must've been the wind. Or the simple fact that Tillie Gingerich had wound him up to where he was hearing things.

One last pat to the dog's head, and Levi shuffled back to his room. Yet before he could go inside, he heard it again, that low sound somewhere between the creak of his barn door and a strangled cry. But he could hear it better in the hallway, and it sent his pulse racing. Was he just being anxious? Or was there someone in trouble?

Tillie.

Somehow he knew. Something was wrong with Tillie.

His heart lodged in his throat as he ran up the stairs and down the hall to where she slept.

He raised his hand to knock on her door. But stopped. What if he was being overly anxious?

The sound came again, and this time it raised the hairs on his arms. It was coming from inside the room.

He knocked on the door, the sound unnaturally loud in the silent house. "Tillie?"

"Levi?" His name sounded as if it had been wrenched from between her clenched teeth.

Something was wrong. "I'm coming in."

She made another noise; he couldn't tell if it was consent or not. Whatever it was, she sounded like she was in trouble, and like she needed someone immediately.

He pushed into the room, his lantern casting shadows across it. He swept the light around the room, stopping when it reached the bed. Tillie was there, hunched up against the headboard. Her knees were raised, her arms wrapped around them. Even in the dim light he could see the beads of perspiration despite the chill in the house.

He stopped.

"The baby," she panted. "The baby is coming."

He had never seen anything like it in his life. His thoughts went in so many different directions, then finally he settled on the one that seemed most logical. He was halfway down the stairs before he remembered they were in the middle of a storm. He had to think this through a little more. He couldn't get the horse out in this. He supposed he could run to his nearest neighbors' and use the phone to call for an ambulance. Though he didn't know if they could get out in times like this either.

"Levi!"

She needed him.

He turned and raced back up the stairs and into the room where Tillie labored. But he could hardly step foot into the room. It was too fully ingrained in him: this was women's territory.

Yet there were no women around.

"I need," she panted. "I need . . . you." She reached out a hand toward him. He stepped into the room and could now see that tears were streaming down her face. Still she beckoned him to come closer.

Unsure of what to do, he hooked a hand under the desk chair and pulled it close to the bed.

Still her hand reached for him. He reached back, offering her his fingers. She clutched them in a deathlike grip, and he felt the bones pop. Then she leaned forward as if bearing down. Never in his life . . .

Was this right? Should he get help? Should he leave her? He just didn't know. "I should get help," he said.

"No. Don't leave." She let out a hard breath between each word and somehow managed to squeeze his fingers even tighter. "There's no time."

How did she know? He supposed that was just another of the mysteries of women.

"You're going to have the baby now?" Again his thoughts tumbled around on top of one another. He couldn't make head nor tail of any of them.

"Yes." It was more of a soft hiss rather than a word. Then a strangled cry and she panted once more.

"I need to get help."

She shook her head. "You have to stay. Please stay."

All thoughts of what was right and what was wrong, of what was accepted as the man's role in the Amish world, would have to be put aside. This was an emergency. A part of him still wanted to run down the stairs and go find help. A woman, any woman, would surely know better what to do than he. But there was no way she was letting go of his fingers, and he was almost certain the only way to escape her grip was to cut off his own hand. Or so it felt.

"I don't know what to do." He had to wait for another of her pains to subside before she answered. They seem to be coming closer and closer together. Wasn't that the way of it? He had no idea. He'd never seen a baby being born. A colt, a calf, even lambs and kids — the goat kind — but never a human baby.

"Stay here," she said on a long exhale.

"I don't know what to do." He could help birth just about any farm animal there was, but he didn't know what to do with a baby.

"I do," she managed before the next pain set in.

He had never felt so useless in his life. He wanted to help, but even as he sat there and watched her labor, allowed her to squeeze his fingers as the pains came, he still wanted to do something more. Go get help. Take away the pain. Something, anything, to make it better. He could only sit and watch.

The labor seemed to take forever. But he knew that it was fast. Women didn't talk about such matters in front of menfolk, but he knew that some women labored for days. It seemed as if Tillie was on some sort of express track to having her baby. He guessed that sometime before dawn the child would be born. The thought left his mouth dry, his heart thumping. Again he wanted to tell her that he didn't know what to do, though at this point he didn't think it mattered. Even if neither one of them knew what to do, the baby was still coming.

"Help . . . me," she managed between her clenched teeth.

Something was wrong. *Please God, no. Don't let anything be wrong.* Even in her tight grip, his hands started to shake.

"What do I need to do? Tell me what to do."

"She's coming," Tillie said. "Help me." She reached out her other hand and he took it in his own. She used her hold on him to raise herself up. "Get the cover."

He looked down at their clasped hands. "Release me."

She let go long enough for him to pull the sheet from the bottom of the bed. She braced her hands behind her, supporting herself, but once the sheet was to her knees, she reached for him once more.

She needed support, that much was certain. He managed to take both of her hands in one of his and arrange the pillows on the bed behind her back.

She gave him a grateful smile. "It's almost time."

"*Jah.*" That he knew as well.

Then suddenly her face changed, grew tense, and her breath caught. She squeezed his hand even tighter, using her hold on him to pull herself up a bit and bear down at the same time.

"She's coming," she panted. Lines of worry creased her face. Sweat plastered her hair to her cheeks. And he was so aware that there was a miracle happening right before him.

"Is it time to push?"

She gave him a tired laugh. "What do you think I've been doing?"

In the golden glow of the lantern light, their eyes met. And it was as if they both recognized this moment as a miracle. A miracle that only they were sharing. He extracted his hands from hers.

"Don't leave me." The weariness was replaced with fear.

"I'm not leaving. The baby is coming." He needed something to wrap the child in. He glanced around the room. On the peg next to the door she had hung the towel she had dried her hair on. It wasn't soft, but it was nearby. It would have to do. He grabbed it and in a heartbeat was back at her side.

"This is it," Tillie said.

Her whole body tensed. She closed her eyes, gritted her teeth, and bore down once again. Levi could only stand helpless and watch.

He looked beneath the sheet just as the tiny baby slid into the world. A feeling like nothing he had ever experienced before came over him.

Tillie lay back against the pillows with a sigh. Her eyes were still closed as she said, "Clean her mouth."

He was frozen in place. He had the towel in his arms ready to scoop up the baby and wrap it in the fabric, but he could only stand and look at it. It was a girl, as she had claimed. A perfect baby girl who waved her fists and tried to breathe this new thing called air.

"I don't know what to do." How many times had he said that tonight?

"Just take your finger and run it around inside her mouth."

How did she know to do that?

He did as she instructed and the baby sucked in a deep breath and squalled like he had never heard before. Her tiny fists shook in the air. Her body was slick and pink and covered in something white. He had no idea what it was, but he managed to wrap her as best he could in the towel. He placed her on Tillie's stomach.

"How did you know it was a girl?"

"Scissors," Tillie said. "We need scissors. Clean scissors. And two clamps. Shoelaces. Something."

He looked around the room as if he would find them there. Then, with a shake of his head, he raced down the stairs. He was back in seconds with a pair of scissors, two clothespins, and a bottle of alcohol. He opened the scissors and used the alcohol to sterilize them and the clothespins as best he could. Then he looked to her for further instructions.

"Cut the cord," she instructed. "You have to clamp it first." She showed him where and he did as she said. He was reeling from the fact that she had just had the baby. She'd had the baby right there in his house. A perfect baby girl.

Tillie looked down at the child she held in her arms. She did it. They had done it. She could still hardly believe it.

So it was true what they said, what the English ladies had told her about childbirth. She had expected to feel uncomfortable with someone else in the room, even worse if that someone was a man, and doubly worse if it was Levi Yoder. She had been reluctant at first, but that had soon disappeared as she labored on. All modesty seemed to fly out of the window in the face of the health and well-being of her baby.

She touched the infant's tiny little nose. Perfect nose. She shouldn't think her baby was perfect, but she was. The tiny creature had come out whole. Ten fingers and ten toes and a sweet little mouth that was eager for her first meal.

The embarrassment had returned a bit when she had to ask Levi to leave so she could pass the afterbirth. Having a baby was a messy business. But worth it. So very worth it.

And she knew then that she was right not to believe the baby was a mistake. How could she?

When it was all said and done, she moved into the chair still holding the baby while Levi stripped the bed and stuffed the sheets into a garbage bag. They were beyond washing, and she promised to buy him some new ones. It was a small price to pay for all that he had done for her. But he waved away her offer as if it was meaningless. Perhaps it was for him as well. After all, birth was truly a miracle.

A small knock sounded on the door, and

she moved to cover the baby's head with the sheet. It was more than awkward. She had a maternity dress, but not a nursing one. And when the baby wanted to be fed, she had to basically strip down to nothing. That was okay, she supposed, for a while anyway. It was starting to turn light outside now, and hopefully soon she would be able to leave. So it would only be a time or two. Maybe just this once.

Levi stepped into the room. "I don't mean to bother you, but I brought you something to wear." He approached the bed slowly. "The shirt's mine. I'm not sure where this skirt came from. It must've been something of Mary's." Though she could tell from his voice if it was Mary's, she had never worn it. For some reason that made her feel a tiny bit better. "This way you can . . . feed the baby."

They had gone back to a little more of the awkward stage.

Tillie smiled at him. *"Danki,"* she said.

He laid the clothes on the end of the bed. "The weather report is not very good."

"The roads?"

He shook his head. "There are trees down. A few of the roads are closed. Everything is still covered in ice. Some of the city streets got sanded and salted during the early-morning hours, but the back roads are pretty much impassable."

"So what do we do now?"

"That's what I wanted to talk to you about. I can go to the neighbors' house about two miles down the road here. That's my closest English neighbor. They have a phone. We can call for an ambulance or the fire department. Whoever we should call and tell them about the baby. I have a battery-operated radio in my workshop. I brought it in to see if there was any word about the storm. It seems there are a lot of accidents on the highway, so if it's not an emergency . . ." He let his words trail off.

It wasn't an emergency. She and the baby were fine. They had made it through the golden hour, that first sixty minutes after birth when things sometimes went wrong. That was not to say that something still couldn't happen, but it didn't seem likely at this point. There was no emergency.

She shook her head. "If no one's coming, it seems a waste to have you tramp out in the ice and cold just to be told that no one can come."

"I could call someone. Maybe your sister? The Mennonite one?"

Tillie nodded. "Or my nephew. They both have phones. We could tell them, but they wouldn't be able to get word to the rest of my family." Was it worth sending him out in the freezing weather just so two people wouldn't worry when the remainder were probably beside themselves? A part of her wished he would go and tell Leah about the baby. But that was just the excitement that comes with birth. She wouldn't ask that of Levi. She'd asked so much of him already.

"I don't think it's worth it," she said.

He gave her a tentative smile, as if he could hear the sadness in her voice. He knew she had big news to share and no one to share with save him.

"Tomorrow," he said. "Tomorrow the weather is supposed to be a bit better. They'll be able to clear the roads. Perhaps get cars back this way. Maybe the next day we can get the horses out." But he shook his head. "I don't know about you riding in a buggy so soon after." He nodded toward the lump under the sheet that was the baby she held.

She wasn't so sure about traveling by buggy right now either. Every part of her was sore, from the obvious parts all the way to her fingers and toes. Her hair was the only part of her that didn't feel like it had been run through the mill. The thought sent a wistful smile to her lips. "Two days," she said, confirming his news.

He nodded. "Maybe three. But after that we should be able to get you home."

CHAPTER FIFTEEN

Levi sat at the kitchen table and watched the second hand tick away. Upstairs in the first room on the right lay a woman he barely knew and the baby she just had. The whole thing sounded crazy. Add in the ice storm outside and it was almost too much to believe. How had he managed to get in the position he was in right now?

The Lord works in mysterious ways. It was what Mamm was always saying.

But could he really believe God was behind this?

Who else would it be?

Mims would say that. She would tell him that he had shut himself off and done his best to forget about the world around him, and this was God's way of bringing him back.

And she might be right. There was no way to know for certain. But it seemed like an awfully big coincidence. But perhaps that just showed that the Lord did indeed work in mysterious ways.

There was one thing he knew for certain. They were stuck there for a couple of days. Thankfully, he had plenty of firewood already cut, stacked, and waiting, and Mims had provided him with enough food to feed half the district. They would be fine. The baby . . . Tiny babies had needs. Diapers and tiny little clothes.

He pushed back from the table and slowly made his way down the hall to the room just next to his. The door was closed, as it had been since the last time he'd been in there. He had tried several times to go in and clean through everything, but he hadn't been able to get past the door. It was just so hard. But the baby upstairs needed the things that he had in that room. And so some good use would be found for them.

With a heavy sigh, he opened the door and stepped inside. Sunlight filtered through the window and landed on the crib. A crib much too big to cart up the stairs. But there were other things. A bag of disposable diapers, a stack of the cloth kind, and rubber pants. Large safety pins, tiny little cotton gowns, minuscule socks, sweet little hats, and a cradle that would be no problem at all to carry.

He packed all these things and a stuffed bunny of sunshine yellow into the cradle. But he stopped before actually picking it up. It made his heart hurt to see those things there, those tiny little baby things that would have belonged to his son. And it hurt even more to think about the son who would never use them. The mother who would never see her child grow and learn.

But there's a baby upstairs who can use them, even needs them.

He sucked in a fortifying breath. Then he hoisted the cradle and carried it from the room. He set it in the hallway and closed the door behind him. For the first time since Mary and the baby had died, he left the room with a lighter heart than the one he went to it with. It seemed almost a miracle. A surprising, astonishing miracle. He missed them; he probably always would. They were gone — he knew that. He had understood it from the beginning, but he had not been able to get rid of the things that belonged to them, Mary's clothes and the various baby items that had been brought over from well-meaning family members and friends. But now these things had a new purpose.

He stopped outside the door of the bedroom where Tillie had slept, where she had given birth, and he knocked on the door.

He waited for her response before he set the cradle down and opened the door for himself. Then he picked up the mess of things he had gathered from downstairs and carried them into the room.

Her eyes grew wide.

She had taken his suggestion and was wearing his button-down shirt. He supposed she also had on Mary's odd skirt. He still didn't know what she had intended to do with it, but that was Mary, always with the ideas.

"What is all this?" Tillie asked.

Suddenly Levi felt extremely self-conscious. He had helped this woman bring a life into the world, and suddenly he was embarrassed over the items he had brought to her. He wasn't sure why. So he swallowed back his emotions, cleared his throat. "Some stuff for the baby. I didn't know what all to bring up. There's diapers, a couple of gowns, a pair of socks or two." He shrugged. "And the cradle."

She looked at the cradle filled with various things for the baby and back up to his face. "Did these things belong to your baby?"

He didn't bother to ask how she knew that his child was gone, seeing as how she had been gone when Mary had died. Someone must have told her, even in the short time that she had been back in Pontotoc. It was the way small Amish communities worked.

"*Jah*," he said. "I haven't been able to get rid of them yet. I guess that was a good thing after all."

"Levi," she breathed his name, and he knew from the sound it was more than a summons. It was closer to a prayer. Suddenly he felt even more embarrassed. "This is very generous of you." She didn't finish. She didn't say the rest, though he knew what she was thinking: how painful it must be for him. But she understood, and that was enough.

Tears pricked at his eyes, and he blinked them back. He cleared his throat once more. "The baby," he said. "Your baby has got to have things. It's just lucky I have those things, I guess."

He could say *I guess* all he wanted, but he knew: This had to be the Lord at work. All of it. From the ice storm to Tillie having her baby on such an inconvenient night, he felt as if God was giving him a big message. It was time to get himself together. And that's just what he planned to do.

"There's more downstairs if there's anything else you need."

She smiled, and to his dismay, tears

formed in her eyes as well. "I'm sure this is plenty. I don't want to take your things."

He shook his head. "They're just things." And suddenly he knew it to be true. The things that Mary had saved, things that she had gathered, their baby didn't need them, and the child before him did.

He looked at the baby once again, how beautiful and perfect she was. Was it okay to think that? But he was sure he couldn't change his thoughts if he tried. She was a miracle wrapped in her mother's arms. In fact, as far as he was concerned, they were both miracles.

"I really appreciate it," she said.

Levi could only nod in response. Then he started to the door. He stopped there, turned back around to face his previously unwelcome houseguest. "I'll go down and get some breakfast," he said. "I figure after the night we had, we could sure use some bacon and eggs."

Tillie started to shake her head, to tell Levi that it wasn't necessary, but he was gone before she could say the words. She didn't want him cooking for her, waiting on her hand and foot like she was an invalid. She had just had a baby, that was all. But she had only had a short nap since the time the baby came. And she was very hungry. Truth was, she wasn't sure exactly how she was going to maneuver the stairs. But that wasn't the first problem on her list. She unwrapped her baby from the dress she had swaddled her in and checked the makeshift diaper she had put on her.

Tillie had found a bandanna in the nightstand drawer. Perfect to use for a diaper, along with two small safety pins. Thankfully the baby hadn't wet yet, but Tillie knew it was only a matter of time.

She loosely covered her baby girl again, then eased off the bed. She winced as the sore parts of her protested, but it had to be done. She stood, and with one hand braced against the small of her back, she started unloading the cradle he had brought up.

It had been no secret that he didn't want her there, and she could only imagine how he felt about having her and the baby stranded due to the weather.

It would be days before the ice would melt, the roads would be cleared, and somebody could get through to them. And despite his gruff and sour demeanor, she knew that somewhere in that big chest of his, he had an equally big heart. There was no other explanation for his extreme generosity.

She unloaded a pack of diapers and pulled the plastic bag open. Her first thought was that she would replace them immediately, but diapers were not something he needed any longer, were they? There had to be something else she could do for him. At least she had a couple of days to think about it.

She quickly uncovered her baby girl and wrapped her in a diaper. And as easily as she could, she pulled one of the tiny gowns over the baby's head. It was a surprisingly good fit, but the baby didn't appreciate being disturbed from her midmorning nap. No matter though. It was cold.

As gently as she could, since she still harbored a fear of somehow breaking this tiny little thing the Lord had entrusted to her, Tillie slipped a hat on the baby's head and impossibly small socks on her feet. She pulled a blanket from the cradle and wrapped her baby inside.

Tillie winced again as she bent over to empty the rest of the things from the cradle. She could only assume that he had brought everything up in the cradle because he intended for her to use it. So she emptied it and laid the baby inside.

She was about to crawl back into bed when she stopped. She'd had the baby with

227

her since the minute she had been born, right next to her, side by side, and she felt a little lost with her even a foot away in the cradle. Tillie supposed that feeling would ease with time, but she didn't want that time to be now. She turned back, scooped the baby into her arms, and climbed into bed once more.

She was just settling in when a knock sounded at the door. She'd been smelling all kinds of great aromas from the kitchen, and she still hadn't figured out how she was going to navigate the stairs, especially with the baby in her arms. And she certainly didn't want to leave her behind. So it was a conundrum.

Levi opened the door and let himself in. He carried a tray of food — two cups of coffee, a large stack of toast, and two plates piled high with bacon and eggs.

"You're bringing breakfast to me?"

"I didn't know if the stairs . . ." He turned a warm shade of pink.

She wasn't sure if it was from the awe she heard in her own voice or the words he was speaking. Trying to speak. He didn't seem to be able to get them out. But no matter; she understood.

"It might be a day or so before I'm ready to tackle the stairs." She gave him a small smile. It was strange how two people could share such an intimate time and still be strangers, unaccustomed to the other.

He placed the tray next to her on the bed and pulled up the same chair he had used the night before. Then he took his plate, balancing it on his lap. Tillie bowed her head and wondered for a moment if he had any intention of praying before he ate. But she would never know. Once she prayed, he followed suit.

What did you expect?

He had lost so much. Was it a wonder that his faith was shaken? Perhaps even gone for a time? She hadn't been through near that much, and her faith warbled like a broken buggy wheel.

"It's good," she said. And it was perhaps the best meal she had ever eaten.

"You're just being kind," he said. "But *danki.*"

"Thank you for the things for the baby."

"You already thanked me for that." He took a sip of his coffee.

"Then I'm thanking you again." She gave him a smile.

He smiled in return but the action looked as if he hadn't smiled in a long, long while. Or maybe she was just making stuff up.

"You have a name for her?" He nodded to

the baby who lay close to her side.

"I don't know."

"You seemed pretty confident before she was born that she was a girl." He shook his head. "Did you have one of those fancy English pictures done?"

"Early on. But too early to know the gender." She wasn't sure she would've wanted to find out anyway. She had the rest of her life to know what the baby was, a boy or girl. But only nine months to wonder and dream.

"So you didn't pick out names?"

It wasn't uncommon or even unheard-of in communities such as theirs that a woman didn't pick out names for the baby until the baby came. Picking out names, buying too many items, making too many plans for a child that wasn't born yet was somehow arrogant, and no one wanted to feel arrogant when it came to such a special matter.

"I was thinking about Michelle," she said. "But she doesn't look like a Michelle to me." And it didn't seem right to name a baby who was born so close to Christmas something like Michelle.

It was a great name. But just not Christmassy sounding.

The baby needed a Christmassy sounding name. Tillie wasn't sure why. She just did.

And they shall call him Emmanuel.

"Emmanuela." She said the name without thinking.

"Emmanuela?" From the sound of his tone she couldn't tell if he thought the name was a good one or not.

Like it matters.

It wasn't his baby. But somehow she wanted him to like the name she gave the baby. Because he helped bring the child into the world? Maybe. Or maybe just because she didn't know what she would've done without him there. And she would've been alone had she managed to stay in the barn all night. It was a thought that didn't bear thinking.

"Emmy?" she said. Emmanuela did seem like an awfully big name for such a tiny little baby, but Emmy seemed to fit just right.

Levi smiled. It was the same rusty one from a few moments before, but it seemed to be getting a little easier on his face. "Emmy," he repeated. "I like it."

The three words shouldn't have filled her heart with such warmth and joy, but they did. And she wasn't taking time now to examine why. "Emmanuela Dawn," she said, trying out the middle name she had been contemplating. The baby had been born in the dead of night, but Dawn had a

231

nice ring to it. There had been a woman she had worked with at the day care center named Dawn. She had been so nice to Tillie, always. Perhaps the nicest person she had met in her time in the English world. And Tillie liked the idea of naming the baby after her. Not that she would ever tell her mother that. Or her sisters, even.

The thought brought a smile to her lips.

"What's so funny?" Levi had finished his food and started to restack the dishes on the tray.

Tillie shook her head, but she was still smiling. "Just thinking about my sisters."

Levi stood and gazed down at little Emmy. "Thinking about what they're going to think about her?" he asked.

"*Jah,*" she lied. But it was okay. She had been thinking about what her family was going to think about the baby girl she just had. Along with some other things that she would rather not think about just yet. Like how someone could consider such a beautiful child a mistake, or a sin, even. It was something she couldn't fathom.

Because it goes against your own desires.

Because she wanted to raise her baby in the chaste confines of the Amish church. But if Melvin decided not to come back to the church, then what other choice did she

232

have but to go back to him? She knew the rules. She had known when she broke them. She just never thought it would turn out quite like this.

Levi picked up the tray and started toward the door. "I'll let you get some rest."

She hadn't realized until he said the words how very, very tired she was. She supposed it was to be expected. The rush she had experienced when she woke up and knew she was in labor had long since passed. She was fine, the baby was fine, they both had food in their bellies and warm clothes. They had a nice bed and a generous, gentle man who she supposed had been called by God to help them. It would be nothing now to lie back on the pillows and get some rest. Much-needed rest.

Levi closed the door behind him, and Tillie skootched down into the covers and lay her head on the pillow. She curled up on one side, Emmy still in the circle of her arms. It was amazing to just lie that way with her baby and not worry about church roles and wayward boyfriends. About her chastising congregation or how hard it was to live among the English. For the time being, all she had to worry about was herself, the baby, and maybe the man downstairs.

Chapter Sixteen

The sun was shining brightly through the window when Tillie woke next. She blinked, unsure of where she was for a second before everything came rushing back. A warmth filled her heart as she looked down at the face of her infant baby girl.

She had left in the middle of an ice storm, she had ended up at Levi Yoder's house, and she had given birth during the night. A beautiful baby girl.

A soft knock sounded at the door.

Levi.

"Come in."

The door eased open, and there he stood, another tray in hand. "I wasn't sure if you'd feel like coming downstairs."

Tillie give her sleeping daughter one more look, then pushed herself upright in the bed. She was sore and achy, but she couldn't stay there forever. She would have to start getting around soon.

"How about for supper? That is, if the roads are clear," she hopefully added. She had taken up too much of this man's time already.

He shook his head, though she couldn't read his expression. Was he remorseful, angry? He couldn't be overjoyed. She was the epitome of everything he had lost. Why had things turned out so twisted?

"Maybe tomorrow?" she asked.

He gave a shrug and came into the room. He set the tray on the end of her bed, his blue eyes straying to where her daughter slept.

It was amazing to watch his features soften as he looked at her. And Tillie felt a surge of pride. She may have gone against everything she'd been taught growing up, but she couldn't help but love this baby. The perfect little baby who came three weeks early in the midst of an ice storm.

"Maybe." Levi shifted his gaze back to her. "I don't figure there'll be many buggies out, but maybe some English cars. I can still walk over to my neighbors' house if you want."

Her stomach rumbled as the smell of the food he had brought in reached her. "That smells delicious."

He nodded. "Mims made it. My sister."

Tillie smiled. "I remember Mims."

Actually, Mims was kind of unforgettable. Like a young Eunice. Forceful and in charge, yet somehow lovable all the same.

"She means well," Levi said with a chuckle.

"Sisters always do," she quipped.

He nodded toward the door. "I'll just . . ."

Tillie pulled the tray closer to her. "You don't have to go. In fact, I'd rather not eat alone."

He stopped, his blue eyes assessing. "I have one of those little soft baby chairs. We could put her in it, if you wanted to come downstairs. I think it's a little warmer down there anyway. Are you up to that?"

Surprisingly, she was. "I'd feel better if you took the baby down." She wasn't sure how strong her legs would be, and she surely didn't want to take any chances. She had thought it would take her a couple of days to get downstairs, but if Levi was willing to carry Emmy, Tillie figured she'd be able to make it too.

He hesitated only a moment before answering. "*Jah,* of course." Then he had gathered up the tray and headed out of the room before she even had her feet on the floor.

Emmy slept peacefully, her little mouth

moving at nothing as if she were eating some invisible treat.

Tillie eased her feet. She could do this. *Jah,* she was a little sore. Having a baby wasn't the easiest thing to do, but she knew the stiffness would pass soon. She had heard enough talk from Amish ladies and English women alike. It was just a matter of time.

There went that word again. *Time.* Everything needed time.

"You're up," Levi said as he came back into the room.

She nodded, trailing her hand around the footboard of the bed. *"Jah."*

He looked down at the baby and back to her. And she could see on his face the second thoughts of caring for such a small creature.

"She won't break."

"Are you sure?" he croaked. His voice sounded strained and a little odd.

She had to admit it was strange, the power such a tiny creature could hold over the adults around it.

She smiled at him reassuringly. "Pretty sure." And then she realized men didn't have the practice with other people's babies that women did. At one time or another, she had held almost every baby in the district. Women were just like that. But men didn't have that prior experience.

"Place your right hand under her bottom," she instructed. "And your left hand under her neck. Support her head. And you'll be fine."

He swallowed hard.

"And hold her close to your chest. If she can hear your heartbeat, she'll feel more secure."

He shook his head and slowly moved toward Emmy. "How do women know these things?"

Tillie shrugged. "I guess the same way men know how to fix roofs and the best way to plow a field."

Gingerly he scooped Emmy into his arms. The look on his face was wistful and a bit sad, and somehow filled with joy at the same time. Only a baby could do that.

"I suppose you're right," he said. The words were more of a breathless whisper as he looked at Emmy. Tillie understood and it filled her heart with joy to see that Levi felt the same way she did. Emmy was a miracle. Not a mistake.

The baby arched her back as he picked her up. She raised a tiny fist in the air.

"She wants to stretch," Tillie told him.

She was amazing, this baby he held in his

arms. And the woman too. Her mother. Simply amazing. Suddenly he wondered if this was how Joseph felt when he looked at Jesus for the first time. It didn't matter that the baby wasn't his biologically; he would do everything and anything to protect it. It was just that precious. And then to know that you held the Messiah?

He didn't hold the Messiah in his arms, but she was something else.

"How does she stretch?" he asked. He had so much to learn about babies. He reined in that thought quick. He would have Emmy and Tillie here for another day or two and that would be it. Maybe one day Mims would get married and he could play with her baby. But for now, this was his chance. No. Not his chance; just another small bump in his life.

"Lay her back on the bed and unwrap her blanket," Tillie told him. "Now lift her back so she has room."

He did as she instructed and Emmy stretched and yawned. Her little arms shook with the motion, and she relaxed back into her previous position. A miracle.

"Now wrap her back up and pick her up like I told you earlier."

He did as she bade him once again and held the baby close to his chest. Her warmth and slight weight filled him with joy. A joy he hadn't felt in a long, long while.

"You first," she started. "That way if I need to rest you won't be stuck behind me."

He nodded and started out of the room. He took the stairs one at a time, a little unnerved to carry such a precious bundle. He had loped down the stairs more times than he cared to admit, but today was different. All those trips up and down the stairs and he never once remembered touching the banister. Now he wanted to hang on to it for dear life, and yet both hands were cupped around the child. So he took it slow.

It seemed to take forever, but finally they made it to the bottom of the staircase, Tillie just one step behind him.

"I put the tray on the table," he said. "Can you get the chair from the baby's room?" He nodded toward the door that Mary had deemed to be the nursery.

Tillie nodded.

A small sense of unease filled him as he watched her make her way to the door and open it. She disappeared inside that sacred room, returning a couple of moments later with the chair he had been talking about. It wasn't really a chair — more a hammock made of quilted fabric with a strap to keep the child safely inside. It was small enough to go on the table, or even on the floor if need be. But for now the table seemed better. He couldn't just put the baby on the floor.

Once they had the baby securely strapped in place on the table, he went to fetch some more stew for the both of them.

"I don't have any bread." He chuckled. "Well, the truth of the matter is that when Mims comes and makes corn bread, I tend to eat all of it. Then I don't have any left for the stew. But I've got crackers."

She laughed, and for some reason sound of that laughter made his heart feel light. For just a moment the worry was gone from her eyes, as if she hadn't a care in the world other than crackers and corn bread.

"Crackers are fine," she said. "Maybe tonight I'll make corn bread for you."

He shook his head. "Only if you're up to it. But you don't have to for sure."

"You helped me deliver my baby," she said. "A pan of corn bread is the least I can do."

"Mims is a good cook," Tillie said. And she wondered why no man had snapped her up yet. Mims was a striking woman, with her dark hair and crystal blue eyes like her brother's. And Tillie seemed to remember

241

there having been a time when she had run around with David. But Tillie had been younger then and hadn't paid it much attention.

"That she is," Levi said. "And for that I'm grateful. Can you imagine if she came over every day and cooked and it was terrible?"

Tillie laughed, then winced.

"Are you okay?" His eyes were filled with concern.

"I'm fine. Really." She gave him a reassuring smile.

Together they stood and carried their bowls and spoons to the sink. Levi went outside to fetch some water, and Tillie set a pan on the stove top to heat it so they could wash up. They performed the chores without speaking. Like an old married couple would do.

They had just gotten water in the pan when a piercing cry came from the direction of the table.

Emmy was awake, and apparently very hungry.

"You should go feed her," Levi said. "I can do this."

Tillie hesitated for just a moment before nodding and unstrapping Emmy from the fabric chair. She carried her into the living room for a little more privacy and wondered

242

at the intimacy of it all.

She sat in the chair close to the window and looked out at the crystalline ice that covered everything. A few drops melted from the roof and fell in front of her. And the trees creaked when the wind blew. Maybe tomorrow she would be able to go home. But the strange thing was that, there with Levi, she felt wholly content.

That's because it's safe here.

There was no judging, no consternation, no bishop to talk to, no congregation of the church to satisfy; the rules had been somewhat suspended. She supposed that was to be expected when a person gave birth in an ice storm.

She switched Emmy's side and looked around the living room at the Christmas decorations she and her *mamm* had left. She knew that Levi had been hesitant for the additions, but she was glad he had accepted them. Even the stinky cedar boughs. She wasn't sure why everyone thought cedar was so wonderful. If you used the wood, trimmed and polished it, it was great. But just having it sitting there was like breathing in smelling salts.

Emmy was starting to fall asleep. Tillie laid her on her lap as she got her own clothing back in place. Then she held the baby close to her shoulder. She rubbed her back gently to release any air. She was so delicate and tiny even her cry was feminine and ladylike. So was the small little burp that escaped her.

Levi came into the room still wiping his hands on a dish towel. "I would say she's got perfect timing."

Tillie smiled. "It seems that way to me. Sorry about leaving you to clean up by yourself. Maybe I'll be able to make it up to you tonight at supper."

He shook his head. "You're my guest."

Uninvited guest, she silently corrected. But he was too polite to say so.

"I don't suppose the roads would be clear tomorrow?" she asked, giving a nod to the window and the ice that still coated everything outside.

He pressed his lips together and shook his head. "I'm thinking maybe English cars. And I can still walk to the neighbors'."

"I hate to ask you to do that." But she needed to get word to her family.

"I can go this afternoon," he said. "You and the baby can have a nap, and I'll walk over and call your sister. The one who owns the store in town."

"Danki," she said. "I really appreciate it. You've done so much for us already."

244

He gave a shrug, as if his help had been of no consequence. But it meant the world to her. And she knew that it had cost him dearly.

Levi pulled his scarf a little farther up on his face but didn't stop walking. Rarely had he gone to his neighbors' house to use the phone. In an emergency only. And this was an emergency. Though he didn't remember it seeming to take this long to get there, or maybe that was the weather.

The wind had turned cold again, and what little ice had melted had refrozen. With any luck, tomorrow the English cars would be able to get out. But he wasn't sure about taking a horse and buggy on the icy, rutted roads.

The best he could hope for was a cop or an ambulance maybe, though if he called either one he was certain Tillie would be madder than a wet hen.

She was something to behold when she held that baby. It was mystifying to him. A miracle. But wasn't that the way of Christmastime? A moment of miracles?

It was a miracle, as well, what happened inside him each time he gave her something for the baby. A blanket, socks, a pacifier that seemed to take up half of her little face.

With each item a little bit of his heart went as well. The strange thing was he didn't mind it at all.

He smelled the smoke from the chimney before he saw the house. Thankfully, that meant someone was home. Levi had lived next to Owen Carson for many years now, and he seemed a good man. It had been Owen who had called the ambulance for Mary. Owen who had given her CPR even when they both knew that she was already gone. And Owen who had sat with him until his family came.

Levi made his way to the back door and knocked. No lights were on. Levi wondered if maybe the electricity had been knocked out by the storm.

He rapped once more, then the door opened to reveal his longtime neighbor.

"Levi?" Owen said by way of greeting. "Come in, come in." He stood to one side to allow Levi to enter. "What brings you out this way?" Owen asked as he led the way to the kitchen.

"I'm sorry to ask, but may I use your phone?"

"Everything all right?" Owen asked with concern.

Levi nodded. "I have an unexpected guest. Well, two, really." He explained about Tillie and Emmy.

"You don't say," Owen said. "That is something else."

"I need to call her family and let them know that she's okay," Levi continued as Owen shook his head in wonderment.

"She's not Amish?" Owen asked.

"*Jah,* she is." Sort of. "But she has a sister who is Mennonite. She runs a secondhand store in town."

Owen nodded. "I know the one. I bought the missus some of their goat milk lotions for Christmas." He placed one finger over his lips as if to tell Levi it was a secret, then he pointed to the table where his cell phone lay. "Sit down if you like. Wanda made some coffee before she went for her walk and the power went off. You want a cup?"

"Thanks," Levi said. "That would be welcome." He pulled out one of the chairs and sat while Owen poured coffee into a mug and refilled his own cup.

Then Owen sat down across from him and tapped a few times on the phone screen. "We turned the house phone off a couple of months ago," he told Levi. "It seemed like only telemarketers called that number anyway. So we both just use our cell phones now." He tapped a few more times, then handed the phone to Levi. "That there's the number for the store. I figure that might be the best way to reach her. Unless you have a number for her personal phone."

Levi shook his head. "No, this will have to do."

Of course no one answered at the store, and he was forced to leave a message. He hated telling Leah the news of Emmy's birth over a recorded message, but he wanted to let her know that Tillie and baby were both fine and doing well. He wondered when she would get the message. Hopefully it would be before Tillie managed to find her way home.

Owen thoughtfully rubbed his chin. "You know what? I bet if we call the nonemergency police number, they might be able to get word to her family. It's a special case, wouldn't you say?"

It was to him. He wasn't sure what the police would think about it. But he handed the phone back to Owen and waited for him to get it ready for the next call.

He took a sip of his coffee and tried to figure out what he would say to the police, but he was saved the trouble when Owen took the matter into his own hands.

"This is Owen Carson," he said into the phone. "I'm calling for my Amish neighbor." He went on to explain the situation as Levi took the time to warm up for the walk back home.

"So you'll send someone out there to let them know?" Owen asked. "Good. Good."

Levi gave him the address, which Owen in turn gave to the dispatch person at the police department.

Owen hung up the phone with a satisfied nod. "There. All taken care of." Then he smiled at Levi. "A baby, huh?"

Levi nodded as a lump filled his throat. Never in his wildest dreams had he imagined having a newborn in his house. Not after losing Mary. "It's something to see," Levi said, a little surprised at his own words.

"Wait till I tell Wanda."

Owen's wife walked daily due to a bad heart. It was nothing to see her on the road at all hours regardless of the weather. Like today. Chilly and icy and she was out walking for her health.

"Maybe y'all can walk over and visit. I think we're going to be in for another day or so."

Owen looked out the kitchen window at the ice that still covered everything. "You know, I think you're right."

Levi drank a second cup of coffee, thanked Owen for his help, then begged his leave.

He trudged back through the icy field, waving at a bundled-up Wanda as he passed her. Despite the weather, despite being iced in, his heart felt lighter than it had in a long, long while. The funny thing was he hadn't realized how much his heart was weighing him down until the heaviness had been lifted.

And he could only attribute the change to Tillie and Emmy — mostly to the child. The baby represented everything he had thought he had lost, and though she in no way belonged to him, he felt a strong kinship to her.

You're losing it.

That's what Mims would say. "Projection" or something like that. She would tell him that he was taking the feelings he had for Mary and their child and pushing them off onto Tillie and her baby. Which was ridiculous. He hadn't known them that long. He didn't love Tillie the way he loved Mary, and it wasn't possible after only one day he would feel that strongly toward a child who wasn't his. Strong enough to love it as if it were his own. That sort of bond came with time.

Time.

He pushed the word away and stuffed his hands a little deeper into his pockets. He was being melodramatic. He supposed that was what happened when a person had someone like Mims for a sibling. Or maybe it was that combined with being somewhat stranded and in a situation that he had never expected.

Perhaps.

He just knew that something had shifted for him. Not a lot, but enough. Every time he gave Tillie something else for her baby, it shifted a bit more. He found more joy, a lighter spirit, and he was starting to like it.

Mary, forgive me, he prayed. But he knew that she did. His wife was nothing if not a sweet, kind, and loving person. She had a heart as big as everything, and forgiveness was second nature to her.

Plus it wasn't like his being stranded for a day or so with Tillie Gingerich was going to change anything for him. Not really. But for now he felt better about it all, and that was worth more to him than gold.

Tillie eased up from her seat in front of the window the moment she caught sight of Levi. She bustled into the kitchen as fast as she could and returned with the pot of coffee she had been heating on the stove. She wanted to give him something warm to drink the minute he walked in the door. It was cold outside and seemed to be getting colder.

But it was toasty in the house. The fire crackled merrily in the fireplace, Emmy slept peacefully in the fabric chair contraption that Levi had offered, and Puddles in all her round, spotted glory was lying on her bed next to the potbellied stove in the kitchen.

All the scene needed was the head of the household to come home.

The door swung open and there he was.

Like a husband coming home. But it wasn't her home and he wasn't her husband. Not the father of her baby. He was just a man who had helped her in her time of need. She needed to get ahold of this fantasy before she made a mess of things.

"Did you get in touch with Leah?" Tillie asked. She poured him a cup of coffee and offered it to him the moment he pulled his coat off.

But he shook his head. "I've already had four cups today. Any more and I won't be able to sleep tonight." He chuckled, and she could tell that he meant no harm by his words, but somehow she was secretly crushed. He had ruined her little fantasy.

She supposed it was for the best.

Levi hung his coat and hat by the door

and removed his ice-covered boots before padding in his sock feet over to the fireplace. "I left a message for Leah at the store number," he said.

"That's good. I suppose the store isn't open today due to the weather."

He nodded. "I suppose you're right. And I called the police."

"The police?" She was more than shocked.

"*Jah.* It was Owen's idea. He's my neighbor. He thought they might be able to stop by and let your folks know where you are. And that you're safe."

"That's a good idea." She figured she had worried her family enough as it was.

"How's the baby?" Levi continued to warm himself in front of the fire but looked over to where Emmy rested.

Tillie had placed the baby seat on top of the coffee table, far enough away from the fire that nothing would pop out and hurt her, but close enough to keep warm. She was wrapped in the little yellow blanket that Levi had given her just after she was born. She looked warm and toasty and quite content.

"I think she is quite well-adjusted for a newcomer."

Levi smiled at her words, and that made Tillie feel a bit warmer inside. It was crazy, and she had to get herself out of this fantasy that she had been creating in her mind.

"I mean, she's good."

He turned his full attention to the baby. "She looks better than good."

His voice sounded a bit wistful, and she wondered if Levi was starting to have a few fantasies of his own.

Was that natural? Healthy? Or were they both getting caught up in the drama of being iced in so close to Christmas?

"A penny for them," Levi said.

Tillie dragged herself out of her thoughts and turned her attention back to the man who was still hovering by the hearth. "I'm not sure they're worth any more than that."

He sat in the chair closest to the fire, and despite his earlier refusal, he picked up the cup of coffee and took a sip. He sighed. "That's good," he said, closing his eyes. "I never can manage to make decent coffee."

"I'll show you how," she offered.

He shook his head. "Mims tried, Mamm tried, Mary tried. I guess I'm hopeless when it comes to coffee."

"Well, you'll have mine for another day or so, *jah*?"

"I believe so. It's going to be at least tomorrow before we can get out, if even then. But I think the day after will be fine."

And if the police could get word to her family, then she wouldn't have to worry about their concern for her well-being. She could relax and enjoy the next couple of days.

Chicken.

She knew she was, but she was simply enjoying the peace while she had it. For soon, very, very soon, all that and the perfect little Amish fantasy she had created would be shattered.

"I told you I would do them, and I'm going to do them."

Levi sighed and sat back in his seat as Tillie took their dishes to the sink.

"At least let me fetch you the water," he said.

She nodded. "I'll let you do that. It's cold outside, and I'm sure you're faster than me."

He nodded, then gave Emmy one last look before hustling out to get Tillie a bucket of water.

"You are quick," she said when he returned just a few minutes later.

He smiled at the compliment, somehow loving it and feeling silly for loving it all in the same moment. "Are you sure you're up to this?"

"I had a baby. I didn't get hit by a bus."

"Fair enough." And if Tillie was doing the dishes . . . He made his way over to where Emmy slept. Once again she was in the little fabric baby seat they had placed on one end of the table while they ate.

"What are you doing?" she asked, her words more like a hiss than a normal question.

"I want to hold her." He really hadn't given it much thought. He had just acted on it.

"She's asleep," Tillie protested.

Levi frowned, though in mock annoyance. "She's always asleep."

"She's a baby," Tillie replied unnecessarily. "They tend to sleep a lot."

"I want to hold her," he said again and started to undo the buckle that held her in place.

Tillie sighed, but didn't argue. She turned back to the dishes, and he gently scooped Emmy into his arms.

"Fine," Tillie said. "But if she wakes up hungry, you'll find yourself in here doing the dishes."

He brushed aside her protests and gazed down at the tiny baby. Would he ever tire of just looking at her?

Like he was going to get to see her at all after tomorrow. She would go back home and that would be that. His life would return to normal.

The thought was paralyzing. Normal was not a state he liked these days. Normal was alone and sad and lonely. As much as he had hated the thought of having Tillie and now her baby in his house, he couldn't imagine them gone. And it had only been a day!

He needed to get ahold of himself, and fast.

In his arms, Emmy woke, her soft blue eyes searching his face for something, he had no idea what. Apparently she hadn't found it, and she puckered up and started to cry.

"Shhh . . ." He tried to bounce her a bit like he had seen the women in town and at church do, but she was so tiny he was still afraid he might harm her. Not on purpose, of course, but she simply looked so fragile.

Except when she was crying. In that moment she looked angry.

Tillie sighed. He barely heard the sound over the baby's wails and his own crooning, shushing sound. Then she dried her hands on a dish towel and held her arms out for her baby.

Her baby.

Reluctantly, Levi handed her over.

257

"Let me feed her, and you can have her back, deal?"

He smiled. "Deal."

She took the baby from him and nodded toward the sink. "The dishes are all yours."

While Levi finished the dishes, Tillie fed Emmy, burped her, changed her, and managed to get her back to sleep.

"You want to hold her now?" she asked as he came back into the room.

He shook his head. "I mean, *jah,* I do, but I want her to sleep as well."

"Maybe tomorrow," Tillie said. Though she knew the next day wouldn't be much different than today. It would be weeks before Emmy would be the kind of baby Levi was dreaming of holding, but that he wanted to hold her at all filled Tillie with contentment.

And that was something she couldn't get used to.

"Wanna play a game?" he asked.

"What kind of game?"

He went to the bookshelf there in the living room and started searching through the shelves. Until that moment, Tillie hadn't paid much attention to what was stored there.

"I've got Rook."

"That needs more than two players."

"Dutch Blitz?"

"The same."

"Sorry?"

She shook her head.

"Trouble?"

"Maybe," she said. How long had it been since she had played a game with family or friends? Since before she left to go to the English world. Melvin wasn't big on board games. He would rather play one of the fancy English games that required a special box, a controller, and a television set.

"Trouble is fine," she said.

He stopped, turned to face her. "That didn't sound fine."

She made a face. "I'm afraid we'll be too loud and wake Emmy."

"Good point." He studied the shelves for a moment. "We could read." He held up his Bible.

"You'll read about Jesus's birth?" she asked. It was one of the things that she loved and admired about her *mamm* and *dat*. He would read the Bible to her almost every night. And at Christmastime the whole family would gather round and Dat would read the story of Jesus from the Book of Luke. She looked forward to it every year. And the way things seemed to be going for her now, this would be the last year she would have that privilege.

"What's wrong?" he asked. "Your whole face changed just then."

She shook her head. "Nothing." Just one more bad habit she had picked up in the English world. Lying. And the lie slipped easily from her lips. But she didn't want to lay all her woes at Levi's feet. He had done enough for her already.

He hesitated for a moment, as if he wasn't sure whether to press the matter or not, then he sat down next to the lantern and pulled on a pair of reading glasses. To Tillie he looked even more handsome. He looked serious, as if this was worthy. And it was.

She sat back and closed her eyes and listened to his rich, deep voice as he read. He didn't miss a word, and she wondered if he could recite most of it by heart. She supposed she could if she thought about it long and hard enough. The story was comforting and familiar. Mary and Joseph on their way to Bethlehem. No room in the inn. Giving birth in the barn. Laying Christ Jesus in a manger.

The story wove around her like the threads of a familiar blanket, until the rest of the world fell away. It was just her, the baby, and Levi. This was what she wanted. This peace and harmony. The feeling of well-being. Was that too much to ask from the people around her? Maybe it was. She had broken the rules.

She supposed that Joseph's Mary had done the same. In her own way, of course. But Mary was forgiven by all because she had given birth to Jesus. Tillie'd just had an ordinary baby. An ordinary miracle.

But she didn't want to think about rules and such as she listened to Levi. She only wanted this moment. The one she was in right then. How many times had she actually spent time in the time she was in? Not enough. She had lived her life thinking about what was happening next or what had happened before. So much so that she never lived in the time where she was living.

The thought was like a lightning bolt. It jolted her.

"Are you okay?" Levi asked.

She must have jerked or jumped. "Just a chill," she lied. Yet another lie on her long list.

Levi placed a piece of ribbon in his Bible and stood. In seconds he had the fire roaring once again. The heat felt good, even though cold wasn't Tillie's real enemy. It was herself. Just how did one go about living in the current moment? She had no idea. Was it even truly possible?

"You're very thoughtful tonight," Levi commented.

"Just listening to the story," she said. She supposed that was mostly the truth.

He nodded, though she wasn't sure that he entirely believed her. That was okay. She didn't entirely believe herself. Though she didn't want to bring it up with him. She might have known him or who he was her entire life, and he might have delivered her baby, a most intimate act, but they were practically strangers.

Strangers who were stranded together for a short time. And after tomorrow, what would happen?

There she went again. Living in the future. She could neither put off tomorrow nor change the past. She needed to live in the time she had been given, the now, for a change. All too soon the opportunity would be gone. The world would encroach and she would be unable to put her worry for the future aside.

"Read me another story."

He sat back down in his chair and adjusted his reading glasses. Then he started reading about God telling Jonah to go to Nineveh.

Tillie relaxed into the couch cushions and listened once again. "Interesting choice," she said when he was finished.

He grinned at her, his face transforming into that of a schoolboy. "It was my favorite growing up."

She could understand that. A fish big enough to swallow a man. Or was the draw the idea of following God's instructions? Levi appeared to have followed God in his life. He had joined the church, gotten married. She supposed that made it all the harder to accept the blows of losing a wife and a child. He hadn't said as much, but she could see it on his face.

"Have you ever thought about leaving the Amish?" She asked the question before she had fully thought it through.

"You mean live with the English?"

She nodded, though now she wished she could take the question back. It was really none of her business.

"No," he said finally.

"Never?" She sat up a little straighter, as if that would help her understand better. "You never once thought about leaving and driving a car, or wearing blue jeans?"

"That's not who I am," he said simply.

The words were so straightforward they took her breath away. And she envied Levi. She had never known who she was enough to make such a quick decision. Or in his case never to be faced with doubts of the life he was living.

But truth be known . . .

"I would have never left if it hadn't been for Melvin," she said. The words fell quietly between them, accented by the crackle of the fire and the sound of the ice-coated trees creaking in the wind.

"And what do you do now?" he asked. "You don't have to answer that."

She smiled and shook her head. "I'm not sure." But she was. She would have to return to the English world. And she would have to return to Melvin. What choice did she have, really? She couldn't make it on her own in the world, and without Melvin as her husband, she wouldn't be allowed to stay with her Amish family. "Except . . ." She nodded toward Emmy, who had started to fuss.

"Hungry again?" he asked.

"Looks that way." Tillie stood and scooped her daughter gently into her arms. "I guess I really should be heading for bed."

He looked to the clock on the mantel. "It's past my bedtime too." He stood and stretched. "I'll see you in the morning." The sentence almost sounded like a question, as if he half expected her to take off sometime during the night.

That wasn't happening. She might have only one more day of putting the world on hold, but she planned to keep it at bay for as long as she could. All too soon she would have to face the reality of the situation she found herself in. But for now she was cocooned in a bright world with a caring man and her newborn. It was cowardly of her, but she planned to enjoy it for as long as she could.

Soon enough the world would come calling.

"See you in the morning."

CHAPTER SEVENTEEN

Tillie watched the melting ice drip from the rooftop to the soggy ground. The sun was out in full force, though she could tell from the frost on the window that it was still very cold outside. But the ice was no match for the sun, and soon the outside world would be at their doorstep.

Except it wasn't her doorstep. It belonged to Levi. And she couldn't pretend otherwise for much longer.

Thank you, Lord, for giving me this time, she prayed. She had needed a bit to clear her head. Not that she had succeeded. She still had nagging doubts and troubling problems, but at least she'd had a bit of respite.

But soon, she thought as the water continued to drip. *Soon.* Her family. The bishop. Decisions.

"It's hard to believe it's almost Christmas," she said as Levi came into the room.

Emmy was sleeping in her little chair, as content as ever. Tillie was so blessed to have such a sweet-tempered baby.

Today was Sunday, and Christmas Day was only a week away. Yet that seemed impossible.

Levi nodded. "I remember when I was little. It seemed forever until Christmas. Now they seem to go by quicker and quicker."

Clouds filled his eyes, and Tillie hated the reaction. "I shouldn't have brought it up," she said apologetically.

He shook his head. "It's not something I can avoid."

"You want a cup of coffee?" She was on her feet in a second.

"You don't have to get me coffee to make up for mentioning Christmas."

She sat back down. "I just know that it must be very painful for you."

He took his usual place by the fire. For a moment she thought he might not answer, then, with his hands clasped between his knees, he gave a small nod. "It is. It was. But . . ." He didn't finish.

But what? she wanted to ask but held her tongue. On that matter at least. "It's so strange being back." With the ice storm and the baby, it hadn't seemed quite like Christmas as usual. When she had come back, that had been heavy on her mind, returning to her Amish home. But it just went to show that things could never go back, no matter how badly a person wanted it.

"Mims usually makes a gingerbread house, but I don't think she did this year."

Tillie thought about it for a second. "By herself?" Building a gingerbread house was something she had enjoyed doing with Jim's kids. It was something of a family tradition for them. But as far as she knew there were no small children in Levi's family.

He chuckled. "By herself. I suppose she should have gotten a Christmas job at the bakery. She could've decorated cakes and such. But she just does the whole house each year, with gumdrops and everything."

Tillie smiled. "I love gingerbread houses. Except sometimes it seems like such a waste. I mean, it sits there for days and gets a bit stale."

Levi looked at her in disbelief, but only after he spoke did she realize he was being silly. "Don't you have an aunt to eat the gingerbread house?"

"An aunt? Like a person? Not little bugs, right?"

"So I guess you don't have that sort of aunt," he said with a nod.

Tillie laughed. "I have one, she just doesn't eat the gingerbread house. But she brings food for everyone, and who knows how long it's been sitting there." She gave a pained smile. "One year she gave me a gelatin mold."

"Gift wrapped?"

"*Jah,*" Tillie said. "Thankfully it was really cold that year and the gelatin had been set away from the fire, otherwise, I think it might've melted all over Mamm's floor."

"It's the thought that counts," Levi said.

"You're right. It is the thought that counts." She shot him a smile to show that she had completely forgiven her aunt for the crazy gift. "She died a couple of years ago." Her voice turned wistful. What she wouldn't give for one of those gelatin molds this year. Wasn't that how it always went?

"My *mamm* always makes a gelatin mold. She says it's a family tradition. It's sort of pretty, I guess — dark red cranberries with oranges and pecans in it." He shook his head. "Nobody eats it but her."

"No one?" she asked. "It sounds sort of good to me. Does it not taste good?"

He shrugged. "I never tried it."

Tillie stopped. "Wait. You won't eat it, but you never tried it because you don't think it'll be good, but yet it looks pretty?"

"Okay, the truth of the matter is I have trouble with gelatin."

"Trouble?"

He shook his head. "You'll laugh."

Tillie eyed him skeptically. "Of course I won't laugh. What sort of trouble?" She knew there were people who were allergic to peanuts and citrus and all sorts of things. Shellfish and such. She'd never heard of anyone being allergic to Jell-O.

"It wiggles."

She stopped again, eyed him to see if he was actually telling the truth. He looked serious enough. "What?"

He sighed. "I said it wiggles. Food shouldn't wiggle."

Tillie couldn't help it; a bark of laughter escaped her. She clamped one hand over her mouth, but the giggles still came. "You won't eat it because it wiggles." It wasn't even a question.

He shot her a stern look. "You promised you wouldn't laugh."

She shook her head as tears sprang into her eyes, tears of mirth and laughter. "I didn't promise. But you have to admit that is really funny. I don't know a soul who won't eat food that wiggles. I guess cold gravy is out."

He made a face. "Why would anyone want

270

to eat cold gravy?"

"Point taken." But she still couldn't help the chuckles escaping her. And all the while she tried to think of other foods that wiggled. "Pudding?"

He held his hand out and tilted it from side to side. "Depends. Some pudding is not so trustworthy."

She laughed again. "Untrustworthy pudding. I've never heard of such a thing."

"Maybe we should go out to eat and I'll show you some."

At his words they both stopped.

"I didn't mean that the way it sounded." His whole demeanor changed. His shoulders had grown stiff and his back like a board as if he knew he had crossed a line.

"I didn't take it that way." But how should she take it? It seemed as if he too had come to enjoy the seclusion that they had. For a time they had locked out the world, not so they could be together, but more so they could be alone. It just so happened to be that they were with each other. What's a person to do about that?

They looked at the other a moment, then Tillie jumped as a knock sounded at the door. They'd been so engrossed in their conversation that they hadn't seen or heard anyone arrive. She whirled around and looked out the window. "It's the police!" she exclaimed.

Levi pushed to his feet and made his way to the door.

She had made it seem like they were doing something they shouldn't be, but she had been surprised that anyone had arrived. How had she been so captivated in a conversation with Levi that she hadn't seen a patrol car pull up outside?

"Levi Yoder?" the uniformed officer asked.

Levi nodded and stepped back to allow him to enter the house.

"I'm Brian Carmichael. I've been out checking on all the Amish folks since the roads have been so bad. I just came to see if you were okay. We have a record that you called the nonemergency number about a Miss Tillie Gingerich."

Tillie jumped to her feet. "I'm Tillie Gingerich," she said.

"Your folks have been worried about you," Officer Carmichael said with a smile.

"Is there a way that you can tell them that I'm okay? I know Levi left a message at my sister's store. She has a phone."

"I've been out to see your folks," Carmichael said. "And they know you're fine. But that doesn't stop a mother from worrying, now does it?" There went that smile

272

again. He was young, maybe in his early twenties, with twinkling brown eyes and slashing dimples. He wasn't wearing a wedding ring, so Tillie figured he was single. But with his sweet demeanor and cute smile, she had a feeling that wouldn't be his state for long.

Tillie returned his smile. "I suppose not."

Carmichael checked his notepad and tucked it back into his pocket. "And I suppose your mother is anxious to see that new baby I heard about. Do you need me to take you to the hospital? I can arrange for an ambulance right now."

Tillie shook her head. "No, thank you. I'm fine. Everything went fine. I'm just anxious to get home." Add that to her list of lies.

"I can arrange a patrol car to come and get you. I still have rounds to make before dark. But someone can get you home if you want."

If she wanted. The one thing she wanted was to stay locked into this fake dreamland she had created for herself with Levi Yoder. It was most ridiculous, and she needed to correct that situation as soon as possible.

"My sister Leah will come get me."

Carmichael nodded. "I believe I still have her number if you would like me to call her for you."

Tillie wanted to yell *No!* She wanted to stay right where she was, and if he could arrange for a couple of feet of snow to go on top of the ice, that would be great. Instead she nodded. "Yes, thank you."

"And you're sure about the hospital? It's no trouble to get an ambulance for you." He looked over to where baby Emmy lay snuggled in her little fabric chair on the coffee table. She had been there most of the morning, sleeping and growing and just being beautiful.

Tillie knew what he was thinking. Everything looked okay, and there didn't seem to be any cause for concern on his part.

"No, I'm fine. My sister will be enough."

"Then I'll let you be. Thank you for calling, and if you need anything else you know how to reach us."

Levi nodded. *"Danki,"* he said and shook the officer's hand.

A moment later Carmichael was out the door and seated in his patrol car, no doubt trying to reach Leah to tell her that Tillie was ready to go home.

The trouble was Tillie was nowhere near ready to leave.

He remembered when he was little taking a bath in a warm tub of water filled with bubbles. Some would rise and he would poke them with his finger. They would pop with small bursts, then disappear. That was sort of how he felt right then. How had he managed to let himself become so ingrained with Tillie and her baby? If anyone had told him two weeks ago that this was going to happen, he would have laughed in their face. Or at least told them to go to the doctor; that they were crazy. Even crazier than his sweet old aunt who ate the gingerbread house each Christmas.

Tillie turned to him with an expression he couldn't read. "I guess I should get my things together," she said. "If I know Leah, she'll be out here in a heartbeat."

He cleared his throat, which suddenly felt tight. "I'm sure your *mamm* is ready to see you and make sure that you and that baby are okay." It was understandable. What mother wouldn't be worried about her child and her grandchild? What mother wouldn't be worried about her grandchild who was born in the middle of an ice storm?

"I'll get you a bag." He started toward the baby's room. But she grabbed his arm.

"I didn't come with anything."

He nodded. "But you're leaving with a baby who has things that she's going to need."

275

She shook her head. "I can't take your things."

"I've been needing to get rid of some of this for a while. I would love for you and Emmy to have it."

"All we need is the blanket and the clothes she's wearing. We'll take care of the rest on our own."

After all she had been through, now she wanted to be prideful? "Please let me do this, Tillie."

At his beseeching tone she stopped, seemed to wilt a little in place. "Only if you're sure," she said.

"I am."

She released his arm and he walked into what would've been his son's room. He was oh so aware of Tillie right behind him.

"I don't suppose you brought any baby things with you when you left . . . Columbus." He couldn't quite bring himself to say Melvin's name. He was disappointed in the man. He had a wonderful woman like Tillie, a beautiful baby like Emmy. Granted, he hadn't seen the child, but he had known she was coming. And he knew that Tillie wanted to leave. So why even after a week was he still not there?

Levi supposed the man could still turn up. It was Christmas, after all, and a season of miracles.

He had known Melvin before. Just a little. And he knew that Melvin was one of those born in the wrong place. Just like some people dreamed of being Amish, some Amish had dreams of the English from the very start. As far as Levi could tell, Melvin Yoder was one of those people.

"No." The one word was small and held more meaning than fit into letters. And he knew without her telling him that there were no things she could've brought. There was no money for them in the first place and no room where she lived. Somehow he knew.

He picked up the black-and-white diaper bag that Joy, Mary's sister, had given her. "It's used," he explained. "But most of the stuff is. Not the diapers, of course. Mary's family brought most of this over when she found out she was going to have a baby." He stuttered over those last words. Not from pain of loss, but simply because pregnancy wasn't something men and women talked about. Not even married couples discussed such matters regularly.

"I appreciate it," she said. From her tone he couldn't tell if she noticed his hesitation or not.

He placed the bag on the fancy English changing table that Mary had insisted on buying at the flea market and began filling it with diapers. "I'm just happy that someone is getting some use from these things now." And it was the truth. Somehow putting these items to use lessened his pain and gave a jump start to his healing.

He added a couple of thin blankets and one made from the soft fleece fabric Mary had bought at the store in town.

"But —" Tillie moved toward him. "That looks handmade."

He knew what she was saying — commercially made socks and little nightgowns weren't as intimate as something that Mary had made for their baby. But that baby was gone and this baby was here.

"I think Mary would want you to have it." Mary's baby was in heaven with her and warm enough for sure.

Tillie swallowed hard, then gave a small nod, and Levi put the blanket into the bag. A couple of hats, the knit kind to keep the baby's head warm, a few more pairs of impossibly small socks, and a stack of what Mary had called onesies. The gowns went in as well.

"If there's anything else you'd like to have . . ."

"You've been more than generous," Tillie said.

"It's been my pleasure." And it was. As strange as it seemed, he had wanted to cut himself off from the world, and he had, but he had thought to do it alone. Instead he was with a woman and a baby who somehow changed everything for him. It was true he still felt the pain of loss, but the thought of Mary and the baby now didn't make his heart bleed. Somehow Tillie being in his house with Emmy enabled him to separate the two: Mary and their baby in heaven and Tillie and her baby here. So strange the difference a couple of days can make.

Or the power of God.

The last was more likely. He hadn't prayed for much since Mary and the baby died, but he was sure Mims had, and he could probably blame all this on her. Then again, she might like that. He smiled.

"What is it?" Tillie asked.

He supposed he looked something of a fool standing in the middle of an unfinished nursery, holding a tiny pair of baby pajamas and grinning like a fool. He shook his head. "Nothing. Nothing at all." He put the pajamas in the bag and handed it all to her. Then he reached down and picked up a package of disposable diapers. "I suppose you should take this too. You're gonna need them, and who knows when you'll be able to get out."

"I never dreamed the baby could go through so many diapers. And I worked at a day care center."

He tilted his head to one side. "That's what you did in the English world?"

She nodded. "I enjoyed it, but it doesn't pay much, and . . ." She didn't finish. And he didn't have to have her spell it out for him to understand. Quitting school at fourteen didn't make for easy transition into the English world, where education seemed to be prized above almost everything else. Employers didn't take into account the home education the Amish kids received after they quit going to school. How Amish girls were taught to be wives and Amish boys were taught in trade, farming, and such. Had his baby been born, Levi would've taught him how to work with leather. Just as Tillie would teach Emmy to can food and quilt and make clothes and all the other things that girls did. Tillie didn't say as much, but he understood. Without Melvin, she wouldn't be able to make it in the English world, and without Melvin, she wouldn't be able to make it in the Amish world. So where was she going to go from here?

CHAPTER EIGHTEEN

"Tillie!" Leah screeched as she came through the front door about an hour later. "My goodness! We've been so worried!"

Leah wrapped her in a bone-crushing hug and rocked them back and forth as she held on.

"I'm okay." Tillie returned her sister's squeeze, then pulled away. "Would you like to meet your niece?"

Leah nodded, then turned toward the coffee table, where Emmy rested in the fabric seat.

"She's perfect," Leah breathed.

Tillie had to agree. She would admit that she was a little biased, but every time she looked at Emmy, it was as if the world was sitting there wrapped in a little yellow blanket, sleeping peacefully. She supposed Emmy was. Her world, at least.

"And you named her Emmanuela?" Leah said. "That's an awfully big name for such a sweet little girl." That was Leah, never holding back.

Tillie was barely aware of Levi hovering behind her as she approached her sister once more. "We've been calling her Emmy."

Leah nodded. "I like that. That fits."

"Just a form of Emmanuel: God is with us."

"Christmas." Leah smiled at Emmy. "I guess she wanted to spend Christmas here this year."

"I guess so," Tillie murmured.

"Baby's first Christmas," Leah said. "Can I hold her?" She was already reaching for the snaps and buckles that kept Emmy in the chair.

"If you wake her up, she'll want to feed."

Leah stopped, but only for a moment. "Is that a problem?" She looked from Tillie to Levi, then, as if sensing her mistake, turned back to Tillie once more. "She's eating, right?"

Tillie nodded. "Like a little pig."

Leah sighed with relief, then continued her mission to hold the baby. "My goodness," she said as she snuggled Emmy close to her. She turned the baby in her arms so she could see Emmy's face. "I can't believe how beautiful she is. So tiny and perfect."

"That's what I said." Levi nodded.

Leah turned to him, still snuggling the baby close to her. "I can't thank you enough for the help you've given Tillie. We'll be forever grateful."

Tillie felt her face heat up, and she knew she was as red as a Christmas poinsettia.

"I'm just glad I was here to help," he said.

He seemed genuine enough. And he acted as if he was glad they were there. Not at first, of course, but now he did. And now they were leaving.

"We need to get her in the car seat, and we'll head out. Mamm wanted to come, but since I was already in town at the store, I didn't run by the house to get her first. She's champing at the bit to see you and this baby."

Tillie nodded. "I'm sure," she murmured.

Leah picked up the baby carrier she had dropped as she walked in the door.

"It's used," she said. "But clean. And I was assured that it's never been in a wreck. So hopefully it will be just fine for this little one." She shook her head. "What am I saying? I'm going to buy a brand-new one tomorrow."

Levi chuckled and shook his head at Leah's antics.

"My goodness," Leah said again. She gently placed the baby in the carrier and tried to strap her in. Emmy, disturbed from her rest, started to fuss.

"Oops." Leah looked to Tillie. "I suppose she wants to eat now?"

Tillie shook her head. "Probably, but she can wait a little bit. Give her the pacifier and see if that helps. Maybe she'll go back to sleep."

"Good idea," Leah said. "Babies love to ride in cars. I'm sure she'll be asleep in no time." She continued to buckle Emmy into the car seat. Levi picked up the diaper bag he'd filled earlier and handed it to Tillie.

"Leah's right," Tillie said. "There will never be enough that we can offer you to show our thanks for helping me. I don't know what I would've done without you."

"You would've been just fine," he said. "But I'm so glad I got to be a part of it." There was a strange light in his blue eyes. Tillie had no idea what it meant. But she had to admit that Levi looked happier than he had the whole time she had known him. She supposed that was the power of a baby and a Christmas miracle.

"Well, thank you anyway," Tillie said. "From the bottom of my heart, I thank you."

Levi just smiled.

She supposed *You're welcome* would be a

little awkward to say in a case like this, but his smile was enough.

"I'll take these to the car for you," Levi said, holding up the half-empty bag of diapers.

"And I'll wash the dress and have it back to you —"

Levi shook his head, cutting off her words. "Keep the dress. You may need it while you're here."

"Thank you again," Tillie said.

This time he murmured, "You're welcome."

Since the time she had arrived, she had been thinking about leaving, and now that the time had come, all she could think about was finding a way to stay. But there was no excuse to stay. And she knew deep in her heart that all she wanted was to postpone the inevitable, to stall the reckoning.

"Are you ready?" Leah asked. "You don't have a coat?"

Tillie shook her head. "Just a sweater."

"Well it's a good thing the heater in the car works. It's not a long drive. You should be fine." And she turned and started toward the door.

Tillie had no choice but to follow after her. And she could feel Levi behind her as they trailed down the porch to the car.

Tillie had watched hundreds of times as moms snapped and unsnapped their babies from their car seats, but it was still something of a mystery to her. She allowed Leah to get Emmy into the car seat base that held the carrier she had brought for her.

Then Levi put the bag of diapers in the back seat next to her and took the diaper bag from Tillie and placed that beside it.

Now is the time to get in the car.

Leah slipped into the driver seat, but Tillie had trouble getting her feet to work. Somehow she forced them to walk around the car. She opened the passenger side door, then she looked at Levi one last time and gave him a small smile. "I'll see you at church," he said.

"*Jah,*" Tillie said. "See you at church."

Mamm was waiting for them on the porch when they arrived. Tillie figured she would swoop in on the baby first, but instead she wrapped Tillie in a warm embrace that brought tears to her eyes. She was sad to leave Levi's; she was happy to be home. But like with everything else, that joy would be short-lived. Somehow she just knew it.

Mamm pulled away and wiped her own tears with the tail end of her apron. "Get inside, out of this cold," she said, as if the cold was what had caused her tears in the first place.

Tillie nodded.

Leah grabbed the baby from the back seat of the car and carried her inside the house. She took her into the kitchen, which always seemed to be the warmest room, and set her, carrier seat and all, on the kitchen table.

"My word," Mamm gasped.

"Isn't she beautiful?" Leah said. "Of course, I know that I'm a little bit prejudiced, but I do believe she might be the most beautiful baby in the world."

"Of course we should think our new baby is the most beautiful in the world," Mamm said.

True to their predictions, Emmy had fallen asleep in the car and had snoozed all the way over to the house. Now that they had stopped, however, she wiggled around like she was about to wake up again.

"I think she might be getting hungry." Tillie checked the clock over the sink. *Jah,* it was getting close to time for her afternoon snack.

"Let me get her for you." Mamm moved to undo the buckles and straps on the baby carrier and lifted Emmy from inside. She fussed a bit and stretched, then looked at her grandmother. She studied Mamm for a minute, then let out a long wail.

Mamm chuckled and snuggled her nose in the crease of Emmy's neck. "Mmmm, babies always smell so good," Mamm murmured, the wistful words mixing with Emmy's screams.

"I'll let your mother feed you, then maybe we can get acquainted in a little bit, *jah*?" Mamm handed Emmy to Tillie, who still wore one of Levi's old shirts and the bottom half of the dress that his wife had made for some reason or another.

"Land sakes, girl. What are you wearing?"

"I got lost in an ice storm," Tillie said. She started to unbutton his shirt with one hand as she cradled the baby in the other. She settled down on the long bench in front of the table and pulled her baby close.

Mamm smiled. "You're right, of course. But we do need to get you some proper clothes."

Another week. She would have to stay at least another week, maybe a week after that. It wasn't like she could go traveling around with the baby. And she was still a little sore. There was a reason why English people took six weeks off when they had a baby. It was a lot of work. But much longer than that and she knew she would have to admit to everyone that Melvin was not coming back, that he would not marry her, and that she would have to leave again. But until that time, she was holding on to hope with both hands.

"Wait till Dat sees her," Mamm said.

Tillie loved her father, but he was a hard man. And she had broken rules. But she had seen the miracles a baby could perform without even trying, without lifting a finger. And she supposed this little girl would have her *dawdi*'s heart without even trying.

"I want to see Anna's face." Leah grinned. "And Gracie. They're both going to be so excited."

"As excited as you are?" Mamm asked. She slid into the bench next to Tillie and ran a finger over Emmy's head as she ate. This would be a good time as any to talk to them about her future plans. But she wanted so to live in this moment and not worry about what was coming. She wanted to live each day between now and Christmas just for that day. She knew she wasn't going to be able to stay. Not unless Melvin agreed. And since he hadn't come after her, she figured he wouldn't agree at all.

"Tomorrow," Mamm said. "Tomorrow the roads should be good enough that everybody can come over."

Another party, just what she didn't want. No, that wasn't exactly true. She wanted to spend time with her family, soaking it all in for safekeeping. Later, when she was back in Columbus and missing her family, she could remember these times and smile. But even though that's what she wanted, it was still very overwhelming.

But the worst thought of all was that she would only have this week. After that she would have to face the reality of what was coming. Whether she wanted to or not.

Levi walked from the living room to the kitchen, looked around for a moment, then turned and walked back. He told himself he was checking on Puddles. The poor dog looked more miserable by the minute, and he figured it was only a matter of days, perhaps even hours, before she gave birth to those pups.

But the truth of the matter was he missed Tillie and Emmy.

His house seemed too big and too empty, and his footsteps seemed to echo when he wandered from room to room. Even with Mary gone he hadn't done this. There was something lively about Tillie that seemed to light up everything when she was around. Maybe it was Emmy. He looked at the little fabric seat still sitting on the coffee table. He should have offered it to Tillie. He should take it to her right now.

He walked over to pick it up, then stopped himself. The police had said the roads were still pretty bad. And since most of them lived out where the roads weren't paved, it was hard on the horse's hooves to drag a carriage through the mud. He would have to wait. If the county held true to what they usually did, there would be graders out working on the roads probably no later than tomorrow. So maybe tomorrow afternoon he could take it to her.

Surely he could wait until then. Maybe Tuesday morning at the latest. He set the chair back down where it had previously been and walked back to the kitchen. How was it that Tillie had only been in his house for a couple of days, and yet she seemed to have left something in every room? Not necessarily her things. She had grabbed them all up when she left. But other things. Things that belonged to Emmy. Things Tillie had used for the baby. A burp cloth, a bib, a blanket, all these things were peppered throughout his house. More and more reminders that once again he had lost something special.

He shook his head at himself. He was making way more of this than he should. Regardless, he wanted to take the chair to her and maybe another bag of the diapers. He'd found one in the closet just after she left. It seemed Mary had things squirreled away all over. He supposed to her, not putting everything in the same place didn't feel quite so much like overpreparing. But that was Mary. She was one of those preparing kind of people. She bought spring fabric on sale in the summer and saved it until the next year. She said she was thrifty. He had always just smiled at her words. He wished now that he had told her she was. There were a lot of things that he wished he could tell Mary, and more than anything right now he wished he could talk to her about Tillie.

That had to be the strangest thought to ever come into his mind. But Tillie had done more than just crash into his life on the night of an ice storm. She had brought him back to the now and given him the chance to start healing.

He could barely admit it to himself; there was no way he could say it out loud to her. But he wished he could tell them both, Mary and Tillie, how having a stranger in his house the week before Christmas had changed everything for him.

A knock sounded at his door, so unexpected that he nearly jumped from his own skin.

Maybe the police again? But he hadn't heard a car. Truth be known, he had been so wrapped up in his own thoughts he hadn't been listening for things like cars. Surely the person who arrived had come by buggy. But if they had, maybe that meant the roads weren't so bad after all. He crossed to the door and opened it.

"It's about time." Mims stomped her feet on the rug outside, wiped them twice, then stepped into the house. "It's freezing out there." She hustled over to the fire while Levi still stood with the door open, his mouth the same.

"Is that a bike?"

Mims turned and gave him an innocent smile. "Yes, I suppose it is."

"Please tell me you borrowed it from your neighbor," Levi said.

"Sure," Mims said. "Let's go with that. I borrowed it from the neighbor so I could come and visit my brother. I wanted to check on you from the storm."

"I'm fine." He held his arms out to his sides as if to say, *See?* Then the thought hit him: he might not be able to talk to Mary, but here was his sister. His best friend. "It hasn't always been as quiet though."

Mims raised a dark brow in a questioning manner. "*Jah?* You have puppies now?" She abandoned her warm fire and rushed to the kitchen. He watched her shoulders slump as she spied Puddles, still round with unborn puppies, lying by the potbellied stove.

"You know you're going to take one," Levi said.

"Not if she never has them."

"I suppose she felt she needs to wait her turn."

Mims whirled around and eyed him carefully. "Why are you talking in riddles, Levi?"

He had wanted somebody to talk to, and now that he had her, he didn't seem to be able to find the words. Where did he start?

"Tillie Gingerich was here." It seemed as good a place as any to begin.

Mims drew back in surprise. "What?" Then she rushed toward him, grabbed his hand, and dragged him over to the sofa. "Sit," she said. "Sit down and tell me everything."

CHAPTER NINETEEN

By Wednesday he could take it no longer. After he had explained the entire weekend to his sister, Mims had squealed, then clapped her hands together as if it was the best news that she had ever received.

He wasn't discounting the fact that it was indeed wonderful news, for Tillie and her baby. But having them around for that couple of days . . . It was as if something had shifted inside him.

Monday after Tillie had left, he started to pick up all the little wayward pieces of her visit, all the reminders that there had been a baby in the house. He washed a load of clothes and then regretted it since it was so cold outside. The items would freeze before they got dry, but he hung them up anyway. Then he ate his solitary supper, washed dishes, and checked on Puddles.

The poor dog still hadn't given birth to her puppies, and before he went to bed, he checked on her. He made sure she was warm and hoped that soon she would whelp. She looked so miserable.

Tuesday was given to a litter of eleven pups, six of which looked exactly like their mother, speckled and mottled as if someone had spilled bleach on a regular dog. Two were solid black, one was black with brown paws, and yet another was white with black dots. The last one had a white face with a black nose, or half-black anyway, and a little white tail with a black tip on the end. He didn't ever recall seeing something like that. Usually the dog had a black tail with a white tip, and he figured if she made it through, he would keep that one for sure.

Puddles looked more than relieved to have had the puppies. Though they couldn't all eat at the same time. The poor dog had more puppies than teats. But she seemed to make sure they all were fed, and none seemed to be in any kind of danger. The rest of Tuesday passed uneventfully. Mims had come by the day before, so she skipped Tuesday.

He walked to the edge of the road and checked the mail. He cleaned the horse stalls, milked the cow, fed the chickens, left food out for the stray cats that came by, and otherwise sat around and waited. For something. He felt as if he were biding his time. Until what?

He had no idea.

And by Wednesday he'd had all he could take. He wanted to go see Emmy and Tillie. He needed to get out. He had been in the house for days — something he never thought would've bothered him before. But for some reason, today it felt so confining. He needed to get out, but he was almost down the driveway when he realized he needed some sort of reason to go to see Tillie. And that was where he was going. But he couldn't just show up on her doorstep.

Couldn't he?

He was reluctant to, anyway. So he turned the buggy around and headed back to the house. Leaving the horse hitched, he loped back up the steps and was inside in a flash. He made his way to the baby's room and looked around for things to take. He grabbed the last bag of diapers and the little yellow bunny that he had placed in the cradle for Emmy.

It was new, and he was certain Mary had bought it for their baby. But he didn't need it. And he thought that it would perhaps bring a little joy into Emmy's life. When she was big enough to realize what it was, anyway. Those items in hand, he hustled back out the door and hopped into his buggy once more.

The weather had warmed up just enough that the road graders had gotten out and smoothed over some of the damage caused by the ice storm. Even so, it was slow going. Or maybe it just felt that way because he was anxious.

As he rode along, he bounced one foot even faster than the clip of the horse's hooves. He wasn't sure why he was so nervous. He just was. Surely he had cause to call on her today. Not just Emmy, but Tillie too. He wanted to make sure that they were okay, that they had settled in, that no other complications had arisen after she gotten back to her parents' house.

And a part of him wanted to know how Melvin had taken the news.

Levi knew in his heart that it was no business of his, but it still plagued him.

Maybe because he knew what was at stake. Because if Melvin didn't come back and live an Amish life, kneel before the congregation, and confess his sins, Tillie would be forced to leave as well. For some reason it just didn't sound right to him. Nor did the thought of her marrying Melvin. But it was really none of his concern. And yet somehow he felt that it was. Maybe because he helped bring little Emmy into the world. He'd been there, and perhaps it should have been Melvin, even if the thought made his stomach plummet to the ground.

It was slow going down the hill on the road that led to the little valley where the Gingeriches lived. Their road hadn't been traveled much since the storm and hadn't been torn up like the main roads. But it was still a little worrisome, heading down that hill. Finally, Levi hopped down from his buggy and walked the horse the rest of the way to their destination.

The day was overcast, cloudy and a bit gloomy, but he was looking forward to the visit all the same. He was only about halfway down the hill when he saw someone in the yard. From this distance, it looked to be Jim, Tillie's oldest brother. Levi knew that he worked with Abner there in the shop making sheds, playhouses, and the like. Most everyone who had a store in front of their house used a shed made by Abner Gingerich. Levi knew he sold the little buildings to the English as well, and he had heard tell that Abner was contemplating getting into the playset business — wooden jungle gyms and the like.

He caught Jim's gaze and waved. The man waved back and was soon joined by David, his younger brother, and Abner.

Jim grinned at Levi as he hobbled his horse and walked over to where the men stood. He could feel eyes watching him from the house and figured the ladies were inside checking out the new visitor. He approached the men first.

"We were wondering when you would show up," David said. He shook Levi's hand. And once again Levi wondered what had happened between him and his sister. David was a nice enough fellow. Never missed church. And he was handsome enough, Levi supposed. David had clear green eyes and sandy brown hair that always looked as if the sun was touching it. And a smile that seemed genuine enough.

But Levi bit back his questions and shook hands with Jim and Abner as well. "I wanted to give them time to settle in." It wasn't entirely a lie, though it wasn't entirely the truth either.

Abner nodded toward the front door. "Go on in the house. I think she'll be happy to see you."

Levi nodded. "I'll just let you get back to work, then."

He started toward the house, and the door

opened before he even got onto the porch.

"Levi Yoder," Eunice greeted him. "It's good to see you out today."

He nodded. It felt good to be out.

Where did that come from? Wasn't he the man who wanted to stay in his house until Christmas was over?

Just another miracle that a baby could perform without even lifting a finger.

"How's Tillie and the baby?"

Eunice smiled. "Come see for yourself," she said. "She and Libby are in the kitchen making candies. Maybe you can try one and have a cup of coffee."

Levi nodded and took off his hat. He twirled it in his fingers a moment before placing it on the peg next to the door. Then he took off his coat and followed Eunice into the kitchen.

He wasn't sure if it was a unique candy-making disaster or if every time Tillie stepped into the kitchen such a mess occurred. He looked at all the items scattered across the table. Powdered sugar, regular sugar, brown sugar, bags of nuts, sticks of butter, mixing bowls, mixing spoons, and various flavorings, including cocoa powder, which the lid was off of. In the midst of it all, Emmy sat in the car seat Leah had brought, content to be close to her *mamm*

301

in the warm, warm kitchen.

Eunice gave a small cough, and Tillie turned. She had a streak of something brown on her face. He assumed and maybe even hoped that it was chocolate. Her apron was dusted with powdered sugar and looked like it'd been smeared in a few places with greasy fingers. Maybe butter?

But she was the prettiest sight he had ever seen. Her hazel eyes twinkled with something he hoped was joy, and she wiped her hands on her apron as she greeted him. "Hello, Levi."

"Hello," he said.

Why did he feel like all eyes were on him? Or maybe it was the two of them. He tore his gaze from hers and looked from Libby to Eunice. They were watching him and Tillie with nearly expectant looks on their faces.

"I brought you some things," Levi said. Nothing like jumping in feet first.

"Danki," Tillie replied. "You didn't have to. You've done so much already."

Eunice nodded. "I don't know how we'll ever thank you enough."

Levi smiled and turned his attention to Tillie's mother. "Leah already thanked me. But I only did what anyone would do." And it was the truth. No one would have left

Tillie out in the barn to give birth alone. No one would have let her remain alone after she had gone into labor. And no one who had the items on hand would withhold them from a beautiful baby who needed them.

Suddenly he thought of Mary and Joseph in the barn, laying baby Jesus in a manger. He supposed there were some people who perhaps would, but he was not one of those people.

"Even so," Eunice said. "We are very grateful."

Levi sat down on the bench side of the kitchen table and looked at the baby amid all the candy mess. "She's quite something, isn't she?"

All three ladies nodded. And he could tell immediately that little Emmy already had the Gingeriches wrapped around her little finger.

"Stay for supper," Eunice said. It wasn't quite a question.

"I don't want to be a bother."

"I don't believe you would ever be a bother," Eunice said.

Tillie turned back to the pot she was stirring on the stove and instructed Libby on how to take the temperature of whatever it was they were concocting.

"As soon as these girls finish up what they're doing, and get the mess cleaned up," Eunice pointedly said, "then I'm going to start dinner. Everyone's coming tonight."

Libby turned and addressed him. "Kind of a welcome home party for the baby. It only seems right that you're here too."

Tillie nodded, but didn't turn away from her pot stirring.

"That's a lot of mouths to feed," Levi protested.

"Then what's one more?" Eunice waved his objection aside. "I'm not gonna take no for an answer."

Levi chuckled, the unsaid *You might as well give in now* still hanging around them. "*Jah.* Okay, then. I would be honored."

"But you may have to help with these peanut butter balls if you want some supper. These girls have been in here since breakfast."

The last thing Tillie had expected was to be making candy with her niece while Levi Yoder sat and watched. So far he had sampled their date balls, their peanut butter balls, their coconut bonbons, and their fondant. "And why are you making all these?" Levi asked.

Beside her, Tillie saw Libby go red in the

face. "Libby wanted to make some candy to give her friends for Christmas." Tillie took the tray of peanut butter balls and set them in front of Levi. Then she handed him a jar of red and white dyed sugar. "Here," she said. "Sprinkle these with this sugar before they dry." Levi did as she instructed, and somehow his compliance made Tillie smile a little inside. Here he was delivering babies and sprinkling candy. She figured he never thought he'd be doing that this year.

"Done," he said, obvious pride in his voice.

Tillie took that tray from in front of him, and Libby slid another into its place. "Next batch," the young girl said with a smile. These were white chocolate, and Tillie handed him the bottle of green and red sprinkles. "And this."

Levi's forehead wrinkled into almost a frown, but he took the bottle from her anyway. "How do you know which ones to add to what?" he asked.

Tillie turned with a smile and tapped the side of her head with her forefinger. "Creative genius," she quipped.

Levi chuckled, and once again she was surprised at how much she enjoyed the sound.

From the baby carrier, Emmy started to

fuss. She stretched her arms out as if gearing up for her cry, then she let out a wail that belied her tiny self.

"Uh-oh," Libby said. "Someone's hungry."

Tillie dried her hands on the bottom of her apron and went to scoop the baby into her arms. They had gotten on a pretty good schedule the last couple of days. Emmy would sleep three or so hours at a time, then demand to be fed. It was working so far. Though Tillie knew that once she left, it would be harder to go to work each day on such little sleep. As it was now, she could rest in the afternoons while the baby napped and get up just in time for supper. Well, to feed the baby first, then eat her supper.

"Mamm!" she called. Her mother didn't answer.

"I saw her go outside," Libby said, her hands covered with white as she rolled the date balls in the powdered sugar.

"Can you stir that?" Tillie asked Levi.

He jumped as if she'd poked him with a cattle prod. "What? You want me to stir it?"

"*Jah,* I think you can handle that." She smiled at him as encouragingly as possible, but she didn't have any time to waste. Emmy was in full-scale fit over not being fed.

"I will just be a few minutes," she said. "Just stir until I get back."

She made her way into the small bedroom that she shared with the baby and quickly undid her dress to feed her. She made it just in time. The baby's cries made her milk go down, and she had started to leak a bit. How embarrassing to do such a thing in front of Levi. Then again, he had delivered the baby. But it was as if things had changed now. She still felt a deep connection with him. Yet on a different level. She couldn't quite explain it, but she knew it was there all the same. And now he was staying for dinner. The thought shouldn't have thrilled her, but it did.

She bent down and kissed the top of Emmy's little head. She couldn't believe that the baby was here. Tomorrow, they were taking her into the doctor's office to have her checked out and get a birth certificate. But Tillie didn't need a doctor to know that her baby was just fine. And she felt she owed thanks for that to Levi Yoder. He still claimed that he did nothing but be there for her, but he would never know how much that meant to her.

She switched Emmy's side. The thing she dreaded most was calling Melvin. She had the number to the garage where he worked written on a piece of paper, and for the last day and a half she had pretended she couldn't find it. The truth was she hadn't looked very hard. She wanted to tell him, she needed to tell him, but she dreaded it all the same.

"Tillie!" Libby screeched. She must've been somewhere in the hallway, as close as her voice sounded. "Come quick! Levi set the candy on fire!"

CHAPTER TWENTY

"Other than church, I don't think I've ever seen so many people in one house before," Levi said to Tillie with a small laugh.

Growing up, it had just been him and Mims and their brother, Daniel. Until Daniel was killed. But three children, no grandchildren, and only one grandparent in the *dawdihaus* made for much quieter family dinners. They would have the occasional cousin come over, but this was nothing like he had ever seen.

"It is something," Tillie returned.

He sat across from her during the meal, and as strange as it seemed, he could hardly remember what they ate. Some of her family members ate at the kitchen table, and the children had a table of their own, so he was thankful to be at the quieter, adult table. And it gave him time to watch Tillie among her sisters.

One thing was obvious. They loved each

other immensely. And Leah was almost as bossy as Mims. Almost, but not quite.

"Mind if I sit?" He nodded toward the end of the couch next to her.

She held Emmy in her arms, but if the previous time he had spent with her and her family meant anything at all, someone would buzz in any minute and whisk her away.

But first . . . "Can I hold her?" he asked.

Tillie looked at him in shock. "You want to hold her?"

He nodded. "Is that surprising?"

She looked down at Emmy and shook her head. "It's just . . ."

Men didn't normally go around asking to hold babies that weren't theirs. But he didn't say it. And she didn't finish.

"You don't trust me after the candy incident," he said.

She shook her head. "That has nothing to do with it."

He sighed. "Libby completely overreacted."

She smiled at him and all his doubts fell away. Then she gently eased the baby toward him so that her neck was cradled in the crook of his arm. Emmy rustled a little bit, stretched some, then settled back down, sleeping peacefully, her mouth moving like she was sucking on something that wasn't there. And she was perfect. He just couldn't believe how beautiful and perfect she was.

"She's a good baby," he said. He had nothing to do with it. He wasn't her father. He'd just stood by while Tillie labored, but he felt a kinship to her all the same.

"Thank you for the diapers," she said. "And the bunny. You didn't have to do that."

"I know. But I wanted to." He could've added the tiny bunny to the memorial he had set up for Mary and the baby, but somehow he felt this was a better purpose for it.

"What does Melvin think of her?" Levi asked.

Tillie's expression turned sheepish. "I haven't exactly told him yet."

"You haven't?" It was beyond surprising.

"I know. I know. But . . ." She shook her head. "Things had changed between us before I left," she admitted.

He jerked his gaze to her in surprise. And she shook her head again. "I don't know why I'm telling you this. But I think I wanted him to come after me, not just the baby."

It was understandable, he supposed. But instead of commenting, he nodded. "So he's not going to come back," Levi asked.

She shook her head. "Doubtful." She fiddled with something in her lap, a string on her apron or some invisible something on the fabric. "He's not going to come back, and I'm not going to be able to stay."

Levi had figured that one out for himself. How had such a sweet girl gotten herself into such a mess? "What will you do?"

"I don't know. Maybe stay with Leah. I think the bishop will find fault with that, but I don't want to go back to Columbus."

"Will you try to get a job at a day care center like you had before?"

"You remember that?"

"Of course."

"I don't know. I'll have to find a job doing something. But with me being a . . . single mother, it might be kind of hard. I know firsthand; childcare is expensive."

Levi had no idea about such matters. "It's really none of my business."

"I just wanted you to know." She shrugged. "I know people have been saying all kinds of things about me. I guess some of it's true. Some of it might not be. I don't know. But I wanted you to know from me what's happening."

"You don't have to explain anything to me," Levi said.

"Thank you."

He lightly traced the curve of Emmy's nose with one finger, then stopped when he realized how calloused his finger was and how rough it must feel against the soft baby skin. But she was just so beautiful. He wanted to touch her. Maybe to make sure she was real.

"Melvin," he said. "Do you love him?" He closed his eyes and shook his head. "You don't have to answer that." He had no right to ask. He had no cause to ask. But somehow it was very important that he know.

"I did," she said quietly.

"There you are." Leah breezed into the living room, where they had managed to sit in peace for a while. But with a house full of people it was only a matter of time before someone interrupted them. "Okay, my turn," she said and reached out for Levi to hand her Emmy.

He wanted to tell her that he wasn't done holding the sweet baby just yet, but a part of him knew he needed to surrender her. He almost felt as if he was getting too attached. And it would do no good to get attached to a baby who was going to be leaving soon and returning to a world he wasn't a part of. Or to her mother, for that matter. It hadn't taken long, but it seemed as if Tillie Gingerich had become quite important to him.

Leah cuddled the baby and kissed her head, then marched back the way she came, calling, "I found her," as she went.

Levi turned back to Tillie. She seemed like she had been about to say more before Leah interrupted them, and he wanted to ask what that might be. But he had pried enough for one day.

"The truth is," Tillie said, "I don't know anymore. If I love him."

Levi swallowed hard. He wasn't sure why those words made his mouth go dry, made him wonder about a lot of things all at once.

"Why is it so complicated?" Tillie asked.

"I don't know," Levi answered honestly. "I really do not know."

"I think I've outstayed my welcome," Levi said. He stood and stretched his legs as Tillie watched, unable to protest if he left now.

What call did she have to claim any of his time? None. None at all. She stood as well and smoothed her hands down over her apron. "*Danki* for helping us with the Christmas candy."

He patted his stomach. "I'm sure it cost me a good two or three pounds, but it was worth it in the end."

She smiled, happy when he returned the gesture. "Isn't that the way of candy?" She turned and headed to the kitchen. "Wait one second. Don't go just yet."

"I won't."

Tillie hustled into the kitchen, grabbed the box of the candy they had made, and ran back to where Levi waited.

"You worked so hard on these; I think you should take some with you." She held the box toward him.

He seemed hesitant, but finally accepted her offering. "Between you and Mims, I'm going to be fat as a pig by the time the new year comes around."

She laughed. "I doubt that very much. Enjoy the candy."

He nodded and headed toward the door. He grabbed his coat and his hat, donned them, and turned back to Tillie. "I know I will."

Tillie stood at the window in the dining room and watched as Levi said farewells to the men outside and pulled himself up into his buggy. Moments later, he was gone.

"He seems like a nice man," Hannah said.

Tillie whirled around to face her sister. "I — oh, *jah,*" she finally managed. "He's a very nice man."

"And he adores the baby."

Tillie shrugged. "I suppose."

"Ain't no 'suppose' about it," Leah said, coming into the room. "That man is crazy about little Emmy."

"Speaking of . . . where is she?"

"Mammi has her. She said she would ring the bell if she got hungry. Emmy, not Mammi," Leah explained. "Though Mammi rings the bell when she's hungry too."

"We got it," Hannah said.

Leah stuck her tongue out at Hannah, then turned her attention to Tillie. "So, anything interesting happen while you were at Levi's?"

"I had a baby," she replied.

"You know what I mean. That man seems smitten."

"It's not that simple."

"It never is," Hannah returned.

"His wife hasn't even been gone three months now. I don't think he has given the first thought to romance."

"That's when it always gets you," Leah countered.

"I'm not staying," Tillie finally said.

Both her sisters gasped. "Not even through Christmas?" Hannah asked.

"*Jah,* but no longer. The bishop . . ." She didn't have to explain what the bishop had said. Her sisters knew the rules as well as

316

she. Tillie couldn't remain in the community if she wasn't married to her baby's
father. It was as simple and as complicated
as that.

"Have you told Mamm?" Hannah asked.

"She knows," Tillie replied. "She was here
with me when Amos Raber came by." But
like the rest of them, her *mamm* would
rather pretend that the end wasn't coming
and enjoy the now. Just as Tillie had been
trying to do when she was at Levi's house.
But it was a lot harder than it sounded.
How was a body supposed to experience
the now with the future looming ahead?

She guessed if it was a good future it
might be easier, but with what waited for
her . . .

"I wanted to ask you," Tillie started, turning to Leah. "Do you think maybe I could
stay with you for a little while? Just until I
get back on my feet?"

Leah frowned. "I'll have to talk to Jamie
about it, but I don't see why not."

"What about Melvin?" Hannah asked.

The question of the hour, as they said.
"He didn't come after me all this time. I
don't see why he would want me back
merely because I've been excommunicated."

"And what about telling him about

317

Emmy?" Leah asked. "You told him all that yet?"

"You know I haven't," Tillie replied.

"Just making my point." Leah dipped her chin as if it were the only answer they needed.

"Which is?" Hannah asked.

"She's withholding information from him and not giving him a chance to prove himself."

"I'm not?" Tillie asked.

"Prove himself?" Hannah asked.

"Right," Leah stated. "As I see it, he would be here in a heartbeat if he knew you'd had the baby."

Which was the exact reason why Tillie hadn't told him yet. She had been holding out the hope that he would come for her. That maybe he missed her and would travel all that way to be beside her, come what may. If she told him about Emmy and he came now, Tillie would always believe that he only came because she'd had the baby.

"As he should," Hannah said.

"But Tillie's not telling him and then holding it against him when he doesn't show up."

She shook her head. "That's not exactly the truth."

318

"It's close enough," Leah said. "You aren't giving the poor man a chance."

The words echoed around inside Tillie's head as she lay in bed and stared into the darkness. Had she kept Melvin's chances from him? Was Leah right that Tillie wasn't playing fair with him? He needed the chance to come see her, see the baby, tell them that he missed them. That was all she really wanted, wasn't it?

Honestly, she wasn't sure what she wanted any longer.

She rolled over and punched her pillow, trying to get it into a more comfortable shape.

It was Wednesday. Christmas was only four days away. Four days and she would have to leave the community. Four days and she would either move in with Leah and her family or she would be forced to go back to the apartment she had shared with Melvin.

Forced. Was that really how she felt about it?

It was one thing to want to stay, to need to be close to her family, but it was quite another to literally dread leaving. And she did. Even if she didn't return to Columbus, she dreaded the leaving. She didn't want to say goodbye, she didn't want to leave it all behind. She had made the mistake of leaving to begin with. Leaving again would just compound it. But what else could she do?

You could try to talk Melvin into staying.

He might. Maybe for her. After all, she had left for him. Perhaps he had grown bored with all the English freedoms. She had learned the hard way that some freedoms weren't all they were cracked up to be. Maybe Melvin was ready to recommit to her and the baby and possibly even join the church. And there was only one way to find out. She had to call him. Tomorrow. She needed to tell him as soon as possible that they had a little girl, a perfect baby girl, and that Tillie wanted him to come back.

Maybe she wouldn't tell him that last part right away. She had to save something for later on. No sense in hitting him with everything at once.

Yes, she decided. It was time that she called Melvin, had him join her for Christmas, maybe. And then he would have the chance to do what they all, including Levi, had already done — fall in love with Emmy.

"So it's a Tuesday normally, a Wednesday when you're busy on Tuesday, and a Thursday if you're busy on Wednesday and Tuesday. Am I getting this right?" Tillie asked.

Once again, she was seated at the dining room table surrounded by overpowering scents and bottles of goat milk lotion.

"Got it in one," Leah said.

"I still can't believe how many orders the website brought in," Gracie said with a shake of her head.

"The Internet is where it's at," Leah said.

"I think next year we should put a time limit on when they can order to have it for Christmas," Hannah said.

"Good idea," Gracie said. "I think. Only what happens if they order after that?"

Leah shook her head. "I'm not really sure. We'll have to figure it all out. But Hannah's right; we need a deadline so that we can start preparing for the next holiday."

"Valentine's Day?" Tillie asked.

"Chocolate-scented lotion," Gracie said. The smile on her face showed how proud she was of her unusual creative streak.

"You know," Hannah said. "That's not quite a bad idea."

"Or we can mix scents and name them after famous couples," Leah added. "Like Romeo and Juliet."

"Samson and Delilah?" Gracie laughed.

Hannah pushed back her chair and stood. "Some of this stuff might be good. I'll go get a piece of paper and pen." She bustled from the room while Leah and Gracie laughed and Tillie tried not to be jealous.

Just a couple more days and she would be forced to leave Pontotoc. Unless the impossible happened — unless she could manage to talk Melvin into staying, confessing, and marrying her.

Like a flash of light in the dark, Levi's face appeared in her thoughts.

It was perplexing, to say the least. Why was she thinking about Levi Yoder at a time like this?

But she knew, in her heart. Levi Yoder was a good man. He had been hurt, practically devastated, by the loss of his wife and child. And yet he had taken her in, given her and Emmy more than they had a right to ask for. She found herself with him never far from her thoughts. But that was an impossibility. Worse than Romeo and Juliet, worse than Samson and Delilah. Even if she stayed in their community — and she wasn't going to be allowed to — but after confessing, going through baptism classes, and finally joining the church . . . Who would say Levi would even want her after all that?

Who said he wants you now?

His loss was fresh. But by the time she went through all those steps, he probably would have already found somebody else.

She shook her head at herself. Her thoughts were going all over the place like one of those super bouncing balls kids get out of the gumball machines.

"What's wrong?" Leah asked.

"Nothing," Tillie said.

Leah shot her a look. "We all know that that's not the truth."

Hannah picked that moment to come back into the room, pen and paper in hand. "What's not the truth?"

"Tillie is claiming that nothing's wrong today."

"I've just got a lot on my mind," she said.

"You say that and it's just like saying nothing at all," Leah chastised.

"Are you going into town to call him today?" Gracie asked.

"I can take you in my car if you like," Leah offered. "We can go to my store and use the phone there."

"And you can take a lot of these lotions with you at the same time," Hannah said. "Two birds."

"*Jah.* I suppose I must." Her conviction of the night before had faded to gray in the morning light. In the dark hours she'd been confident that calling Melvin and telling him about Emmy was the greatest idea ever. Now she merely felt like it was the only idea she had. The only *choice* she had.

She supposed it was. The man deserved to know that his child had been born. But for Tillie it was more than that. Would he forgive her for walking out? Would he want to take her back? Would he help her raise Emmy? And the biggest one of all, could they do it Amish?

Chapter Twenty-One

"I really appreciate this," Tillie said. She and Leah had just pulled up into the parking space behind Twice Blessed. Still, the thought of contacting Melvin made her stomach plummet like it had the time she rode the roller coaster when the fair came to town. But she was excited to see her sister's secondhand store.

Leah pocketed her keys and together they walked around to the front of the building. "We park in the back so there's plenty of space out front for customers," she said. "And the Amish bring their buggies back here so their horses aren't on the main street," she added.

Tillie had been surprised to see a buggy parked behind the shop, but it wasn't like horse and carriages were unheard-of in Pontotoc. Any time of day there would be two or three parked at Walmart. It was simply a part of life. But she hadn't considered the idea of her Amish friends and neighbors shopping at Leah's store. The thought made her miss her community all the more. It was ridiculous, but there it was.

"You don't go in the back door?" Tillie asked as they rounded the corner to the front facing Main.

"Sometimes," Leah said. "But since there's a buggy in the back, I figure there's an Amish person in the storeroom looking at the Amish exchange clothes."

Her sister went on to explain how she kept Amish clothing in the back in a special place so people could come and take as they needed and give back if they wanted to. She charged nothing for the service. It was just something Leah wanted to give to the community where she had grown up.

Tillie looked around as they stepped inside. But her perusal was interrupted when Brandon caught sight of them.

"Tillie! And Leah!" he greeted, walking to the front of the store as he spoke. "I wasn't expecting you today. Isn't it cousins' day part three?"

Leah affectionately patted him on the cheek. "You should be glad I like your sass," she said. She passed him her car keys. "There are two boxes of lotions and soaps in the trunk. One needs to go to the back where we can get it ready to ship and the other one needs to come up front for the shelves. They're marked."

Brandon took the keys from her and nodded. "You just like my work ethic. Because you know you can treat me like a slave."

Leah smiled at him and shook her head. "Buy you lunch?"

"Boondocks Grill?"

Leah rolled her eyes. "You're going to turn into a fried green tomato," she said.

Brandon grinned. "I'll take my chances."

Tillie watched the exchange between aunt and nephew. They really were close, and it had all happened in the time that she had been gone. And if Melvin . . . She stopped that thought. She couldn't think that far in advance. She had to keep her perspective. First thing was to tell him about the baby, second thing was to hope that he came to visit. And the third thing was praying that everything fell in line from there.

"The phone's over there when you have a mind," Leah said, pointing to a charging station with a cordless phone in the cradle. "Or do you want a tour of the store first?"

Tillie nodded. "*Jah,* please." She did want to see her sister's store and all the hard work she put into the enterprise, but it didn't hurt that it delayed, even if for just a bit, her calling Melvin.

"So you can see the shelves where we keep the lotions and soaps. We have a lot of people come in from outside just out of curiosity."

"And they come in just for the lotion?"

"Sometimes. I think the red labels help. Brandon and Shelly designed it for us. I think they did a good job."

"Me too," Tillie agreed. "And they're not . . . ?" She didn't have to finish the sentence.

Leah shrugged. "They say not, but I think they're really good together."

"Well, the display does look pretty."

Leah had constructed wooden shelves on which to stack the bottles of lotion and cakes of soap. Most were stored in mismatched baskets, a display that somehow had a country charm even though it lacked consistency. The bars of soap were wrapped in cellophane and tied with a red bow. A deep red crimson, like Christmas. The label itself had a logo with a curly-cue *G* and *S* intertwined.

"Gingerich Sisters," she said.

"Or Glick," Leah added.

Gracie might not be their sister by birth, but she was as close as.

"I try to keep hot ticket items toward the front. This time of year, it's small appliances, books, sweaters — things that people can give as Christmas gifts. It all shifts come the next holiday or if I see something is in good demand."

"In demand?" Tillie had no idea second-hand items could come into demand.

"Yeah. June is good for dishes, due to all the English weddings. Picture frames and that sort of thing for May, with the graduations. And then sometimes things go in demand just because. Like microwaves."

"Microwaves?" Tillie asked. They'd had a microwave at the day care center and used it to reheat things, mostly coffee that had gotten cold while they were working with the kids. It was a convenient something to have, but Tillie couldn't imagine it coming in "demand."

" 'Mine is not to reason why,' " Leah quipped. "The rest of the household goods are behind the front area, clothes behind that, and then the Amish in the back. That way Amish can come in through the back door and leave and not have to worry any with the front, and their horses are safe behind the building."

"It's a good setup," Tillie said. She was proud of her sister. And impressed. Briefly she wondered if Leah might have a place for her on staff. But could she really stay so close to home and not be a part of the community she loved and missed?

As much as she wanted to say yes, she knew the answer was no. If she couldn't stay in Pontotoc, if she couldn't live with the Amish, if she couldn't join the church and be a part of the community where she had grown up, she was going to have to move away. It would just be too painful to be so close and an outsider.

Voices from the back of the store reached her. Brandon was coming in the back with the lotion and soaps that he had gotten out of the car. He must have stopped to talk to the Amish woman whose buggy was parked out back. Her voice sounded familiar, but with so much tumbling around inside her head as she took in Leah's store and tried not to think about calling Melvin, Tillie couldn't quite place it.

"Let me check," Brandon said. A moment later he appeared from the back of the store carrying the box labeled *DISPLAY*. "Aunt Leah, the lady in the back wants to know if you would be interested in adding any baby furniture to the section."

"The Amish section?" Leah asked.

"You want to talk to her?" he asked.

Leah nodded and walked to the back of the store. Unsure of what to do with herself,

Tillie followed behind.

"Hi," Leah greeted the woman. She turned and Tillie was surprised to see that it was Mims Yoder.

"Tillie! It's so good to see you." Mims's greeting sounded genuine enough, yet Tillie couldn't help but wonder what the chances were of running into her at Leah's store.

"You too," Tillie murmured.

"You wanted to talk about furniture?" Leah asked. "Baby furniture?"

Mims cast a hesitant look toward Tillie, then answered. "My brother has some furniture." Tillie knew the exact moment when Leah realized who she was talking to. A change came over her sister, not good or bad — she just held herself differently.

"I'm so sorry," Leah replied.

Mims nodded. "I just didn't know if maybe someone could use the things, and I wanted to make sure that it got to the person who might need them the most."

"I don't normally trade furniture, but if you would like you can put it in the store on consignment. I'll keep a small portion and help you sell it and get it out of the house, if that's something that you need, and I'll keep it until it sells."

"I was thinking more of a donation to a person," Mims said. "There's a beautiful changing table and a crib."

"I've got an idea," Leah said. "We have a small staff here, and we communicate well. We could put a tag on it and try to sell it. That way if somebody needs it and they can afford to buy it, they can. But if somebody has a need for it and can't purchase it, then we will add it into the exchange. When they're finished using it, they can bring it back for a second round. Or pass it on. You know, pay it forward."

Leah, with all her brashness and sassy attitude, never ceased to amaze Tillie with her generosity.

Mims visibly relaxed. Tillie knew right away that she liked the idea. "That sounds great. I'll talk to my brother about it." Then she turned to Tillie and held out two tiny dresses and an impossibly small prayer *kapp.* "I found these back there. I thought you might could use them." Then she turned to Leah. "I didn't leave baby clothes, but I left a couple of dresses of mine that have gotten a bit snug." She tugged at her trim waistline. Where she put a couple of extra pounds Tillie had no idea. At this rate she never thought she would get rid of the bulging belly she still carried. It was another thing no one told you: after you have the baby you still look like you are going to have a baby. For much longer than any woman wants to.

"Danki," Tillie said, and told herself not to cry. It seemed Levi had a sister much like her own. Mims could be just as sassy and bossy as Leah, but they both had hearts as big as everything.

Mims turned back to Leah. "I'll let you know," she said.

Leah smiled and gave a small nod. "I'm looking forward to it."

With a small wave, Mims turned and made her way into the back of the store, to the back door where she had entered before.

"Well, isn't that interesting," Leah said.

"I don't want to take these dresses," Tillie said. It wasn't that baby Emmy couldn't use them. They were poor, but not destitute. She didn't want to take from someone who might need them more than she.

"She came out of the back room with those," Leah said. "Before she knew you were here. She came here looking for something for your baby. I say you keep them. No, I insist."

"Danki," Tillie said. "Though if Melvin doesn't come . . ." She didn't finish that sentence. If Melvin didn't come, then she surely wouldn't stay, and if she didn't stay, Emmy would not need the dresses after all.

"Consider it a beacon of hope," Leah said.

Tillie ran her fingers over the fabric and let out a rueful chuckle. "Beacon of hope. Got it."

"Are you ready to call now?" Leah asked.

"*Jah,* I suppose. As ready as I'll ever be."

Once again Leah nodded toward the phone.

Tillie's palms grew damp as she walked toward it. There was a stool behind the little desk where the phone sat. She supposed she could sit there if her knees got weak. Got weak? They were already trembling like a sapling in the wind.

How could one phone call hold her entire fate? The decision of one man decided where she lived and even how she lived. It didn't seem fair, and yet those were the rules.

"There's always room at my church," Leah said softly.

Tillie sat on the stool and smiled at her sister. She knew what Leah meant. There was always an answer. It might not be the answer you wanted, but there was always an answer.

She took the slip of paper from her pocket, the one where she had written down the number to the garage where Melvin worked. She picked up the phone and dialed. Her mouth went dry, and her hands trembled like her legs as she waited for someone to pick up on the other end. Three long rings later, someone finally did.

"Garage," the man barked. Behind him she could hear the clank of metal against metal and the whirring of the different machines.

"I'm looking for Melvin Yoder," she said, her voice small and hesitant.

"What? I can't hear you. Can you speak up?"

Tillie cleared her throat. "I said, I'm looking for Melvin Yoder."

"He's not here today," the man hollered back.

Tillie wondered just how loud it was in the garage. No wonder Melvin liked peace and quiet when he got home. A person would think he would want to watch TV all night since he'd been denied it his entire life, but he would rather sit and read the paper with no sound other than the ticking of the clock and the running of appliances.

Of course he wasn't there. "Can I leave a message?"

"Hold on, let me get a pen." The phone clanged as if he had dropped the receiver on the desk or table. He hollered something to someone around him.

Tillie could feel Leah watching her. What she really was going to tell Melvin that he had a baby over a telephone message, not even directly? It seemed a bit heartless, but it wasn't like he didn't know she was pregnant to begin with, right? And he didn't need to know that news in order to determine if he wanted to come and visit. Or so she had thought.

The phone clattered again, then the man's voice came back on the line. "Okay," he said. "What's the message?"

"Please tell him that Tillie called and that he has a baby girl."

She couldn't see his face over the phone, of course, but she could sense his change in attitude. "A baby girl?"

"Yes. And please tell him that we're at my parents' house. If he wants to come." She closed her eyes. Why had she said that last part? If he wanted to come, he would come. She didn't need to invite him. He knew he was welcome. Why else would she have called? She just didn't want to sound like she was begging for his attention, and somehow that's exactly how this felt. Maybe if she didn't need him so much right then . . .

"Got it," the man said. "Melvin comes in tomorrow, but if I see him before then, I'll give him the message."

"Thank you," Tillie said. And she hung up the phone. She sighed and looked to Leah.

"Okay, that's done." Leah's normally sassy tone was filled with a little bit of hope and even more despair.

Tillie couldn't blame her. She felt the same. What a mess she had made of everything. And what a mess she was putting her family through so close to Christmas.

"I should just go," Tillie said.

"I thought we were going to get supper," Leah said.

Tillie shook her head. "Back to Columbus. I should've never come here." Tears rose into her eyes. It was hopeless. Why did everything end up so hopeless?

"You cannot leave before Christmas," Leah said. "It would break Mamm's heart."

Tillie knew it would.

"And even better than that, you're going to go with us to the buddy bunch Christmas celebration tomorrow night." Leah held up a hand as Tillie started to protest. "Hup," she said. "I will not hear any objections. Everyone who's anyone is going to be there."

Tillie blinked back her tears and smiled at her sister's very English vocabulary. "No

337

one's going to talk to me. No one will want me there." Just one of the joys of excommunication.

"They let me come," Leah said.

"You don't have a baby without a husband either," Tillie replied. She would not be remorseful about her baby. She could not.

"Even worse," Leah quipped. "I'm Mennonite."

Tillie did her best to keep her spirits up on the drive home. She had thought that by calling Melvin she would feel better about the situation. She was wrong. Now she felt even more nervous and anxious than ever.

It was crazy, what a person hoped for even when they knew they wouldn't get it. And more than anything, she hoped that Melvin would say he was coming back, that he would come back, and they would live the Amish life she always thought they would. But then she thought of the troubles they'd had before she left Columbus. Lack of money, too many arguments. There was no guarantee those troubles wouldn't leach into any life they had, Amish or English. And most definitely they would be present if they left to go live with the English again.

Yes. There was no doubt about it. If Melvin wouldn't come back and marry her in the Amish church, then she would have to go. She would have to leave Pontotoc. It was as simple as that.

The worst part of it all is she knew Melvin didn't want to come back. Did she want him to come back solely for her? And be miserable? Or should she just accept what she had done and be miserable and English and raise her baby by herself? It was a no-win situation.

"Well, look who's here." Leah parked the car next to a very familiar buggy.

Levi.

Tillie was glad Levi was there, even though she knew she shouldn't be. There could be nothing more than casual friendship between her and Levi Yoder. But she wanted that friendship if at all possible.

Tillie grabbed her purse and got out of the car, then she slowly made her way into the house. She was glad that she would get to see Levi again.

He is just a friend.

And that's all he would ever be to her. Her life was about to drastically change, even more than it had by giving birth to Emmy. She figured right now she could use all the friends she could find.

She opened the door, Leah right behind her. "Mamm, we're home!" Leah shouted.

Tillie shushed her. "If Emmy is asleep, you'll wake her up."

"Sorry." Leah shot her a sheepish grin. "I'm not used to having a sweet little baby in the house."

Mamm hurried into the living room from the kitchen, carrying a fussing Emmy.

Tillie looked to her sister. "See?"

Leah shot her an apologetic look. "I didn't mean to."

"You didn't wake her," Mamm said. "But I think she wants to be fed. You came back just in time."

Tillie and Leah shrugged out of their coats and bonnets, and Tillie placed her purse next to the couch. Then she reached out her arms for her mother to hand over her baby.

"I see Levi Yoder is here," Leah said.

"He's in the kitchen helping me make Christmas cranberry bread."

Leah and Tillie both turned to their mother. "What?" they asked together.

Eunice shrugged. "He came in when I was just starting it. He said he wanted to help, so he's in making cranberry bread." Their mother said it as if it was the most natural thing in the world.

Tillie smiled and shook her head. "I got to feed this baby."

Mamm nodded. "I'll let him know."

"I'm sure he's figured it out with all that crying," Leah said as Tillie turned toward the bedroom. It was the easiest place to feed Emmy, out of sight from any male eyes, and it gave her a measure of privacy with her baby. It was a bonding time and she loved it, probably more than she should. She would miss that time when she had to go back to work.

After Emmy ate her fill, Tillie burped her baby, straightened her clothes, and laid her down in the small crib Mamm had brought down from the attic. "Sweet dreams, precious girl," Tillie said. She ran one finger over Emmy's tiny ear, then eased out of the room. She shut the door behind her and made her way to the kitchen.

Hearing it was surprising enough, but seeing it was almost more than she could stand. "You really are making cranberry bread," Tillie said.

"It's almost done. Would you like a piece?" Levi asked. He seemed very satisfied with himself. Maybe learning to cook would be another healing activity for him. Tillie was certain it would take a lot of work off Mims, and even his mother. That was, if Levi didn't get remarried soon. The thought sent a pang through her belly. She didn't know

341

why it mattered to her whether Levi got remarried or not. The fact of the matter was it wouldn't be to her. There was no chance of it. None at all.

The timer dinged.

"That's it," Libby said. "Time to take it out." She handed Levi the pot holders.

Tillie almost laughed at how domesticated he looked. Blue shirt, black pants, green apron that must've been something her father used at one time or another. It was the kind that went over the head and had a bib. It tied around the back like the ones she had seen cooks wear when they had some kind of festival in town.

"Can't cut it yet," Mamm said. "It will need to cool first."

"Put it on the porch," Leah said. "It'll be ready to eat in a heartbeat."

Libby nodded and grabbed the pan. "That's a great idea." She bustled from the room to take the bread to the porch to cool. Though the ice had disappeared, it was still very chilly outside. Cloudy and gray, a little too much like her thoughts, to be sure.

"I'll check on Emmy," Mamm said.

Leah hopped up from her place at the kitchen table. "I'll go with you."

And just like that Tillie found herself alone with Levi Yoder once again.

"So what brings you out today, Levi?" Tillie asked. "I know you didn't just come over to make Christmas cranberry bread."

He slid onto the bench seat opposite her. "I did have a good time making it though." He grinned, and she realized that she had missed his smile. "I brought you some diapers." He nodded toward the package at the end of the table. With all the baking supplies still out and scattered around, Tillie hadn't noticed them until he pointed them out.

"You didn't have to do that."

"I wanted to."

"These are new diapers." She hadn't meant for her voice to sound so accusing.

"*Jah.* Maybe."

There was no *maybe* about it.

"You can't continue to do this, Levi. As much as I appreciate it."

"I know, but I need to do it now, while I can."

"Levi." There was a world of emotions in her word. Regret, remorse, resignation.

He shook his head. "I failed Mary, and I failed the baby. Please let me help you. I don't want to fail you too."

Chapter Twenty-Two

"I'm telling you what I heard," Mims said.

Levi pressed his lips together and frowned. "Why are you so concerned that she called Melvin? He is the baby's father."

"I know, but she invited him to come here. Don't you find that interesting?" Mims shot him an inquisitive look.

Levi wasn't sure exactly what his sister was getting at, but he had a clue. "She needs to be with Melvin," Levi said. "They need to be a couple. An official couple. Married," he said before she could interject anything else.

"That doesn't bother you?" Mims pushed.

Did it bother him?

Yes, yes it did. But there was nothing either of them could do about it. Tillie would have to marry Melvin if she wanted to stay in Pontotoc. There was no other way. She couldn't marry someone else, not having had a baby with Melvin. But if Melvin didn't return to the Amish, Tillie would be forced to leave, excommunicated. She would take her baby with her and it would most likely be the last he ever saw of her. "What bothers me and what doesn't bother me has no part in this." As much as he hated to admit it, that was the truth. "And even if it did," he told Mims, "it's too soon."

"Too soon?"

"Mary's only been gone a little over two months. And I admit Tillie brought me back from a dark place. Her and the baby. And for that I will always be grateful to her. But gratitude is not and should never be mistaken for anything more."

Mims propped her hands on her hips and gave him a stern look. "Levi Yoder, you are one stupid man."

"Did you just call me stupid?" He asked the question though he was certain he had heard her correctly.

"I'm your sister," she said. "I'm entitled."

"I'm not stupid. In fact, I think I'm trying to be very smart about the whole situation." Though smart where the heart was concerned was not always a possibility.

"So that's it. You're just going to lie down and give up without a fight?"

Well, he was Amish. But even fighting for love was hard.

"It's more than that. You know the rules. If she doesn't come back and marry Melvin, she has to leave."

Mims seemed to wilt a bit, and her starchy attitude softened. "I know, but —"

"Besides, why are you fussing at me when you didn't fight for David?"

Mims drew back and sniffed. "It's not anywhere close to the same."

"I beg to differ."

"I'm not going to talk about this anymore," Mims said.

"Your love life or my love life?"

"Neither," she replied.

"Good."

"But you have to promise me that you'll go with me to the party tonight."

"I do not want to go to a party." In fact, it might be the very last thing that he wished to do. Tillie may have helped him get out of the dark place where he was living after Mary and the baby died, but that didn't mean he was ready for all social interaction. "You forced me to go to the wedding, and I did. But I can miss the party."

Mims shook her head. "No, you can't. Because I said you can't. And it will be fun. It'll be good for you. And maybe Tillie will be there."

"You're not going to give up, are you?"

"Never." She smiled. "So say you'll go, and that will be that."

Levi sighed. "Fine," he said. "I'll go."

"I insist," Mamm said. "Now redo your hair and get ready for the party. Express your milk and I'll watch the baby."

Tillie looked from Emmy, who was sleeping peacefully in the baby carrier, to her *mamm.*

"Come on," Leah said. "Everybody's going to be there."

"So you say." She bit her lip. "It's just . . . She's never eaten from a bottle before. What happens if she doesn't take it?"

"If she doesn't take it," Mamm said, "I'll get in my buggy and bring her to you at the party."

Tillie looked down to her baby once again. She hated the idea of Emmy eating from a bottle. But she supposed it was necessary. Soon she would have to get a job. Hopefully the day care center would let her keep Emmy there. Maybe at a reduced rate. She hoped so, anyway. And there would be times when she couldn't be with her, and Emmy would have to be fed with a bottle then. There was no way around it.

"Okay."

Leah jumped up and down and clapped

her hands.

"I'm going to run into town and get Jamie and Peter," Leah said. "Then I'll be right back."

Tillie stopped. "Peter's going?"

"No, he's staying with Mamm."

Tillie looked to her *mamm*. "Can you handle Peter and a baby? I should stay here."

Mamm propped her hands on her hips and shot Tillie a disbelieving look. "I took care of Jim, David, Leah, Hannah, and you all at the same time, and you don't think I can handle a baby and a wonderful seven-year-old?"

"I'm guessing the answer to this is 'Not at all'?" Though she didn't bother to point out that Jim was practically out of the house before she herself had been born. She wasn't sure Mamm was up for that logic tonight.

"Shoo," Mamm said. "Go to your room and change your clothes. I got this."

Tillie almost smiled at her mother's language, then turned to go into her room. She stopped in front of the mirror behind the door and took a hard look at herself. She was still wearing the nursing dress that she had borrowed from Anna. It was blue and of a nice enough material. But it was Amish.

This whole time she had been kidding herself that she might get to stay Amish. She had called Melvin the day before, and she had heard nothing from him. She should have left Leah's number with him. But it wasn't like he didn't know the name of the store. He could've looked it up himself. But he hadn't bothered to call. He hadn't bothered to show up. And her hopes of remaining in Pontotoc were truly dashed.

She unpinned her prayer *kapp* from her head and set it on the desk by the door. Then she shucked out of her dress and hung it in the closet next to the purple maternity dress that she had borrowed from Anna as well. Then she pulled out her own skirt and shirt and put them on. She redid her hair in a more English-looking bob, or bun, as they called it, without any twists and a little higher on her head. She pulled on her boots and made her way back to the front of the house.

Mamm's eyes widened in surprise. "You're not going like that? Are you?"

Tillie didn't bother to even look at herself. She nodded. "I am." Because it was time that she accepted this was who she was now and probably always would be.

It was just as she had suspected. Even in

English clothes the people around her hadn't forgiven her for her transgressions. Technically she supposed she hadn't asked for forgiveness. When someone moved too close, they cast her a look and sidled away. Tillie felt a little like one of those poisonous frogs from Africa that she had seen at the zoo. They were different looking, with bright colors and black markings, and their skin was so poisonous a person couldn't even touch them without dying. That was how she felt, as if people thought that if they got too close to her, her sins would somehow rub off on them. No matter. Tomorrow was Christmas Eve, and the next day Christmas. And on Monday she would talk Leah into taking her back to Columbus.

The only place you have to stay in Columbus is with Melvin.

And that would never work. Maybe she should distance herself from him. Maybe start over in Tupelo. Or Corinth. Somewhere else. She supposed if she tried hard enough, she could start over anywhere.

"Is this seat taken?"

She looked up and smiled. "Levi."

He nodded toward the space beside her on the couch. Around them a party was happening, people being merry, drinking green-colored punch and eating Christmas cookies, and wishing good cheer upon one another. Most everyone wore a necklace made of shiny garland or a crown fashioned of the same. It was festive and fine, but she was in no way a part of it.

"Sure," she said. "If you dare."

He sat down next to her and raised an inquisitive brow.

"I think everyone here thinks I have cooties." She was completely making too light of the situation, but it was either that or wallow in it, and she really didn't feel like wallowing anymore. She'd made her bed and all that.

"I don't suppose it would do any good if I told them you don't," Levi asked.

"I'm afraid it would only damage your reputation as well."

"That sort of thing is very important around here."

Didn't she know it. Yes, she did. She knew it when she left and she knew it when she came home. But she had foolishly allowed herself to be molded by Melvin into what he thought they needed to be. He wanted to be a young and hip English couple. Amish-turned-English couple, rather. But to look at him no one would ever suspect that he was Amish. Unless they were Amish too. He wore ripped blue jeans and sneakers, T-shirts with a button-down thrown over it and the sleeves rolled up. His hair was cut in a more English style, shaggy around his eyes and ears, a little too long in the back. He thought it ridiculous for them to have to get married in order to live together. They'd run away together. And she was his girl.

Well, she had been for a while.

"Are you having a good time?" she asked, hoping to change the subject.

Levi looked down into the plastic cup he held. "Would it be terrible of me to say no?"

"You're talking to the resident pariah," she said, once again making light of it all.

"Mims insisted I come."

Tillie gave him a sympathetic smile. "I understand." She understood that Levi was still healing, something that Mims seemed to have trouble identifying. "Maybe since I was at your house and you've been coming over to see the baby, Mims thinks you're ready to really socialize. That's why she insisted you come tonight."

Levi drained his cup of green punch and swallowed before answering. "Mims just likes bossing people around."

Tillie couldn't help the laughter that spilled from her. It drew a couple of looks, and she immediately sobered. "I like Mims," she said. "I always have."

"She likes you as well," he said.

She almost asked Levi what had happened between Mims and David, but he spoke again before she could.

"You're dressed very . . . English tonight."

She picked at an invisible spot on her skirt. "I thought I'd better get used to it again."

"There's no chance of Melvin moving back?"

She pressed her lips together and shook her head.

"You called him . . . Told him about the baby."

"*Jah.* Yes. I had to leave a message. Hopefully he got it today." But he hadn't tried to call or get her a message in any way. And that could only mean one thing: he wasn't overly concerned that she'd had the baby.

She tried to soften the thought, even in her own head, but it was still harsh. She had known Melvin for so many years, and never would she have thought he would forget what was important. He just wasn't like that. Yet the only answers were that he didn't get the message or he didn't care.

"Maybe he didn't get the message," Levi said, echoing her thoughts.

Tillie's eyes filled with tears, and she

blinked them back. No good crying at a Christmas party. No good at all. "I suppose." *You hope, you mean.*

"Do you think he'll come here for you?" Levi shook his head. "What am I saying? Of course he will come here for you. Surely you know that."

She would like to think that he would. But the Melvin she had fallen in love with was very different than the Melvin she had left in Columbus. This new Melvin . . . she didn't feel like she knew him at all.

Whose fault is that?

It was no one's fault; both of their faults. Or maybe it simply was what it was. She had heard her *mammi* say that from time to time. *It is what it is.* An easy way of saying *God's will,* she supposed. Sometimes things were a certain way because they were that way.

She wondered if she and Melvin were one of those things.

"So I guess I won't see you if you move back," he said.

"When," she corrected.

"Pardon?" he asked.

"When I move back, not if," she said.

He frowned. "Will you be able to come visit?"

"I doubt it," she said. Then she shook her

354

head. What was she expecting? A change in the *Ordnung* just so her *mamm* could visit with her grandchild? "I mean, no." There, she had said it. And the world hadn't collapsed. It even continued on as if she hadn't said a thing. "You know the rules as well as I do."

He nodded.

"I'm sure Mamm will come when she can, but . . ." Who knew how often that would be and how long it would take before someone tried to put a stop to that as well? Dear Lord, what a mess she had made of things.

"Then I suppose I should tell you now," he said. "Merry Christmas, and I wish you well."

"Merry Christmas," she echoed.

He looked as if he wanted to say more, but he didn't. He just stood awkwardly and stretched his legs. "I'll just go get some punch. You want something?"

She shook her head. Her stomach was in such knots that she wasn't sure she could keep anything down.

She watched Levi cross the room and wondered if it would be the last time she would ever see him. And she knew; the chances of that were great.

■ ■ ■ ■

"Who could that be?" Eunice asked no one in particular when a knock sounded on her door. She wasn't expecting anyone. Tillie was gone to the Christmas party, Libby was with Mammi, and she was coloring a picture with chatty Peter.

"Just a minute, and I'll be right back," she told Peter, who barely stopped his own rattling speech to acknowledge her words. It seemed to Eunice that he was making up for all the words he had missed saying in those first years after his family had died.

That wasn't it, of course, but sometimes she wondered.

"Coming," she said as the person knocked again. It had to be someone they knew. They sat too far off the road for anyone in trouble to wander down for help.

She wrenched open the door, expecting to see a familiar face but not prepared for the one that was there. "Amos!" Her voice sounded unnaturally high. "Come in, come in," she said, standing aside and motioning him into the house. "It's too cold these days to linger on the porch."

He nodded his head and removed his hat and coat. "I don't suppose you have any coffee still warm."

"I can make you some."

"I don't want you to do all that," he said.

But how could she not? He was the bishop. "It's no trouble at all." She led him through the dining room, where Peter was still coloring, and into the kitchen. Maybe she shouldn't have walked him past her grandson. After all, Peter was one of the ones that got away. He and Jamie had converted to the Mennonite church so that Jamie and Leah could be married right away. Once they realized that the one thing Peter needed most in order to heal was a stable, loving home, they knew they had to provide him with one as quickly as possible.

Eunice figured some of the doctrines also struck with Jamie but it wasn't something the two of them ever talked about. Leah hadn't joined the Amish church before she left for the English world and landed with the Mennonites, and she wasn't tradition-ally shunned. Eunice was certain that Amos wasn't happy that she had managed to drag two more of his members with her, but again, it was something they just didn't talk about.

"What brings you out on a night like tonight?" That was the question she asked, when she already knew the answer. A woman could hope. And pray. And she had prayed a lot that something would happen that would allow Tillie and baby Emmy to stay there with the community. Yet she knew. Rules were rules, and the Amish had a very strict and strong set of them. Still Eunice hoped that maybe there was something they had overlooked. Wishful thinking. That was all.

"We need to talk about Tillie."

She nodded, poured him a cup of coffee, and gestured toward the container of cranberry bread on the table. "Would you like a piece?" she asked. "We try to make it every Christmas." She was babbling and needed to stop.

"Where's Abner?" Amos asked.

"In his workshop." He seemed to spend most of his time there these days, working on a late Christmas order. At least she hoped that was the real reason for him to be there, and it wasn't that he was avoiding them all and what was to come.

"I think he needs to be here for this."

Eunice popped back up and went to the dining room, where Peter still sat. "I need you to run to the barn and get your *dawdi*."

He looked up from his drawing. "You want me to run?" he asked. "Like really fast or just sort of fast?"

358

She hid her smile at his so-serious question. "Sort of fast is fine. Just tell him that the bishop is here."

Peter nodded, dropped his crayon, and headed for the door.

Eunice returned to the kitchen, where Amos Raber waited. "He should be here in a minute," she said. And she sat down on the bench side across from him.

Amos shot her a tight smile.

Eunice tried to return it. "Are you sure I can't get you a piece of cranberry bread?" she asked. "It's got pecans." Perhaps that was the dumbest thing she had ever said to the bishop. Maybe to anybody. But the air seemed thick and heavy with what was to come.

Amos drummed his fingers on the tabletop. "No. *Danki.*"

Where was Abner? Perhaps she should have told Peter to run really fast instead.

Eunice jumped to her feet. "Can I warm up your coffee?" She already had the pot and was pouring it into his cup before he could even answer.

Where was Abner?

She almost wilted with relief when she heard the front door open and close. Peter's running footsteps mixed with Abner's steady ones, and a moment later he appeared in the kitchen.

"Amos," her husband said by way of greeting.

The bishop stood, reached out a hand to shake.

"I'll get you some coffee," Eunice said. She grabbed another mug and poured her husband a cup. He sat down next to the bishop, and she eased back to the bench across from them.

"I suppose you know why I'm here," Amos started.

Abner nodded. That was her husband, a man of few words.

"Tillie and the baby," Eunice said.

"I've been patient," Amos started. "And I've tried to be fair. But some things . . ."

He didn't have to say the words for Eunice to know what he was talking about. The rules were the rules. Explicitly spelled out in the *Ordnung* or not, they had to be followed.

"I know it's Christmastime," Amos continued. "But after . . ."

"I understand," Abner said with a firm nod.

Eunice understood too, but she didn't like it. "When?" she asked.

"Tuesday at the latest. I'll give you Christmas and second Christmas, but any longer and I'm afraid it will start to affect the district as a whole. And your own standing with the church."

It was a nice way of saying that if Tillie stayed she would be shunned, and her family would be as well. It would affect them all, from Libby and Mammi all the way over to Jim and Anna just across the way. Hannah and Aaron, David, Gracie and Matthew, and everyone in between.

Tuesday. They had until Tuesday and Tillie would have to go back to wherever it was she had gone in the first place. Eunice hoped against hope that perhaps she could stay in Pontotoc, but even then, Eunice wouldn't be able to have much contact with her. That was all a part of it. The thought broke her heart. She had lost her daughter for good.

At least they would have this one last Christmas.

"Did you have a good time?" Leah asked on the way home.

"Not really," Tillie said truthfully. But it was no matter. It wasn't like she was staying very long. Soon she would have to decide what she was going to do. Though in truth she felt like Melvin had already made that decision for her. She would go back and somehow make it on her own. Perhaps she would have time after Christmas to call Dawn or Cindy at the day care center and talk to them about coming back to work and whether Tillie could get some kind of deal on childcare for Emmy. And she would have to go talk to Melvin whether he wanted to talk to her or not. She would need a place to stay.

"If I can't get in touch with Melvin," Tillie started, "can I stay with you for a little while? You and Jamie. I know it's asking a lot," she said. "But if I can't talk to him, then I don't have a place to go back to. You know I'm going to have to leave soon."

"But —" Leah started, but Tillie shook her head.

"We both know I'm not going to be allowed to stay. Not unless Melvin comes back and decides that he wants to be Amish once more. And you and I both know that's not going to happen."

Leah sighed. "I suppose you're right."

"But I probably shouldn't stay with you. It might bring a lot of trouble to you." Tillie shook her head in despair. "Maybe a friend?"

Leah reached over across the console of the car and patted Tillie's leg. "We'll figure out something." Then she gasped. "The apartment above the store. Brandon is going to move into it soon, but you could stay in it for now."

"But my job is in Columbus." At least she hoped it was.

When had everything turned so blessed complicated? It seemed as if every life choice and decision was weighing heavy on her heart. When would it ease up?

"So that's not our answer." Leah put both hands back on the wheel and turned her full attention to the road. "We will find an answer. There is an answer, and God will give it to us. We just have to pray."

Tillie wished she had Leah's positivity. She had been praying for a long time now, and it just seemed as if God wasn't answering. She wondered if she'd made such a mess of things that He was leaving her to her own devices.

You know better than that.

And she did.

"Uh-oh," Leah said.

"What?" Tillie asked.

"I think that was the bishop," she said as she turned her car down the drive.

"Amos?"

"Is there any other bishop?" Leah asked.

"No." She supposed there wasn't. And they both knew that if the bishop had been to their house visiting the night before Christmas Eve, it was something important. And she could guess what it was. It was all about her and the shame she had brought her family.

Leah pulled her car to a stop in front of the house. "I've got to go in and get Peter, but if you want, I can stay."

Tillie shook her head. "Jamie's expecting you back," she said. "Sorry he wasn't feeling well tonight."

"He just has a case of the shunning blues."

Tillie hadn't thought about it that way. Jamie was shunned by the church, excommunicated. But she knew that most of the district overlooked it, considering he did it for a little boy — left the church, that was. His only sin was caring for someone else. And most could overlook a lot for that very reason. But when they looked at her, they didn't see love but transgression. Though love was in there somewhere. Even if it was gone now.

Was it gone? "He could have sat with me on the couch."

Leah palmed her keys and got out of the car. "Next to Levi, or on the other side?"

"Cute."

"I think he likes you." Leah smiled and headed up the porch steps and into the house, leaving Tillie to trail behind. Levi might like her. She liked him. Maybe even more, or it could be, given half the chance. But there wasn't even a quarter of a chance, a sliver of a chance that they could have. Like it or not, it didn't matter.

Peter was coloring at the dining room table when they came in. Leah stopped to admire his picture, and Tillie headed into the kitchen where she figured her *mamm* would be. She passed her *dat* on the way in. He frowned at her, grunted, but didn't say a word. It was a sure sign that he was angry. He had barely spoken to her since she'd been back. His own brand of shunning. It hurt. It broke her heart. But she understood it. Her dad was old-school. And that's just the way it was. The church and God came first. Even the love for a child was after that.

Mamm sat at the table, wiping tears on the end of her apron. She dropped it quickly when she saw Tillie. She sniffed and tried to act like everything was just fine.

Tillie's heart broke all over again. The mistakes she had made were so great and the baby she had was so beautiful. She couldn't understand why it all still seemed to be such a mess. "I'm so sorry, Mamm."

"I love the church," Mamm said with another sniff. She gave Tillie a reassuring smile that didn't quite hit the mark. "And I love you. More than you will ever know."

"How long?"

"Tuesday."

Tillie felt as if the giant hand squeezed her heart and stole her breath. Tuesday. Could she figure it all out by Tuesday? Probably not. Maybe Wednesday, but that was still pushing it. Tomorrow was Saturday and Christmas Eve, Monday second Christmas and a holiday for all the Amish. She might be able to make it into town to Leah's store and call the day care center, then that didn't give her much time to get things together for Tuesday.

"You think I can have till Wednesday?"

"I'm sure Amos will understand."

Tillie certainly hoped so. It was only a day. One day to figure out her life.

She collapsed into one of the kitchen chairs and braced her elbows on the table-top. She cradled her head in her hands and tried to catch her breath. She was used to things moving as fast in the English world, but not in the Amish. Yet here she was.

"It will be okay," Mamm said. "Sometimes it isn't okay in the way we want it to be, but it always ends up okay."

Tillie raised her head. "You're right, of course." Mamm usually was.

A knock sounded at the door. Mamm looked to Tillie, who shrugged.

"Who could that be at this hour?" Mamm bustled out of the kitchen to the front door. No good came from late-night visitors, that much was certain.

"Oh my!" her mother cried.

The visitor replied. Tillie couldn't understand the words, but she knew the voice.

She was on her feet in a heartbeat. She rushed out of the kitchen, through the dining room, and to the front door.

"What are you doing here?"

Mamm stepped back as Melvin Yoder crossed the threshold. He gave Tillie a sheepish smile, then his gaze dropped to her waistline. "I came to see my baby."

CHAPTER TWENTY-THREE

I came to see my baby. The words washed over Tillie in a cold wave. He hadn't come for her. Only for Emmy. Or maybe she was reading too much into it.

"She's asleep," Tillie said. But she led the way to the room where the baby was resting in the cradle. Every unsaid thing that needed saying trailed behind them.

Not now, she told herself. It would all be spoken soon enough.

Melvin crossed the room and looked down at the baby. He sucked in a breath, and she immediately understood.

"She's beautiful."

"I know."

He reached out a hand as if to touch her but stopped short. "I want to hold her, but I don't want to wake her."

"She pretty much sleeps all the time. She's newborn, you know."

"I know," Melvin said.

"I didn't mean for that to sound the way it came out. Just that she sleeps a lot. In a couple of weeks she'll be more alert, looking at things around her and staying awake more instead of just sleeping all the time. Right now she's just adjusting to the world."

The world she isn't going to get to stay in.

"I can hold her tomorrow?" Melvin asked.

"Of course."

Melvin gave Emmy one last wistful look and backed away from the cradle. Together she and Melvin walked from the room. She gently closed the door as not to disturb Emmy before it was time to eat.

"She should sleep for another couple of hours," she told Melvin. "If you're still here maybe you can hold her then."

"I plan on staying," he said.

Tillie told her heart not to hope. He didn't say how long he was staying and he didn't say if he was staying to be Amish. Only that he was staying.

She wanted to ask, wanted to find out if his words meant what she wished they did, but she bit back the questions. She hadn't seen him in almost two weeks.

Mamm stuck her head into the hallway. "Come to the kitchen," she said. "I've got coffee and cranberry bread."

Tillie nodded, though just the thought of

369

cranberry bread brought Levi to mind. Him in the kitchen wearing a cook's apron, covered in flour as he baked with her niece.

She looked back to Melvin, then he turned and made his way to the kitchen. She couldn't imagine him doing anything so domesticated, so tame.

Nothing about Melvin had ever been tame.

His black hair was slicked back in a new style for him. He wore frayed English blue jeans, lace-up motorcycle boots, and a black leather jacket. More than anything, he looked dangerous. Or maybe that was because he held her fate in his hands. The worst part of all was that he knew it. The question was, what would he do about it?

He sat down at the kitchen table like he had done countless times before. Tillie sat across from him and opened the container that held the cranberry bread.

Mamm laid out a napkin for each of them and brought down three mugs.

Tillie knew that it meant her *mamm* was staying in the kitchen with them. So much for talking things through. It was the one thing Tillie knew had to be done, but she dreaded it all the same. Every time she and Melvin had tried to talk something out in these last few weeks, they just ended up in an argument. Christmas Eve was tomorrow; she didn't want to argue with him now. Maybe they should postpone any serious talks until after the holiday. But could she stand having him close and not knowing his thoughts for three days?

Why not? She'd had no response in weeks. What was a few more days?

"I don't know why I'm doing this," Mamm said. "Well, I do. But I'm sure I'll have to confess this all the same." She was talking about welcoming Melvin into their home.

"Can I sleep in the barn? I had the driver drop me off here," he said. "But I still have a cousin on the other side of Randolph. I can go see him tomorrow. He might let me stay there. But I don't really have a place to stay tonight."

Tillie knew he didn't have the money for a hotel, even one of the cheap ones in town.

"I'll have to talk to Abner. Maybe you can stay with David?"

Tillie wasn't sure how David would feel about having such a rebel in his house, but David was always sweet and welcoming. If she were guessing right, she would say he wouldn't bat an eye at having Melvin stay with him.

Melvin shook his head. "It's late. I don't want to disturb him. I've rattled everyone

371

enough already."

"It'll be too cold in the barn. If you don't want to bother David, you can stay on the couch here."

"Thank you," Melvin said.

"That way you'll be close."

Why did Mamm want him close?

"As soon as the bishop finds out you're back, he'll be here to talk to you," Tillie said.

Melvin took a sip of his coffee and a bite of the cranberry bread before answering. "I know."

"It's getting late," Mamm said.

As if to prove her words, the front door opened and closed. The sound of footsteps grew near. Dat. He looked into the kitchen and saw them. He let out a guttural sound that Tillie knew was a mixture of disgust and disappointment, then he made his way down the hall. He was going to bed. One other thing was clear: Melvin had stopped by the barn before he had come to the house. Tillie wondered if he had asked for permission to approach them. Her *dat* must've given it, for Melvin was seated at the table and her father didn't say a word. He wasn't much of a talker, but even he would break his silence for something as big as the return of Melvin Yoder.

Tillie picked up her coffee mug and stood,

only then realizing that she hadn't taken even one drink of the brew.

"Good night," she said, dipping low to kiss her *mamm* on the cheek. Childish as it was, that was one of the things she missed most when she left home, saying good night to her mother. She only had a couple more days, and then she would miss it again.

She barely cast a glance at Melvin, then she made her way to her room. She didn't know what to say. There was almost too much to say. Too many ideas and questions that went in three different directions. Most important to her was the one that had him staying, marrying her, and living Amish. It would take care of their transgressions. Almost wipe them clean. Almost. But she would get to raise her daughter Amish. Not in the hard English world.

But do you want to be married to Melvin for the rest of your life?

There was a time when she had. A time when that was all she thought about. And maybe with time she would feel that way again. But somehow when she thought about marrying Melvin, it was Levi who popped into her head. She thought that the English had a word for it when a person fell in love with their rescuer. She didn't know what it was called, but surely that's what she was experiencing. And it seemed as if Levi might be experiencing something similar.

She sighed and undressed, then pulled on her nightgown. The floor was cold, and she hurried to the bed, jumping into the covers. Then she sat up and looked over into the cradle where Emmy was resting. She was warm and toasty, wrapped in pink fleece and sleeping peacefully for the time being. In a couple of hours she would be ready for a feed. And Tillie would check to see if Melvin was still awake. If he was, she would let him hold her, meet his daughter truly for the first time. The thought clenched her heart and made her stomach feel like it had fallen to her toes. She would have to explain why she didn't call him right after she had the baby. Or even right after the roads had gotten clear enough for her to go home. But any excuse was just that: an excuse.

She watched the rise and fall of Emmy's breath for a moment and lay down on her side, still facing the cradle. Could she do it? Could she go out into the English world alone with the baby to care for? Would she be able to get her job back? What would she do if she couldn't? And the biggest question of all: where would she live? So many pressures. Too many.

She raised up and turned off the lantern. The room went dark. But the questions still remained.

"I can't believe how tiny she is," Melvin said the next morning as he held his daughter for the first time. He had been asleep when she had woken for her midnight feeding, and Tillie was loathe to wake him. Truth be known, it had more to do with all the questions she knew he was going to ask once he held Emmy. Tillie really wanted a little sleep before she got to all those. So she fed Emmy and placed her back into her cradle to hopefully finish the night.

Emmy was a good baby and slept a long while at a time. Four hours was her maximum. Getting up at four o'clock wasn't too bad for Tillie. She had grown up Amish. The thing she hated was that it was dark outside, and it seemed to be forever before the sun rose. She and Gracie used to sit on the back porch and watch the colors in the sky changing from black to orange to pink and then gold and finally the beautiful blue.

"Her eyes are blue," Melvin said in awe.

"All babies have blue eyes," Tillie said.

"I hope they stay that color."

She supposed that would be beautiful. Emmy had already started to favor her father, especially if she kept his blue eyes and the dark hair she was born with.

Tillie knew that most of it would fall out and grow back. The question was, would it grow back dark blond or Melvin's raven-wing black? They would just have to wait and see. On the eyes too.

"Melvin, we have to talk soon."

He looked from Emmy to her, his expression one of love that changed to remorse.

"I know. But not now. Maybe later." It was Christmas Eve, and later there would be a lot of family ruckus as usual in a household their size.

It seemed as if Melvin dreaded working through their many problems as much as she did. Ignoring them wouldn't make them go away, but he didn't want to talk about such matters on Christmas Eve. Or Christmas Day. She couldn't blame him.

"We have church tomorrow," Tillie said. Christmas Day on church Sunday. It was a rare event. "We should talk before then." If they were going to bend their knees and confess their sins, the quicker they did it, the better. And the quicker they could go about healing and forgiveness.

Melvin swallowed hard. "Tonight, then. We'll talk tonight."

He told himself he was a fool, even as he gathered up a few more baby things to take to Tillie and Emmy. And even more a fool for staying up late and making Christmas gifts for them, but he had done that too.

She was leaving, probably in just a couple of days, but he wanted to see her one last time. And Emmy. He would miss them both, so much.

And it was Christmas Eve. He wanted to see them on Christmas Eve.

He hitched up his buggy and headed toward the Gingeriches'. There was a definite chill in the air, mixed with the scent of woodsmoke. It smelled like Christmas. Suddenly he wished he could take her out for a sleigh ride. But sleighs could be quite tricky and needed a certain amount of snow. Too much and they wouldn't go, too little and it was like dragging something behind the horse. The right amount, which was about the coverage when it snowed in Mississippi, was what was needed. But snow was rare, and it didn't do to store a sleigh for the odd times when it happened. She would like that though, he knew. Tillie would like to go for a sleigh ride, and he would like to take her.

That will never be.

He might as well get it out of his head right now. He was going to visit them today, and that would be the end of it.

Last night should have been the end of it.

It should have, but he wanted to see her just one more time. He missed Mary and his own baby, but being stranded with Tillie and helping her deliver Emmy had created a bond that he hadn't expected. One he had never even dreamed was possible. He pulled his coat a little tighter around him and his collar up a little bit higher over his nose and urged the horse to hurry just a bit.

Jah, he was cold. But every minute he spent in the buggy was a minute he didn't get to spend with them.

Levi pulled his buggy down the drive that led to their house, past the little cabin, and on down into the valley.

Jim stuck his head out of the barn as Levi was hobbling his horse. Levi pointed toward the house so he would know that he was going inside. Jim gave him a wave of understanding and disappeared back into the workshop. Levi fetched the gifts out from the back of his carriage and made his way to the door. He was halfway up the porch steps when the front door opened and he saw Tillie standing there.

She looked frightened, like a scared rabbit cornered by a beagle. The look stopped him in his tracks.

"What's wrong?" he asked.

Tillie swallowed hard before answering. "Melvin is here."

Levi felt like one of those blow-up yard things he had seen in the co-op, but with all the air let out. Deflated, defeated, useless.

It took him a moment to catch his breath, get his thoughts back in order. Melvin needed to be there, just like Levi had told Mims. Melvin needed to marry Tillie, whether they lived an Amish life or an English one. They needed to marry, provide a family, a mother and father for Emmy. There was no room for Levi in that picture.

He tried to smile. "Good, good," he said. "It's been a while." Then he held up the bag of gifts that he had brought. "Merry Christmas," he said.

Tillie looked behind her as if Melvin was going to appear there at any moment. Then she turned back to Levi. "Come in. Mamm's got some coffee on and some of that cranberry bread you and Libby made. It really is good. You're not a half-bad baker."

"And you're not a bad candy maker," he returned with a smile. And suddenly everything felt a little easier between the two of them.

He followed her into the house, a bit leery of what he might find. Melvin was somewhere inside, or so he figured. Or maybe he was out visiting. If Levi remembered right, Melvin still had some cousin on the other side of town.

Tillie led him to the kitchen, and the mystery was solved. Melvin sat on the bench side of the kitchen table, a cup of coffee in front of him. Another sat across from him, and Levi figured that was Tillie's spot. Somehow he knew; the setup had all the earmarks of a serious discussion. One that he had interrupted.

"I'm intruding," he said. "I'll just leave this here." He put the sack at the end of the table, but Tillie shook her head.

"No, no. We have time for friends. Don't we, Melvin?" The sentence made it seem more and more that they were a couple.

They were a couple. As much as he hated to admit it, and as much as he wanted to be part of her life — he would never be. Amish or English. It didn't matter. The situation was hopeless. What a cheery thought for Christmas.

"Yeah," Melvin said. "Sure." He half stood and nodded toward the chair next to Tillie for Levi to sit. "It's been a while."

Hadn't Levi just said those same words?

He slid into the place at the kitchen table and nodded uncomfortably while Tillie poured the coffee.

"So I hear you delivered my baby," Melvin said.

Levi felt himself turn as red as the bows he had tied around the Christmas presents he'd brought. Men just didn't discuss such things. Then again, the sort of things they were discussing normally didn't happen.

"*Jah.* It was just a matter of being there. I didn't do anything special." Though it had felt special at the time. And it would always be special to him. He'd just done what anyone would do. Tillie had done all the work.

"She seems pretty special to me," Melvin said.

Levi didn't know if he was talking about Tillie or Emmy.

Tillie returned from the stove and sat down next to Levi.

The air around them seemed to thicken. One cup of coffee and he would go. She had been hospitable enough to offer it to him, and it would sure help warm up his insides for the trip back home. He took a sip and reached for his sack. "There are a couple of baby things in here that I thought you might could use," he said. "And a Christmas gift for you both."

He wasn't sure if they would be taken in the same spirit he was giving them. He could only hope and pray that they would.

"Danki," she said. She accepted the flat package he handed her and the smaller rectangle one, then she placed them in front of her.

"Go ahead," he said. "Open them."

She picked up the smaller one.

"That one's Emmy's," he said.

She tore off the plain green wrapping paper to reveal a box that came off the bottle of cough syrup. His trepidation doubled.

"I didn't get you medication," he said.

She popped the tape on the box and smiled at him. "I didn't think you had."

That sizzle of connection seemed to be there for a moment when their eyes met, then she looked away and it was gone. Perhaps he had just imagined it.

She pulled the tissue paper out of the box, bringing the present with it. Then she unfolded the paper and stared at the gift.

"It's a pacifier holder," he explained. "You clip it to her gown so she doesn't lose her pacifier." It was something he had been thinking about making for a long time now, but this was the first one he had ever actually fashioned. He had tooled the leather strap with tiny little flowers and figured he could use baseballs or puppies to have embellishments more fitting for boys.

"I know what it is," she said. "And it's lovely, thank you."

It was simple, really: a strap of leather with a snap and the clip attached at one end. But right now, there was not another one like it in the world.

Tillie wrapped it back up into the paper and set it in the middle of the table. "We'll have to try it out when she wakes up."

Levi nodded. He probably wouldn't be here for that.

Tillie reached for the bigger package, the flat one. His heart sped up a bit. Suddenly he wanted to snatch it from her hands and tell her that he had made a mistake, but he managed not to. He tried to breathe normally as he sat and watched her open it.

At least he had found a normal box to put this one in. Some kind of shirt box that Mary must have squirreled away in the linen closet.

Tillie slid the lid off and gasped. "Is this what I think it is?"

He nodded, swallowed hard once again.

"It's a baby book."

She pulled it from the box and laid it gently on the table in front of her. It looked so right there that he knew he hadn't made a mistake.

He had hand-tooled the cover with the same flowers he had used on Emmy's pacifier holder, but these were surrounding an ornate letter E. He was proud of the work. Not only for what he had done, but for the sentiment as well. He had wanted something extra special to give Tillie, and it seemed as if he had succeeded.

"It's beautiful," she said with a sniff. She delicately wiped at the tears threatening to fall.

"Tillie?" Melvin took that time to interrupt their conversation. He said no more than her name, but there was a wealth of meaning to it.

Levi cleared his throat. "I hope I haven't overstepped."

Tillie shook her head without saying a word. She placed the book back into the box very primly. She put the lid on and patted it as if the job was well done. Somehow he knew she was as uncomfortable as he.

"That's very nice of you," Melvin said.

Levi turned toward the other man. For just a moment he had forgotten Melvin was sitting there. But of course he was. *"Danki."*

He wanted to ask her if she had made any plans for after the holiday, but he had no right. Melvin was back, and that changed everything for her. Or at least it had the potential to.

She had been planning to return to the English world, but now that Melvin was back, perhaps she was holding out hope that he would still come back Amish.

Levi didn't have any doubts. Melvin's intention was obvious in the way the man was dressed. He was English from his haircut to the tips of his motorcycle boots. At least that's what Levi thought they were called. Tillie was dressed English as well. In the same clothes she'd worn the night before. He had a feeling that when she had left the apartment she shared with Melvin, she had the clothes on her back and nothing more.

Tillie turned to Levi. *"Danki,"* she said. "Thank you." Saying it twice almost like she didn't acknowledge the Pennsylvania Dutch. She was already slipping away. But she had never been his to start. Whether she left or stayed. But he would be forever grateful to her for helping him move past the crushing grief he'd had when he saw her that cold, icy night in the barn.

"I'm sorry," Tillie continued. "I don't have a gift for you. Except for maybe some more cranberry bread."

"I didn't give you a gift to get one in return." He hadn't, even though she had given him the best gift of all.

He stood. "I should be going."

"Would you like a coffee to take with you?"

He shook his head. It was just one more thing to have to bring back when the time came.

"You could put it in your buggy and bring it back to church tomorrow."

"Are you going to church tomorrow?" Levi asked.

She looked ready to dive right back into the English world. He knew how badly she wanted to stay Amish, but like her, he knew there was no way. It just wasn't possible. Unless Melvin came back.

"Maybe," was all she said.

And that meant this could very well be the last time he would ever talk to her, ever see her.

He wanted to peek in on Emmy, just one last time, but it was hard not to recognize that he didn't have that right. Anyone should be able to look in on the baby, but his feelings weren't so innocent. It was time he let it go.

"You take care of yourself, Tillie Gingerich."

She gave him a sad smile as she walked him to the door.

"I'll be seeing you, Levi Yoder."

He loped down the porch steps even as he knew her last statement to him was nothing but a sweet lie.

CHAPTER TWENTY-FOUR

"Where's Melvin?" Tillie asked a little while later. She had managed to keep everything together while Levi was there, but once he left, she went to her room on the pretense of feeding Emmy and allowed herself time to cry. Then she really did feed the baby as she pulled herself together. Melvin was back. He may have only come back because of Emmy, but he was back now, and everything had changed.

"He's outside in your father's workshop."

Tillie met her mother's steady gaze. Her father was what the English would call a workaholic, but even he would take Christmas Eve off. Normally this time of day he would be over with Jim and Anna visiting and making up for all the times he had been working instead. But if he was in the workshop now . . .

"I should go —" Tillie was on her feet before Mamm shook her head.

"Sit back down," Mamm sternly said.

Reluctantly, Tillie returned to her seat at the table. Her *mamm* set a bowl of potatoes in front of her and handed her the peeler. There was a lot of work to do between now and supper.

"But I —" Tillie started to protest, though her voice was weak.

"What did you expect?" Mamm asked.

She was right. Wasn't Mamm always right?

"I guess. *Jah.*" But she had never expected that she would be in the situation she was in right now. She never expected that she would have a baby without being married. She supposed she was lucky — or maybe Melvin was lucky — that Dat hadn't talked to them both long before now.

But she had hoped that she and Melvin would have a little more time to talk to each other before he was subjected to her *dat*.

She picked up the peeler and started to work on the potatoes.

They hadn't had any time to figure out what they were going to do. She hadn't had a chance to ask him why he had come back, other than to see his daughter. He knew the rules of their community as well as she. If they were staying, they would have to be married.

There had been a time when she wouldn't

have thought twice about Melvin's intentions toward her. She had known from the time that they were in school till now that she would one day be Melvin's wife. That assurance had been shattered. He had changed while they were gone, and admittedly she had changed since she had been back. They needed a little time to get some of that straightened out before they had to deal with her parents. But it seemed that wasn't the way it was going to pan out.

"Mammi Glick says she's ready for another round of celery," Libby said, coming into the kitchen with a tray of stuffed celery stalks.

It was a Gingerich tradition from way back. Tillie wasn't even sure who had started it. But they always had stuffed celery. Stuffed with ham and cheese; pimento cheese; pineapple and cheese. The kids loved it, Mammi Glick was the official stuffer, and it made for smiles all around.

"Right there." Mamm nodded to the next tray of celery just waiting to be filled.

Libby set down the tray she was carrying and picked up the next one. She started back toward the *dawdihaus.* "Was that Levi Yoder's buggy I saw here a while ago?"

"Jah," Tillie murmured.

Libby shot her a questioning look. "He's

not staying for — oh." She stopped as if realizing what she was asking. "I guess we'll see him tomorrow at church."

"I suppose," Mamm replied.

Libby nodded a bit awkwardly and made her way out to the *dawdihaus.*

"Levi's a good man," Mamm said.

Tillie nodded. Just not the man for her. "He is," she managed to reply.

"It was kind of him to bring gifts for you and the baby."

It was more than kind. And they both knew it.

"Ask me," Tillie demanded.

"I have no call to question you about Levi Yoder."

But Mamm wanted to know her feelings toward Levi. Well, that was something Tillie herself would like to be privy to, but the truth of the matter was she had no idea how she really felt about him. Her life had been nothing if not topsy-turvy over the last couple of weeks. She had thought that she might be growing feelings for Levi, but now that Melvin was back, did it even matter?

"Melvin's here," Tillie said as if that explained it all. Melvin was there. He had been her boyfriend for as many years as anyone could remember. They might have run off to the English world. They might have even had a baby together out of wedlock, they might face shunning and excommunication, but he was still Emmy's father. And no matter how she felt about Levi Yoder, the only way she could stay in Pontotoc, in her Amish home, would be to marry Melvin. And that, as they say, was the long and the short of it.

When Melvin came into the house sometime later, Tillie couldn't tell from his expression what had happened. He looked as he always did, a little dangerous and cavalier. He smiled at Tillie, then bent into the baby carrier to give Emmy a gentle kiss on the forehead. After that he went to the icebox for a drink of water.

"Supper will be ready here in a bit, Melvin," Mamm said. "So for now, go get with the menfolk and stay out of my kitchen." She shooed him out the side door.

Tillie wanted to laugh and cry all in the same moment. It was so much like so many times in the past when Melvin had come for one holiday or another, but it was so different as well. He didn't have on his typical Amish clothing or his black hat. He had on some of the clothes she had helped him pick out when they had gone shopping at the Goodwill store. His hair was different, but his smile was the same, and for the life of her Tillie couldn't figure out who was the real Melvin Yoder. Did she even know anymore?

"Do you want me to start taking the food to the table?" Libby asked.

Mamm nodded, and Tillie stood up to help as well. They were having a larger than normal supper tonight, on Christmas Eve. Tomorrow was church service with the typical Sunday fare, but the real supper would be on Monday, Second Christmas. It was traditionally a time for visiting and such, but they had planned to gather into the same house once more and celebrate together.

Mamm continued to stir the gravy but stood to one side when Tillie came back in for the green bean casserole. It was one of her favorites and Tillie figured Mamm had made it especially for her. The thought once again sent tears to her eyes. She had heard the hormones were supposed to slow down a bit since she had already had the baby. But it seemed that wasn't the case. Or maybe her life had been just a little too much lately.

Once the table was set, the food ready, and the glasses of water poured, Mamm rang the dinner bell.

Gingeriches appeared from everywhere. It was just those who lived in the house tonight. Hannah, Leah, and Gracie and their respective families were all having Christmas Eve suppers at their houses. Jim and Anna had their own dinner planned, but as usual David was eating at the main house. Tillie could handle the smaller scale of the meal so much better. Strange how being around so many people had never bothered her before. And part of her wondered if she was merely uncomfortable having so many people there seeing her shame all at one time. They were family, and that should ease the censorship, but it didn't. Maybe it even made it worse.

Dat and David had come in from the workshop, Libby reappeared from taking a plate to Mammi Glick, and Mamm had just returned from changing her apron. Tillie stood behind the chair where she usually sat. Emmy had been fed and was resting nearby in the baby carrier. Now all they needed was Melvin.

"Sorry," he said, grinning at them as he came into the room. Everyone stopped and looked at him. Tillie couldn't believe her eyes. Gone were the T-shirt and jeans. He now wore a traditional blue shirt and black pants with suspenders. Tillie couldn't take it all in for a moment, his Amish dress and English haircut. What did it all mean? At least his smile was the same.

"Uh, sit down," Mamm said.

Dat gave a firm nod of agreement and everyone took their places at the table.

After the time of silent prayer, Tillie looked to Melvin seated across from her, hardly able to believe her eyes. The shock must have worn off everyone else, for they started back up in conversation, David telling Mamm about something that had happened in the workshop and Libby and Mamm laughing in all the right places. Tillie could only stare at Melvin.

He had talked to her *dat*, something she had known would happen from the minute she saw Melvin again. The thing she hadn't expected was the change in clothing. And that could only mean one thing. Melvin was coming back to join the church.

CHAPTER TWENTY-FIVE

"What did Dat say to you last night?" Tillie asked as she and Melvin drove to church with David and Libby. They had promised to talk the night before, but they could never find time alone to discuss the important matters. Then before she knew it, it was time for bed.

David was driving and Libby was sitting in the front seat next to him. Her niece was facing front, though Tillie could tell she wanted to look back at them and chat.

Her father had told Libby that it was Christmas and a Sunday and they had church so it was a solemn day and she should treat it as such.

Secretly Tillie wondered if he didn't want her riding with Melvin. Or maybe that's why Libby was with them and not Joshua. Jim obviously wanted to keep Melvin away from Joshua at least until one of them joined the church. The problem was twofold. Joshua liked running around a bit too much and Melvin had yet to state his intentions toward her.

Since he was dressed Amish once again and riding next to her on their way to church, Tillie had a feeling he was staying, but she wanted to hear him say it all the same.

"He asked me what my plans were. You know, in coming back."

Her heart beat a little faster in her chest. "And what did you tell him?"

Melvin cast a quick glance at David and Libby. Or rather, at the back of David and Libby's heads. Then he reached over and twined his fingers with hers. She looked down at their hands and back up into his eyes. Had he really checked to see if anyone was watching before he held her hand? The good Lord knew they had already been way more intimate with each other than holding hands in the back of a buggy, but Tillie couldn't help but note how being back among the Amish changed his attitude. That was the power of community, she thought to herself.

"We gotta make this right, Tillie," Melvin said. He lowered his voice till even she could barely hear it over the rattle of the carriage and the whir of the wheels.

"Tell me," Tillie said. She wanted him to say the words. She needed him to say them.

"We're going to get married." He squeezed her hand and smiled. For a moment she thought he looked a bit pained, then whatever it was disappeared, and it was just Melvin again.

"Married," she breathed. The thought should have made her heart light, but there was one other thing she needed to know. "Here?" she asked. "We're going to get married here? Among the Amish?"

He nodded. "Isn't that what you want?"

For her entire life that's all she wanted, yet why did she not feel as excited as she should? "I'm glad," she whispered back to him. And she was, truly. Just not . . . excited. "You know what all that means," she asked him.

He nodded.

"And you're okay with all that?"

He squeezed her hand again, that same smile still curving his lips upward. "Anything for you, Tillie."

To say they got some curious looks as they walked into the bishop's house, where church was being held today, was a grand understatement. She had left the baby at home with Mammi Glick, though it was even suggested that Tillie not come to church at all since it hadn't been long since she had Emmy but she wanted to come. It was Christmas. Any discomfort she suffered on the buggy ride over would be well worth it.

Especially with Melvin at her side.

Of course, especially with Melvin at her side. But it wasn't like he could sit next to her during church. She sat between Hannah and Mamm and did her best to listen intently and not shift too much in place. Everyone seemed to be more concerned about the buggy ride over being what was the hardest for a woman having just recently given birth, but hard benches and three hours of singing, praying, and preaching was the hard part.

She leaned over to her *mamm.* "I'm going to move to the back," she whispered.

Mamm nodded, and Tillie eased from her place and tried not to disturb too many people on her way to the back.

There were always seats in the back for the old and infirm. She really didn't feel like either, but she would need some sort of padding in order to make it through the service. This was the best she could do. She eased down next to Ellie Byler, perhaps the oldest person in their entire district. She was also one of the sweetest people Tillie had ever met. She gave Tillie an encouraging smile as she eased into the seat. She hoped Ellie was thinking what everyone else in the room was thinking, that she and Melvin had showed up together and things had changed. Their hearts had been moved. And they were getting married.

But that's what's going to happen.

Right. She knew that. And she was happy about it, even if she wasn't excited. What was excitement anyway? Having a baby in a snowstorm was exciting. Perhaps that's why this didn't seem quite the thrill she had thought it would. For her entire life this was all she had ever wanted, to marry Melvin Yoder and start a family. Okay, so they went about things a little bit backward and they were going to have to make up a lot of ground with the church and other members. The people who had known them their whole lives. But it could be done. A year, maybe two, they would be right on top. Right where they needed to be. Again, the thought should have made her happy, but it only made her sigh in relief.

What was wrong with her? Overly tired, maybe. Christmas blues, maybe. She had heard about people getting sad at Christmastime. Maybe now that she'd had Emmy, she would be one of those people. She knew all sorts of things changed in a woman's body after she had a baby. Maybe that was one of the changes she would have to face.

But she didn't want to be sad at Christmas. Not when everything was going exactly the way she had wanted it to. She should be happy. Ecstatic. Excited.

She looked across the room, her gaze colliding with Levi's. Only the slight dip in his chin told her that he acknowledged her look. There seemed to be a bit of sadness about him today, but she supposed that was understandable after everything he had lost. It was a wonder he wasn't hiding under the bed at home, still trying to work it out.

She gave him a small smile in return and looked back at her hands in her lap. The last thing she needed to do was be making eyes at Levi Yoder during church. That would surely cause a stir.

She turned her thoughts away from Levi and back to the sermon. As expected, it was about the Christmas story. Mary, Joseph, Jesus. As she listened, she realized that she had heard it so many times in her life that she took it for granted. She wondered how many people in the room felt the same without even realizing it.

She looked up once again, this time catching Melvin's gaze. He didn't smile or nod. He just looked back in his lap as if whatever was there was the most important thing in the world. And he looked uncomfortable. She supposed that was one of those to-be-expected things as well. She was uncomfortable in more ways than one, but it wouldn't be forever. One day soon they would be back in good standing. And once that happened, she wouldn't feel this heavy weight pressing down on her. She would be able to be light and joyful, hum a little tune while she cooked like Mamm was prone to do. Now more than anything she wished for a light spirit today. Christmas Day. Jesus's birthday. Perhaps the best day ever to be in church.

Once again she allowed her gaze to rest on her lap and was surprised to see the gnarled hand of Ellie Byler come her way. Ellie squeezed Tillie's fingers where they laid in her lap. "It will all be clear soon, dear," Ellie said.

It was on the tip of Tillie's tongue to ask what she meant, then she realized Ellie had watched her look from Levi to Melvin. Tillie wanted to explain. But she didn't have the words. Maybe because she couldn't explain it herself.

Instead, she squeezed Ellie's fingers, then

stood as the preacher bade them to do so.

As they sang, a dozen questions started floating around inside Tillie's head. She should be singing about the beautiful night when Jesus was born, but all she wanted to do was ask Ellie Byler how long she'd been married to her husband before he passed. It was something like seventy years, maybe. It had only been a couple of years since he died. And before that, the two were inseparable. Did their love come first? Was it always there? Or did it grow in the time that they spent together? What if you thought you loved one person and maybe you were really in love with somebody else?

And what did it matter for her?

She centered her attention back on the song, but still she was only going through the motions. They knelt and prayed and church was dismissed. Still her mind was wandering. But she had to push it all aside. It was Christmas Day. It was cold, but the sun was shining bright, a beautiful day to have church, a beautiful day to be alive. And she needed to soak in that moment then instead of worrying about everything else. It had already been decided that Melvin was coming back. They would be married. They would kneel and pray and ask for forgiveness and eventually life would move on. And if the thought didn't fill her with the greatest joy of perhaps the best Christmas present she could ever receive, then that had to be due to exhaustion and hormones. Nothing more.

"Do you want me to come in?" Mims asked.

Levi shook his head. He tried to smile, but from the look on Mims's face, he knew it was a poor attempt. She gave him a worried smile back. "I don't mind," she said. "I could even spend the night if you want."

Levi hopped down from the buggy. He lifted the grocery sack full of leftovers from behind the seat and tried that reassuring smile for his sister once more. He wasn't certain, but he had a feeling that this attempt wasn't any more successful than the time before.

"Levi —" Mims started.

"I'm fine," he said. "Get on home. It's cold out here."

Mims pulled the blanket a little closer around her legs and seemed as if she wanted to say more. "I'll come by in the morning to pick you up."

"I have a horse and buggy that works. You know that, right?"

"Funny," she said. "But if I drive, I know you have to come."

His sister! Levi chuckled. Despite his melancholy air of the day, Mims was always able to make him laugh, even if just a little. "I see how it is. You come and get me, then I have to go to whatever function it is that you think I need to go to."

She clicked her tongue at him and pointed her finger. "Got it in one."

Levi shook his head. "Of course. Now get on home."

"I'll see you in the morning."

Now why did that almost seem like a threat?

Levi lit the lantern sitting on the porch and took it into the house with him. The worst thing about coming home in the wintertime: it seemed to get dark so early. Normally he would be home way before sundown, but since his family had wanted everyone to get together after church, he had gone back to his parents' house. They had cookies and coffee and opened presents. They laughed and told stories and visited until a little later in the afternoon. That was why he was getting home so late.

He made his way into the kitchen. He checked on Puddles and her puppies, then put all the leftovers his *mamm* had sent home with him in the icebox. He placed the lantern in the center of the table and sat down. His house had never felt emptier than it did in that moment.

He saw them together today, Tillie and Melvin. And them together was exactly how it was all supposed to be. So why did it bother him so? Why did he give it a second thought, a second look?

Because on some level he didn't think that was how it was supposed to be.

How was that for seeing things that weren't there? He had known Melvin was back, but he had held out the hope that —

Hope that what?

Anyway he sliced it, Tillie and Melvin needed to be together. If they stayed English, if they came back to the Amish, whatever their decision was, for baby Emmy, the two of them needed to make a family. And he was no part of it.

"You had your chance at a family," he told himself.

From her place by the stove, Puddles whined and thumped her tail. Little puppies tumbled around, their eyes still closed as they tried to find something to eat. To have that the only of life's problems. Something to eat.

"Merry Christmas, Puddles," he said, then grabbed the lantern and headed for the stairs.

CHAPTER TWENTY-SIX

"Mamm!"

Tillie looked to her mother, who was still standing at the stove flipping pancakes like a short-order cook.

"Is that Hannah?" Mamm looked to the clock above the sink. "She said nine, right?"

Tillie nodded. And it was a little after that. Hannah must've lost track of time. Tillie scooped up the last bite of her own pancakes and took her plate to the sink. "I'll do the supper dishes," she promised.

Her *mamm* gave her an indulgent look.

Just then, Hannah came into the kitchen. "You wouldn't believe!"

"What happened?" Mamm asked.

"Did you walk?" Tillie asked.

Hannah looked to Mamm. "I don't know." Then she turned to Tillie. "Yes. Kind of."

Tillie shook her head. "That doesn't make any sense at all."

"I started to come down the road, but that tree in front of the cabin . . ."

Mamm wiped her hands on her apron and nodded for Hannah to continue.

". . . it was across the road completely. So I had to park the buggy and walk down from there. It wasn't a long walk, but not a very comfortable one when it's under forty degrees."

"Did you tell your *dat*?" Mamm asked.

"*Jah*," Hannah said. "I stopped by the barn first. He and Melvin and Jim are going to go up to take a look at it. Apparently David promised to paint this new shed that they've been building. But he painted with the opposite colors than those the customer ordered. It's supposed to be a green house with cream shutters and he painted a cream house and green shutters. Dat's making him redo it."

"Well, thank heavens Melvin is here to help," Mamm said.

Tillie murmured something she hoped sounded like a positive response. She was glad that Melvin was there to help. Wasn't she? There were just too many other things intertwined for it to be that simple.

Mamm handed them containers of cranberry bread.

Hannah looked at it and tried to hand it back.

"We're just going to Gracie's."

Mamm put her hands behind her back so she couldn't take the bread from Hannah. "Gracie's got growing kids. If nothing else, it'll give the adults something to eat," she said.

"If you say so. But don't let Levi hear you say that," Tillie said. "He helped make it."

Hannah smiled. "Good for him. But I think I just lost my taste for cranberry bread. You know how it goes."

"It used to be your favorite when you were a child."

"I still like it," Tillie said. But she understood. How come so many things had to change?

"Is that who I think it is?" Hannah asked as they pulled up in front of Gracie and Matthew's.

Levi Yoder.

Tillie had forgotten that he and Matthew Byler were cousins, but what were the chances that she and Hannah would come visit when Levi was here as well?

It was as if God just kept putting him in front of her, perhaps to remind her of what she would never have.

Surely God wouldn't be that cruel.

Tillie swung down from the buggy, and Hannah hobbled the horse. Then they gathered a basket of goodies from the back seat and made their way up the steps and onto the porch.

Gracie opened the door before they could even knock. "It's so good to see you two today," she gushed, as if she hadn't just seen them yesterday. But since Gracie had spent most of her life living with the Gingeriches, Tillie supposed that the shift to married life had been a little strange.

And she wondered then where she and Melvin would live once they got married. Maybe they would build a house on the other side of David's so they would be close to the rest of the family.

"We're sorry to intrude," Hannah said. "But we just wanted to bring you some goodies and see you today. And say Merry Christmas again."

Gracie moved aside so Tillie and Hannah could step into the house. She smiled at them prettily in her so-Gracie way. "Merry Christmas," she said in return.

"Merry Christmas," Mims called from the living room.

When they entered the room, Levi was standing by the fireplace next to Matthew.

Until that moment Tillie hadn't realized how much they looked alike. They were both big men, broad with dark hair, crystal blue eyes, and burly beards. Standing there next to each other in almost identical outfits — blue shirt, black pants, and suspenders — they looked like a pair of bookends. Or at the very least, brothers.

Levi nodded his head and averted his gaze.

Tillie wished she hadn't let Hannah talk her into coming over today. But how was she supposed to know Levi and Mims would be there?

"We were just about to play a game," Gracie said. "You want to join us?"

"Jah," Hannah said as Tillie shook her head no.

Gracie looked from Tillie to Hannah and back again, her brow puckered into a frown. "Okay."

"We can't stay that long," Tillie said. She elbowed her sister. "Right, Hannah?"

"But we can be persuaded to stay long enough to have a coffee and a piece of cranberry bread. It's cold outside," Hannah said.

"We've got that too." Gracie grinned. "Have a seat. I'll be right back."

"I'll help you," Hannah said, ever so helpful. The problem was it didn't take three of them to get a couple of cups of coffee and saucers for the cranberry bread. That left Tillie hovering uncomfortably.

She eased around the sofa and perched on the edge. Mims sat across from her in a rocking chair looking perfectly content.

"Where's the baby?" Mims asked.

"Mamm's got her," Tillie answered. "That's one reason why we can't stay too long."

"May be, but you really need to warm up for the ride home," Gracie said, coming back into the room. "Even if you won't play a game of cards with us." She set the tray on the coffee table next to the one already there. There was plenty of coffee and cranberry bread to go around.

"I take it you're staying?" Mims said with a nod to Tillie.

She looked down at her Amish dress. Second day in a row she'd been dressed this way. Once again it was starting to feel so natural and yet so strange at the same time.

"Mims!" Levi and Matthew said at the same time.

The men were still standing by the fireplace.

"Come sit down," Gracie said. "You're blocking all the heat."

The men did as they were asked. Matthew

plopped down next to Gracie, while Levi took the place next to his sister.

Mims shrugged. "What's the harm in asking? I just wanted to know."

This was the way it was going to be; either people would ask outright or they would just stare and wonder. Tillie wasn't sure which one was better.

"Yes," she said. "Melvin and I are staying."

Gracie and Hannah smiled at each other.

"That's so wonderful," Gracie said.

"We still have to talk to the bishop yet," Tillie said before anyone else could ask more questions.

"I suppose after the holiday," Hannah added.

And that was tomorrow. She was sure he would come tomorrow to ask them about their plan and explain to them what they needed to do in order to remain there in the community. It wasn't as if they didn't already know. But that was the bishop's job, making sure it was clear. They would have to confess in front of the church, kneel and state their sins, spread it all out for everyone to see. After that, then they could begin the process of getting back in good standing with the church. It was what she had wanted all along. Her and Melvin, married and raising a family. So why did the thought not comfort her?

She had no idea. But her gaze strayed to Levi Yoder once again.

He was watching her as if trying to figure out who she was and what she was there for. The look was strange, inquisitive, yet familiar. And Tillie gave him a small smile, but it was hesitant. A little shaky. Then she looked back into her cup of coffee and plopped in another sugar cube. It was really sweet enough, but she needed something to do with her hands.

"I, for one, think that it's marvelous," Gracie said.

"Me too," Hannah agreed.

"Of course I make it unanimous," Mims said. "It's just baffling to me."

"Baffling?"

Mims shook her head. "That's not a good word. It's just amazing the things we do in order to find our place. God sets us all on a path and it always makes me wonder when someone leaves the church or the community. Is that part of God's plan? That they leave? Or are they deviating from the plan to begin with?"

"Why would God plan for somebody to leave the church?" Matthew asked. "I don't think the church would want that at all."

414

He shifted uncomfortably. "I don't think we will ever know."

"Did you know that Levi helped make the cranberry bread?" Hannah asked.

Way to change it, sister, Tillie thought, as she hid the trembling in her hands. She needed to get used to these sorts of talks, because it would be a long, long time before anyone forgot her transgressions. Forgiving was just part of the Amish way of life, but forgetting was difficult indeed.

Levi did his best not to stare at Tillie and concentrated instead on his saucer and the cranberry bread that he had helped make. How utterly random that he had come to visit his cousin at the same time she had come to visit hers. It was as if once again God was trying to bring them together.

But her place was with Melvin.

"Levi?"

He shook himself from his thoughts — though he had a feeling it wasn't the first time Mims had spoken his name.

"Jah?"

"Hannah asked how the puppies are doing."

Levi cleared his throat and tried to get himself together. Puppies. *Jah.* "They're good," he said. "They haven't got their eyes open yet, but they all look strong and healthy. Puddles is a good mom. You want one?"

Hannah nodded. "Maybe. Aaron and I have been talking about it. It would be a good present for Andy, give him some more responsibilities and a companion. They may fight like cats and dogs and be as opposite as black and white, but at least Essie and Laura Kate have each other."

Levi smiled. "Every boy needs a dog."

"I think it's great that Leah is getting one for Peter. I know she wished that she could have had it for yesterday, but he knows and was so excited," Gracie said.

"What about you, Tillie?" Matthew asked.

Levi shot him a look, but the other man just shrugged it off. "A girl could use a dog too," Matthew said in defense of his stance. "Besides, I'm trying to help you get rid of them. Don't you have twelve?"

"Eleven," he corrected, but what difference did it really make? He was probably going to end up with four or five of the little mutts himself. But seeing as how lonely his farm had gotten since Mary and the baby died and Tillie and Emmy had left, four or five puppies sounded like right good company.

"I might know some people," Tillie said.

"If you don't mind them going to English homes. They're good homes," she added.

English homes. It didn't matter to him as long as they had good owners, but bringing up the English world just served to remind him that she'd had a life elsewhere. She and Melvin had shared an apartment and they had that life to go back to and correct before they could come back and join the church. But it wouldn't be long before he got to see her all the time. As Melvin's wife. It was not a comforting thought. And it should have been. They were doing what God had intended, what He had planned. Maybe a little late, maybe a little backward, but that was it. They had a baby; they should be married. Husband and wife. It was just the way it was.

Levi wasn't sure how he found himself alone with Tillie on the front porch some time later. Hannah was still inside saying her goodbyes, and this was the first time he'd had a chance to talk to her alone in so very long.

"I'm very happy for you and Melvin," he said. It wasn't an outright lie. He was happy for them. But something about it bothered him all the same, though he couldn't lay his finger on just what it was.

417

Maybe it was just that strange connection he felt to her and Emmy, and he wanted to protect her. Like a big brother.

Jah, that's what it was like. A big brother thing. It couldn't be more than that. And it probably never would be. But he just wanted to make sure that Melvin made her happy. It would be a long time before Levi himself would remarry. And why that thought followed the idea of Tillie and Melvin getting married was beyond him. When he got remarried didn't matter a hill of beans. Only that Tillie and Melvin and baby Emmy were happy.

"Danki," she said. Though he could hear the strangled quality in her voice. Did she feel as he did, that the situation was somehow off?

No. It couldn't be. It was turning out just the way it was supposed to be. Tillie and Melvin. They had been a thing for a long long time.

"I'm sure your *mamm* is very happy. And Abner." He knew as well as any that Abner was a hard man. He was fair and he was caring, but he followed the *Ordnung* above all else. God was his compass. And that was just the way it was. Levi couldn't imagine that Abner would be very flexible about a daughter coming home the way that Tillie had. He would never stop loving her, but there were some things that were harder to accept. Melvin marrying Tillie would correct all that, and over time he could be just a father again.

"They're happy." But she didn't sound happy about that.

He wanted to ask more, but Hannah stepped out onto the porch, still chattering away about the benefits of whipped butter over not.

There was something more he wanted to say to Tillie, but he just didn't know what it was. It hovered in the back of his mind like a bee buzzing around one's head. He would reach out, trying to catch it, but it would slip away, only to return a moment later to start the process all over again.

She turned to him and gave him a pretty smile. Her hazel eyes twinkled. She would be happy. Melvin would make her happy, and that was all that mattered.

"Merry Christmas," she said.

He cleared his throat, doing his best to talk past the lump there. "Merry Christmas," he returned.

"Are you okay to walk down to the house by yourself?" Hannah asked as they turned down the lane leading to the Gingeriches'.

"I'm fine," Tillie said. The exercise would be good for her. She was still a little sore, but that was to be expected. It had only been a couple of weeks since she'd had the baby. But as they pulled closer, they noticed that someone had moved the tree from the road. Not all the way, just pushed to the side enough that a buggy could get past. And that meant one thing for certain. The bishop was coming.

Tillie's heart thumped in her chest. It was to be expected. It would be uncomfortable and even hard, but they would get through it. She and Melvin because they had been a team from the get-go. They were parents now of a beautiful baby girl. They had shared a lot together out there in the English world. But thankfully, *thankfully,* they were returning home. And it would take a while to smooth out all the rough edges of the mess they had made, but soon, so very soon, they would be living the life they had dreamed of for so long. The thought should have been comforting, but somehow it felt almost impossible.

And for the life of her she couldn't figure out why.

"The bishop's coming to dinner tomorrow," Mamm said over their evening meal.

Tillie lost her grip on her fork, and it clattered to her plate. She shouldn't be surprised; she had known it was coming. But somehow it all seemed a little shocking as well. Tomorrow.

"Are you okay?" Melvin asked. He had been the epitome of gentlemen, a caring, loving father.

"Jah," she said.

The bishop was coming and that meant that sometime before the beginning of the year, she and Melvin would make the trip back to Columbus. They would get their things from the apartment they had shared and close off what they had of an English life. Then hopefully by January they would be able to start their new life together.

The life she had always dreamed of. So why wasn't the thought as reassuring as it should have been?

She couldn't answer that question. The more she thought about it, the more it made her head ache. So she pushed the thought away and concentrated on her supper. But soon, very soon, she was going to have to figure out what it all meant.

"What are you doing out here?" Melvin asked. "It's cold."

Tillie pulled her blanket a little closer

around her as she rocked the porch swing with the heels of both feet. "I'm warm enough. I just needed some air."

"Why do I feel there's something more?" Melvin asked. He shoved his hands into his pockets and made his way over to her. She stopped the swing so he could sit down beside her.

"I don't know. It's just a lot of changes right now. I think that's all." And hormones. They seemed to be getting the best of her on a regular basis these days.

"Tillie, we've known each other all our lives. Why are you picking now to start lying to me?"

"I'm not —"

"Don't even," he said with a shake of his head.

She exhaled, relaxed her stance, only then realizing how tense she had been. She had been lying. Lying about a lot of things. The truth was she did know what she wanted, but it was something she knew she couldn't have.

"I'm sorry," she said. "But I don't think I can marry you."

Melvin drew back a bit. "Maybe we should have this conversation someplace a bit warmer."

He was right.

422

Tillie stood. "Where?" she asked.

"Surely there's someplace in the house where we can have a measure of privacy."

Tillie nodded. "Follow me." She led the way into the house through the dining room and back to the sewing room. It was chilly in there since the door was always closed, but at least there was no wind and no people to hear what they had to say to each other.

"You don't think you can marry me?" Melvin asked a second after she shut the door behind them. "Why not?"

Tillie's heart pounded in her chest. She wanted to call the words back as much as she needed to explain them. "I can't see you staying here for the rest of your life."

She could tell from the look on his face that she had hit her mark.

"You want to stay here, don't you? Raise Emmy among the Amish? In order for you to have the life you want, that's what I have to do," he said. The words held an ominous ring.

"But if you marry me, you won't have the life you want," she pointed out.

He didn't say a word, just looked at her.

The situation was hopeless and she had just now allowed herself to admit it. "So what do we do?" she asked.

Melvin gave her a sad little smile. "What do you want to do?"

It wasn't that simple. She wanted to stay with her family, but she couldn't . . . she *wouldn't* do that to Melvin. He was so very happy in his new life. She might not love him any longer, but she surely couldn't see herself making his life miserable. What good would that do either of them?

"I promised I would marry you. Stand by you," he said. "But it has to be what you want. I thought it was what you wanted."

"Me too," she said. "But I need to know what you want."

"I asked you first."

Tillie flopped down on the bed, letting out an exasperated sigh. A box of fabric fell to the floor, but she didn't bend to pick it up. "Don't do this, Melvin. Have that much respect for me."

"You think I don't respect you?" he asked. "I love you, Tillie."

But not enough to stay with her and raise their daughter in the lifestyle and community where they had been brought up.

"But I don't think you love me anymore," he said.

"I do," she promised, but it was different now. She didn't have to tell him that. She knew he could tell. Their time in Columbus had changed that love. His new lifestyle, his new priorities, his new everything had caused a riff between them. One she didn't think she could ever bridge.

"What's it going to be, Tillie?"

She shook her head. There was no sense in prolonging it further. "I appreciate the offer," she said, sounding like a true English girl. "But I won't marry you."

"You won't marry me anywhere, or you won't marry me unless I come back to the Amish?"

"Melvin." His name was a plea on her lips. That wasn't fair. She would have to marry him in order to return to their community. There was no way around that one. And despite that stipulation she still wanted to return. But not with that stipulation. Sometimes the things we want remain the things we wished we had.

He shook his head. "Don't do this, Tillie. Have enough respect for me now to answer that question."

"You don't want to stay Amish, so there's not a point in answering."

"I like being English," he said, even though it was obvious.

"I don't," she said.

"You never took to it, Til. You dress like a nun and don't want to go to parties."

425

"I only left here for you." And she knew how miserable that had made her. If she made Melvin come back, then he would be just as miserable. If she went English, or even Mennonite, she might be able to see her folks from time to time. Shunning wasn't quite as strict as it had been in the past. She might not be able to live as the Amish live, but that didn't mean she had to make both of them miserable.

Because if she made him come back — and she knew he would for her; well, for Emmy — then she would hate herself, and he would hate her too, eventually. What good would that do anyone?

"I don't know what I want."

"I don't think that's the truth," he said. His voice was sad, gentle, and a little prodding.

"I can't have what I want." It was the truth, at least. She wanted to raise her daughter in their Amish community. She wanted people to stop staring at her when she went places, and she wanted to go back to before she had made all the mistakes that had changed her life so drastically.

No. That last one wasn't the truth. Going back would mean no Emmy, and that was something she couldn't imagine.

"Then what's the plan?" he asked.

She gave a one-shouldered shrug. "Go back, I guess. I'm going to try and get my job back."

"But you don't want to marry me." The words almost formed a question.

"Do you want to marry me?" she countered.

He blew out an exasperated sigh. "Do you think for a moment that we can stop talking in riddles?"

"I'm sorry," she said. But the truth was so much harder to say. "I know your English friends talked you out of marrying me."

He shook his head. "It wasn't them so much. I was just trying to break away from everything." Amish rules, he meant.

"You had almost nine months to marry me. And you didn't. Why the rush now?"

"Because I thought it's what you wanted."

There had been a time, a long while, when she had wanted to be married to Melvin, had dreamed of nothing else. But those dreams were shattered now, lost in the light of a new life and the ashes of an old life she could never return to.

"I guess that's my answer," he said.

Maybe she was more English than she realized.

"I'll take care of you and Emmy," he said. "Give you money and such."

She nodded.

"You can stay with me until you find a place to live. I'll sleep on the couch," he said before she could turn him down. She was grateful for the addition. She had been worrying about what to do, where she and Emmy were going to stay.

"But when you move out, you'll still let me see her, right?" he asked.

"Of course. I wouldn't keep her from you."

His shoulders slumped in relief. "I've got a buddy who hasn't seen his son in two years."

That was terrible, but she had no plans to keep Melvin from Emmy. He was her father, after all. "You can see her whenever you like."

"So it's settled, then," he said.

She drew in a deep breath. "It's settled."

"Are you going to tell your parents?"

"Not all of it," she replied. "Just that you and I are going back to the English world." The thought unsettled her stomach, but it was done. It was what had to be.

So why did Levi Yoder once again pop into her thoughts?

"It's Second Christmas," he said. "I don't suppose we need to say much else. It might ruin the holiday spirit."

She nodded. "That is one thing we can agree on."

She should tell them all, right now. There was no sense in going through all the talk with the bishop tonight, no sense in putting her family through all that stress. But she couldn't bring herself to say the words. Her *mamm* was so happily bustling around the kitchen, getting things ready for supper.

Tillie couldn't bring herself to kill that jovial mood and break her heart.

"Dat told me to come in and tell you that we're going to move the tree," David said from the kitchen door.

"So the man's here?" Mamm asked.

David nodded.

Their father had rented a tractor for the day to move the tree from blocking the road to the house. The ice storm had gotten the better of it and, mixed with disease, hobbled mighty oak. Part of it was still good and could be chopped into firewood, or maybe even a tabletop for the English. She had heard her father talking about it the night before. Just one more thing for the Gingeriches to discuss with the bishop.

"Melvin's already on his way up there. I told everyone I would stop and tell you

429

where we are. Just in case you need one of us."

"*Danki,*" Mamm said.

David gave them both a smile and disappeared back to the front of the house. Moments later they heard the screen door slam. Mamm shook her head. "I never did manage to get that boy to shut that door quietly."

But that was just David.

From her place on the table in her snug little baby carrier, Emmy started to fuss.

"I think it's that time again," Tillie said. She unbuckled the baby and picked her up. Emmy stretched like she was prone to do.

Mamm turned from the stove, waving a hand in front of her nose. "Phew! I think it's time to change her too."

Tillie wrinkled her nose with a small nod and a smile. "I think you're right."

She took the baby to the other room to change her diaper and feed her. In a couple of days she and Emmy would move to Columbus with Melvin. The thought was perplexing; it made her happy and sad at the same time. She was happy for Melvin, and she knew that eventually she could be happy in the English world, but she knew that her leaving would once again break her *mamm*'s heart. Someone's feelings would

430

have to be sacrificed. She was just not so happy that it was her *mamm*'s. But Mamm was tough; tougher than Tillie. It might take a while, but they would all heal.

She took a clean and fed Emmy back to the kitchen, where her *mamm* was still bustling around. Tillie was certain Mamm hadn't cooked this big of a meal for Christmas, but Tillie knew that she wanted everything to go off without a hitch. A well-fed man was a little more yielding.

But the problem was she didn't need to go to all this trouble, and Tillie should tell her now. She supposed she could talk to her *dat* about it when they got done with the tree. But tonight's dinner would not be about Tillie and Melvin joining the church; instead, it would be about her father and his plan to build stools and sell them to the English.

"Mamm," she started as she settled Emmy back into her seat on the table. "I think I should tell you something."

Her *mamm* turned around slowly, as if she knew she wasn't going to like what Tillie had to say. "You think?"

"I mean, I know. There's something I need to talk to you about."

Mamm wiped her hands on her apron and waited for Tillie to continue.

She just didn't know where to find the words. How could she, when she knew what she had to say would break her *mamm*'s heart in two? She inhaled, opened her mouth to speak, but nothing came out.

She tried again, but this time her effort was interrupted as her brother David rushed into the room. His face was red from the cold, his nose running, and his eyes filled with tears. "Come quick," he hollered. "There's been an accident."

432

CHAPTER TWENTY-SEVEN

A funeral was always a solemn occasion, but a funeral at Christmastime was especially sad.

It was a gray and drizzly day when they buried him, the crowd a sea of black umbrellas as they laid him to rest. Tillie could only stare at the mound of dirt in shock. Mamm stood next to her, dabbing her eyes. Hannah, Leah, and Gracie stood on the other side of her. She just couldn't believe it.

Back at the house everyone was bringing food, more food than the family could ever eat, but they wanted to pay their respects even if Melvin had never joined the church. He may have left to live with the English for a while. But everyone believed he was coming back to stay. Even his parents.

They had driven down from Ethridge and were staying with Melvin's cousin who lived on the other side of town.

Tillie was surprised they didn't want to bury their son in Tennessee and instead laid him to rest with the other members of their family there in Pontotoc. The thing she hated the most, other than losing Melvin himself, was the pitying looks she received. No one knew what they had planned. They only knew the first plan: to ask for forgiveness, join the church, and live in the Amish community forever. But it was a secret that Tillie would take to her grave. So she endured the pitying looks. She would accept them as his friend. They had been friends for so long. And she would miss him terribly even if they had decided not to get married.

And the saddest part of all for her, the part that was hardest to get over, was that she had wanted so badly to stay in the Amish community. With Melvin gone, there was nothing standing in her way.

Be careful what you pray for.

Wasn't that what Mammi Glick was always saying? Of course, Mammi Glick said a lot of things. Sometimes she got them a little off, but for the most part, she got them right. This one was too correct.

Tillie had wished for a way that she could stay in Pontotoc and raise her daughter Amish. But never in a million years would

434

she have wished Melvin gone in order to do so.

It's out of your hands.

She knew it. And she knew she was not responsible for his death. She didn't cause it to happen. Most would say it was God's plan. God's will that he was gone. Even at such a young age. And she wasn't sure she would ever get used to the idea of never seeing him again.

"Can I get you some tea?" Hannah stopped near the chair where Tillie sat. People came in, set food on the table, then came over to tell her how sorry they were and how much they wished that things were different. But God had a plan and they needed to stick to it. She'd heard the speech a hundred times today if she had heard it once, but these good people believed that Melvin was coming back to his Amish home, and there was no way she would tarnish him in their eyes by telling the truth. No matter how hard it was to keep to herself.

"Chamomile," Hannah continued. "It might help you sleep."

Sleep. She was tired. It seemed like she hadn't slept in days. Something had kept Emmy awake as well, crying in the night, fussing and restless as if somehow she knew

435

her father was gone. So Tillie had spent both nights soothing her baby and wondering what was going to happen now.

Emmy.

"Where's my baby?"

"I think Leah has her. Do you want her?" Hannah asked.

Did she? No, she would share her daughter's company. "Only if she's tired of her. Or if she starts fussing and needs to eat." They would have the nights to stay awake and mourn together. Let her visit with other family for now.

"Tea?" Hannah prompted again.

Tillie nodded. "That would be great, thank you."

Hannah gave her sister a smile, squeezed her fingers reassuringly, and moved on toward the kitchen.

She watched Hannah go, so many thoughts tumbling around inside her head. She envied her sister, and then she didn't. Hannah had had a tough time of it in the English world and was glad to be back with the Amish. Tillie was too, but it came at a high cost.

"Tillie?"

She looked up. "Levi."

"How are you?" he asked. He took the seat next to her and scooted it a little farther away. Whoever sat there last had been a family member. They had reached over to hug Tillie, scooting the chair too close for propriety when it came to her and Levi.

"As well as can be expected."

"I understand."

Of all the people gathered around to mourn Melvin's passing, she knew that Levi understood more than most.

"I brought you something," he said. He reached into his pocket, pulled out a long thin envelope, and handed it to her.

"*Danki,*" she said as she stared at the envelope. Whatever was in it was flat, and not very thick — a letter maybe? She had no idea. Why would Levi write her a letter, then hand it to her? She really needed to get some sleep.

"You can open it now," Levi said.

"I can?"

A lot of sleep.

"Of course. I'd like to see you open it."

"Okay." She tore the top of the envelope open and pulled out a strip of leather embossed with Melvin's name. Beautiful tool work, just like he had done on her baby book for Emmy and on Emmy's pacifier holder. "It's really supposed to be a book-mark. You can put it in your Bible if you have a mind. Or you could put it in a

437

shadow box with some of his other things." Levi shrugged as if he didn't know what else to say. "I wanted you to have something for him."

Tears rose into her eyes. She wanted to throw her arms around Levi and hold him close. She wanted to be held as she shed the tears that had been threatening for so long. Levi would understand.

Or would he?

She would have to hold her secret forever.

Tillie dashed her tears away with the fingers of one hand and tried to smile at Levi. *"Danki."*

He smiled in return. "I didn't mean to make you cry."

"It's okay." Within a heartbeat the tears were all dried up. She didn't want to cry. She didn't want to show emotion, because if she did the dam might break, and everything would come flooding out. She couldn't have that, not with so many friends and family around. She wanted to be able to talk to somebody, but she just couldn't imagine who. Hannah? Leah? Gracie? As much as she loved them, she didn't think they would understand. Not completely.

"I'm really sorry," Levi said. He stood and she grabbed his hand to stop his leaving.

Then she dropped it, realizing the impropriety.

"We're friends. Right?" she asked.

He nodded. "*Jah.* I guess *friends* is a good enough word."

"And maybe I could come talk to you sometime?" she asked. "As friends, you know."

"Or I could come see you," he said. "And Emmy. Just as friends."

She nodded, then sat back in her seat as Hannah approached. "Thank you, Levi."

He gave her a tight smile, then walked away.

"What was that all about?" Hannah asked.

Tillie shook her head. "Nothing."

Levi made his way into his house and through the living room. He stopped there, noting the wilted cedar boughs that Tillie and her *mamm* had placed there. And the fat white candles. They had brought Christmas pillows and an afghan. Though they had claimed that the afghan was a gift from Mammi Glick, he wasn't sure about the rest. Maybe he could take it to Tillie tomorrow. As friends.

Not the cedar boughs, obviously. But the other things. He should return them just in case.

439

And he could visit Emmy and Tillie and see how they were.

But you saw her today.

At her fiancé's funeral. Not the best time to talk about anything other than Melvin.

Levi sighed and grabbed the tree limbs from the mantel. He took them to the back door and threw them out into the yard. Maybe he would move them tomorrow when it was daylight once more. But it was getting dark now. Hopefully no one would come visiting. He wasn't in the mood for company. He wanted to work out some things in his head.

Back in the living room, the fireplace looked bare without the limbs. Even after he started a fire to warm the place. He should have put the boughs in the fire. But he hadn't thought about it at the time.

The kitchen was still warm from the potbellied stove, where Puddles and her pups had their bed. He should have checked on them when he went through to the back door.

It seemed he should have been doing a lot of things.

Like telling Tillie that she looked good and would make it through. It would seem impossible the first few days, maybe even weeks, but each day got a little easier to bear.

He knew it because she had been the one to help bring him home.

And he wouldn't know what to do without her.

But those were things he shouldn't say.

Not now.

Not yet.

Maybe not ever.

New Year's Eve and she was in mourning. It was fitting. She mourned Melvin and all that he had been and all that he was yet to be. She mourned their love that had made such a sweet child and then faded away.

The world around her was preparing to have lock-ins and sleepovers and all sorts of fun events. A few years ago, Hannah would have arranged for them to have a sisters/cousin time, spending the night eating popcorn and waiting for the clock to turn over to midnight.

But those days were gone. Just one more thing for her to mourn.

Since it was a holiday, her sisters had called off their cousins' day. That just meant more work come the next week. But there had been too much going on that day with the road being blocked off and all.

But she was in mourning for a man who wasn't her husband and would never be. Would never have been even if not for the terrible accident that took his life.

The men had been trying to lift the large tree using a tractor and chains. But the chains broke and the tree fell, landing squarely on Melvin's chest.

She had asked, then begged David to tell her about it. No, he didn't suffer much or long and his last words were of her and Emmy.

"He said something strange though," David recounted just after the funeral.

"What was that?" Tillie asked. She wanted to know everything about his last moments. She wasn't sure why it was important, just that it was. She wanted to know for certain that he was happy, or at the very least not *un*happy before he died.

"He told me to take care of you and Emmy," David said.

"That's not strange at all." In fact, it seemed like a very Melvin thing to say.

"Then he told me not to let you go. Made me promise and everything." His forehead wrinkled into a frown. "I don't know what that means. Go where?"

Tillie knew. Melvin didn't want her to go to the English world. He knew that she wanted to stay with the Amish, and he made her brother promise to keep her there. In his last breath, he was concerned for her.

But for now she would do what she had to do. She shook her head. "Me either," she said at the time, but knew that she would cry herself to sleep that night. What little sleep she got.

New Year's Eve, and she was worn out.

However she wasn't in the mood for any parties. Wasn't sure she would be in that mood again for a very long time.

Emmy was napping in her cradle, and Tillie had settled down on the bed with a book. It was good enough to keep her attention, but maybe not good enough to keep her awake. Especially if her baby stayed asleep. Then she might even be able to get some rest as well.

A knock sounded at her door. "Tillie?" Mamm called. "You have company."

Emmy arched her back and let out a squall.

Tillie sighed, placed the leather bookmark Levi had given her between the pages of her book, and stood. He had given her the bookmark to have a reminder of Melvin. But every time she looked at it, she thought of Levi.

Which seemed very disrespectful of the dead.

"Coming," she called. She grabbed the baby's pacifier and started from the room. She gently bounced Emmy in place, cooing to her all the while she walked. "You don't need to be fed just because you're awake. It's only been a little while since you ate. You can wait a bit more." She didn't want Emmy to get into the habit of wanting to eat every time she woke up for the times like this when she truly didn't need to but only thought she did. So Tillie gave her the pacifier instead. It had taken Emmy a little while to get used to it, but it had been a couple of weeks and she was like a natural now.

Tillie almost stumbled as she made her way into the living room to find Levi Yoder.

"Hello, Tillie."

"I wasn't expecting you," she said. She wasn't expecting anyone, for that matter.

"I thought I would drop by and bring you back all the Christmas decorations you left at my house."

She rocked the baby and shook her head. "You didn't need to bring them back."

He shrugged and looked down at the sack. "They're yours."

"*Jah.* I suppose."

He set the bag down on one end of the sofa and clasped his hands together. He released them, then clasped them together once again. It was as if he had just gotten them and he had no idea what to do with them yet.

"Thank you for trying to cheer up my holiday," he said. His voice sounded unused and a little rusty.

"We all have to do what we can for one another."

It was the Amish way.

"*Jah,*" he said. "But I still appreciate it. And what you said yesterday, about being friends . . ." He stopped as if he wasn't sure how to continue.

Tillie patiently waited.

"I want that very much," he finally continued. "And maybe I might one day want more than that."

"Maybe?" That didn't sound very confident. But it was better than what she had fifteen minutes ago.

He closed his eyes as if he'd messed it all up, then slowly opened them again. "I'm pretty sure. See, I haven't been widowed that long."

"I know."

"But when I think of never seeing you or Emmy again it makes my heart and my stomach ache. When I thought about you marrying Melvin, it almost killed me. So I'm pretty sure."

"I don't know what to say," she whispered. Was he proposing that they might have something more one day? How did a woman respond to that sort of talk?

He might not have been definite, but she was thrilled all the same.

"Say you'll be my friend," he said. "You'll ride home from church with me and go on picnics with me in the spring. Tell me that you want to see if there's more to us than what we're seeing right now."

"I'm in mourning."

"Me too. But I'm willing to wait if you are."

She smiled at him as her heart soared. It wasn't true love, not yet, but he wanted to be with her. Well, he was pretty sure he did. And seeing everything that they had been through over the last few months, pretty sure was all right with her.

"I would like that," she said.

"But for now we can be friends," he said, outlining a little more of their relationship. "I do want you to come visit. And I want to come visit you. I know Melvin hasn't been gone but a few days. And — I'm making a mess of this."

She shook her head. "You're doing just fine."

"We can take our time," he said. "Get to know each other."

"That sounds like a great idea."

"And who knows," he said, casting a loving look at her daughter. "A couple of years from now, we might have ourselves another Christmas miracle."

With a little bit of hope and a whole lot of prayers, she felt certain they would.

CHAPTER TWENTY-EIGHT

Two years later
"Tell him I need to talk to him," she told Hannah. "I need to talk to him now."

"Calm down, sister," Hannah said. "I'm sure whatever it is it can wait until after the ceremony."

Tillie shot her sister a look that could have wilted bitterweed out in the fields. "If it could wait, I wouldn't be asking to see him now. So will somebody go get Levi?" Her voice was getting louder. She needed to talk to him. Now. Before the wedding. *Before the wedding* was very important.

Leah nodded at Hannah and disappeared out the door of the upstairs room at their parents' house.

It had taken a year of mourning, getting to know each other, and making good with the church before Levi felt comfortable enough with their relationship to ask her to marry him. Last year's Christmas had been filled with making plans to get married. This year it was all about the wedding.

But she couldn't marry him until she told him one very important thing. Really important thing. Not even a small wedding such as theirs. It was his second wedding, and as far as the church was concerned, hers as well. She may not have married Melvin in an official way, but they'd had a child together, and that counted for a lot where Amos Raber was concerned. Second marriages were half-day affairs, not full days like first weddings, but that was fine with Tillie. She'd had to wait two years to marry Levi, and she didn't want to wait any longer to start their life together.

After she talked to him, that was.

An eternity passed before Levi eased into the room, Leah right behind him.

"What's wrong?" he asked. His brow was puckered into a frown.

Tillie cast a furtive glance at her sisters and grabbed Levi's elbow. She pulled him closer to the window. It would've been better if it was just the two of them alone, but she couldn't make her sisters go out of the room. Well, she could, but if she did, they would forever be bothering her about what she said to Levi right before they were supposed to get married.

"I need to tell you something," she said.

He drew back a bit, his eyes growing hooded.

"No no no," she said, shaking her head. "About Melvin."

His expression remained carefully guarded, though he gave her a quick nod.

"Before he died," she started, "we talked about our plans."

"I know that."

She swallowed hard. "Yes, but what you don't know is that we weren't staying Amish."

His expression puckered into a frown. "You wanted to leave?" He shook his head and closed his eyes as if trying to put everything in the proper perspective.

She was making quite a mess of this. "No, that's not what I'm saying. We weren't going to stay Amish, because we weren't staying together."

He exhaled through his nose. "Now I really don't understand."

"There was a time when I loved Melvin with all my heart."

"Again, I know that," he said.

"But that time wasn't just before he died. I mean, I loved him as a person, and the friend that he had been to me all those years. But I wasn't in love with him anymore. In fact, I think I was already in love with you."

"What are you trying to tell me, Tillie? This is making me a little nervous."

"You think I'm gonna back out now?" She gave him a reassuring smile, but it didn't change his concerned expression. "I just wanted you to know that we were leaving the Amish, but it wasn't because I didn't want to be here. It was because I didn't want to be with Melvin. I wanted to be with you."

"And now?" he asked.

"I'm marrying you, aren't I?"

He nodded, and small twinkles shone in his eyes. "But I want to hear you say it."

Tillie was all too aware of her sisters watching, and though she was certain they couldn't hear what was being said, they weren't about to miss any of the action. "I love you, Levi Yoder. You're my best friend," she continued.

"I love you too."

"And I'm so glad we're getting married today. On Christmas Eve. It seems fitting."

"More than fitting," he agreed.

Tonight they would begin their new life as husband and wife. Tomorrow, on Christmas Day, they would wake up together, open presents, and spend time with family and friends.

Some might not say that it was a Christmas miracle, but as far as they were concerned, it was. And they were looking forward to many more Christmas miracles in their future.

ABOUT THE AUTHOR

Amy Lillard is an award-winning author of over forty novels and novellas ranging from Amish romance and mysteries to contemporary and historical romance. Since receiving a Carol Award for her debut novel, *Saving Gideon* (2012), she has become known for writing sweet stories filled with family values, honest characters, a hometown feel and close-knit communities. She is a member of RWA, ACFW, NINC, and the Author's Guild. Born and bred in Mississippi, she now lives with her husband and son in Oklahoma. Please visit her online at www.AmyWritesRomance.com.